Doris Piserchia

Doris Piserchia was born in West Virginia in 1928. She graduated from Fairmont State College in 1950 and joined the American Navy, in which she served until 1954. While working towards her Master's Degree in Educational Psychology, she discovered science fiction and began to write short stories, which were published in *Fantastic, If* and *Orbit*. Her first novel, *Mister Justice*, was published in 1972. *Star Rider* is her second novel. Her other works include *A Billion Days of Earth*, *Earthchild* and *Spaceling*.

DORIS PISERCHIA
STAR RIDER

The Women's Press
sf

This book is dedicated to my parents,
Viola and Dewey Summers

First published in Great Britain by
The Women's Press Limited 1987
A member of the Namara Group
34 Great Sutton Street, London EC1V 0DX

First published in the United States by
Bantam Books Inc, New York, 1974

British Library Cataloguing in Publication Data

Piserchia, Doris
    Star rider.
    I. Title
    813'.54[F]   PS3566.I7

    ISBN 0-7043-4071-2

Reproduced, printed and bound in Great Britain
by Hazell, Watson & Viney Ltd, Aylesbury, Bucks

Chapter I

Out of the D-2 void we came to stand on a barren
asteroid in a sky full of hot bits of debris. Hinx had
made a rough landing to show me he was insulted by
my long silence, but I paid him no mind. It was good
to be real and solid again.

I jinked my mount from the top of his head to the
soles of his four feet. Hinx and I together were something going somewhere. Separated, we were stranded
wherever we landed. He couldn't go anywhere without a jak on his back and a jak needed a mount under
him to take a trip.

I thought about not having a mount, looked up at
the stars, imagined how it would be to have to stay
in one place. The longing for those lights hit me like a
fist, clawed deep down into my brain and stirred up
things sleeping under the debris.

I said to myself: They're yours, gal, any time you
want them, so what are you aching for?

I knew the answer. It was raw hunger. I had to have
a beckoning light and a mount to carry me there.
That was a jak.

"Settle down, Hinx, you'll throw me," I bawled.

Startling the heck out of me, he stuck his nose
straight at the sky and let out the weirdest howl I
ever heard.

"What was that for?"

"Don't know," he said. "Something came over me."

"I'll come over you, right across your rump with an
old-fashioned beating."

"Do you mind if I do it again?"

He didn't wait for an answer. His nose tilted up

just as a big cinder whizzed by, and the next thing I knew we were in D-2 with me hanging on by a tuft of his fur.

"Sorry," said Hinx, as we landed on a bigger asteroid.

"What'd you come here for?" I yelled. I wanted to dismount, but there were flashing cinders here, too, and he might spook again and catch me unaware.

"You worried about being left behind?" He sounded as if he might be grinning.

I settled back, let my feet dangle at his sides and began picking my teeth with the straw I always carried behind my ear. "Hunters all over the place. Hitch a ride any time I want. Of course, if that happens, I get myself another mount. If you can't trust a mount, you might as well commit suicide. Damn things go loco once in a while and then it's the pasture for them."

"Do that to me and I'll never speak to you again."

"Kind of tired of you. A lifetime of your bellyaching has been enough to make me gag. What's the matter with you?"

"Told you I was hungry."

"We ate a while ago. You forget that planet we stopped at?"

"Not that kind of hunger."

I leaned on his neck and scowled. In some ways, Hinx had more jink than I. Usually, a half-grown mount was frisky and dumb as a rock, but Hinx was a serious thinker and could jink things far away.

When you jinked, you got a thing up close and swarmed all over it with your mind. You didn't go after it to look it over; you dragged it close and pawed it up one side and down the other. Naturally, you didn't pull the actual thing to you, just an aura of its essence.

"We're nowhere near anything interesting," I said. "What the heck can you be jinking?"

He sat so far back on his rump that my own backside almost touched the ground. "Don't know. A powerful hunger's building in me."

"Wish you'd quit dumping us in D so fast." I spoke neither too gently nor too harshly. He was a good

2

mount and there was love between us. I didn't know it then but the clawing longing I'd had a minute ago had gotten under his hide. He didn't know it, either. Time, place, circumstance; those were all it took to make a miracle, or a hell of a mess.

Anyhow, I sat there and he sat there and suddenly the odd tilt of his shaggy head made me feel creepy. I said, "One of these days I'll be slow getting my shield tight around me and the danged vacuum on one of these rocks'll pinch my whistle permanently."

The nose of Hinx quivered. Straight up it jutted. Howl? Enough to give me the shudders.

"I gotta go, love," he said, and I automatically gripped him tight. Bang, D-2. That space-busting maniac under my seat took me like a babe and I made up my mind to have him psyched if I ever got the chance. He needed his brains cleaned out, needed to be put to pasturing and pleasuring on one of those resort planets for blown mounts.

"Whoa," I said, but he paid me no mind. "Damned nag," I swore, and with good reason. He was climbing a string of asteroids as if they were a pile of rocks. My guts jiggled and my brains rattled as I hung on and cussed him to galaxy's end and back. Bang, D-3, with his feet on an asteroid. Bang, D-2, with the wind of nothing in my ears and the black of perdition tearing at my throat. Bang, D-3, with his feet reaching for that little piece of ground ahead, and the son of a clumsy bitch slipped and threw us into D-2 so fast I thought I was a goner.

He finally hit one of those rocks solid, but did he stop and apologize to me, who hung onto his mangy fur for dear life? He did not, just tippytoed across that stone fancy enough to give me scrambled internals, then stuck himself up on his hind legs and gave a bloodcurdling shriek.

"Hot damn, this is it," he said, and licked his chops.

Flat on his back, I lay flat on my back, seeing stars, different bunches with each eye. That day I had crazy vision.

Thought I, if he takes off into D-2 now, I've had it, because I couldn't hang on to a feather, let alone him.

"Hinx, don't do it," I croaked. "We been together. . . ." I couldn't finish, I was that pooped. The stars over my head, long might they prosper, but I wished they wouldn't swarm all over the sky that way.

"Ahooeee. Hot damn."

My breath was back, so I sat up and took hold of his tail. Weaving in the saddle like a drunkard, I mumbled, "Go ahead, let's go."

"Where?"

I grabbed his tail tight. It wouldn't do me any good, though. When he jumped, I was going to go flying.

"Gotta think it out," he said. "It jinks so good I can't stand it."

Fumbling behind me with one hand, I got hold of the long hair on his neck. "You're fixed?" I said. "Not going? You're sure?"

"Sure."

"Okay, then, damn you, we're gonna square off right now and have a tussle. You almost lost me."

He didn't sneer but he sounded as if he wanted to. "Couldn't lose glue, could I?"

"All I had was a couple of hairs to hold."

"That's enough if they're mine. Jinked you all the way. Ready to go either direction to stay under you. We're together in this."

"All the way, but I'm boss."

"Let's argue about that."

"Don't intend to argue," I said. "You know I'm the boss."

"Fine, be the boss. I'm just sitting here. Give me an order."

Of all the stubborn . . . "I got no orders to give you right now. You told me you jinked something. Well, jink it out of your system."

"You don't fool me. You're curious."

"Of course I'm curious."

He forgot what he had been about to say. "Hot damn," he whispered eagerly. He sniffed. He pranced. "Something, something, but what is it? The old blood sings and I just naturally have to poke my nose in the air and go. . . . Ahooeee."

I got off him and walked on that asteroid. Put my hands on my hips. Looked around. Nothing there.

4

Jinked another asteroid way off. Nothing there. Overhead the stars were white freckles on a dark kisser, an ugly face unless you were a jak.

"I'm gonna jink me that star over there," I said.

"Ahooeee ..."

Jinked that star. Piddling little old thing. Jinked those planets. Eight poor dead hulks. Knew 'em by name, knew 'em down to their sterile atoms.

Again I felt that star. Old as hell. Of course, everything was old, except for living creatures. We jaks hadn't been around too long. Think it was only millions of years ago that we started.

"Hinky," I said suddenly.

"Don't call me that."

"Hinx, you feel that star?"

"What for?"

"You feel those eight planets?"

"What for?"

Loud as I could, I yelled, "You bust my brains leapfrogging these asteroids, now you say you don't want to bother jinking anything."

"Already jinked something."

I glared at him for a long minute. "You know this system same as me. One sun, eight planets, no moons and enough asteroids to choke a giant."

He wagged his big head, dug his haunches into the hard rock and sat like a lump of lead.

"Kind of restless," I said. "What say we light out for Veraka? They got blue grass and big crowds. We can panhandle a couple days to get a stake."

"No, thank you."

Cranky, I walked toward him. "How about Adrax? You like all those spooky caves."

"Seen 'em a hundred times."

I was sick of yelling so I said softly, "What do you want to do?"

"Excuse me, sweetie, but something around here smells."

"Not to me."

"You're blind when you're mad. Me, I never get mad so I'm never blind. What say you relax awhile and get the feel of the place, and then if you don't jink anything, we'll take off?"

5

That sounded reasonable so I walked away to do what he said. Felt uneasy, I did; jumpy as a young mount hitting D-2 for the first time.

Me feeling strange wasn't usual. Needed thinking about. Sat down on the ground and considered it.

Nothing on this asteroid to cause Hinx to lose his mind. Chunk of rock so small I felt light even with my shield in place. I had taken some atmosphere from the last oxygenated planet we landed on. Hinx had done the same thing. Carrying along an environment wasn't difficult to do, in fact it became more or less automatic to a traveler after he had practiced it a few times. The mind formed a cage of force around the body, and the atmosphere was captured inside. Its density was determined by the amount of gravity on a planet and by the mass of the traveler. There wasn't any gravity on an asteroid like this one and my shield was so dense that its outer side lay a fraction of an inch away from my skin and just barely covered the hair on my head. I could use the shield I had for about ten hours, after which I'd have to pick up some fresh atmosphere.

I was twelve when I took off on my mount to hunt for the legendary planet. Doubleluck was its name, and I was still hunting for it. Good old Doubleluck. With one hand clasping the long hair on Hinx's neck and the other dug deep into the fur on his rump, I sat in the depression in his back and rode like a fiend. For two years.

How many times I'd promised my mount, "We'll get there first." The devil could take the others, we'd find the place and make it ours. Everyone would throw their hats in the air and shout that jaks were kings of the universe.

If only the universe hadn't been so small. If only we could have gotten out of our galaxy and reached that other one way over there across a big ocean of black space.

That was the real reason Hinx and I rode, only I didn't know it at the time.

The mind could do anything, and mind was just about what a jak was. Mounts, too. Both species climbed the evolutionary ladder close together and

6

though there were animals all over the galaxy there were none like us.

The mind could soar but not the body. I had a good body but it couldn't take me to the stars, nor could Hinx's body take him. Our minds could do it. Linked, we became D-2, a thing that had no depth, created no friction and was unaffected by vacuum or inertia.

Now I sat on a hard rock in the middle of nowhere and wondered what was the matter with my mount.

My mind, it went out. Calm now, no longer mad at Hinx, I let it go. Out. Up. Sideways.

That star up there; pretty little furnace all red and white; worked hard for a long time just so jaks could come and see it.

Eight planets; two little ones close to the furnace, five bigger ones farther out and another little one, that last one packed in ice and getting colder every day.

Moon . . .

Click.

"Hold on, mount, I jink."

Hinx glanced at me across the gray rock. "What?"

"Quiet. Needs thinking on."

What was it about numbers? Not much at math, I counted on the fingers and toes in my mind. Went down deep to do that counting.

"At least one heavenly body in this system is missing," I said over my shoulder. "Recollect there ought to be—"

"My recollect's as good as yours and none are missing."

"Jink me," I said. "Count with me."

"One, two, three, four. . . ." He finished the count after I did.

"Where'd you get those two extra ones?"

"From your mind."

I got up off the ground. "I'm in my own mind. Know what's there and what isn't."

"Archetypes," said Hinx. "Hey, that popped into my head."

"Pop some more."

He growled and scratched his ribs with a hind leg. "Can't. Jinked it for a second and then blooey."

"Archetypes out here in this dinky dump? Even if you're spelling it out right, why should any aura reach you? You mounts originated in the Bowkow Point, sure as hell not in this bunch of backwoods islands."

He grinned. "Sure as hell you didn't come from here, either. You come from the Ridge Cluster, you can't even talk good jak, and damned if you didn't teach me the same. Only how come I can read something in your mind you can't read?"

"Let me think about it some more."

Went away to consider. Sat down again, leaned back on my elbows and dreamed me a dream of stars and gold.

Out of the dim tunnels in my mind came a trailing thing; god, how slow and loggy was it, sneaking up back paths through high canyons, hollow as a reed and its name was Memory.

"Point," said I, and the wispy thing grew a finger. It said, "There," and behind me Hinx said, "Oops," and a second later nobody sat on that asteroid but me.

"Where'd you go?" I yelled, standing up to look around.

"Damn if I know," Hinx answered.

No matter where he was, he couldn't get away from me if I held on to him, and I held on tight. "Come on back," I said.

"Pull me. I hate this place. It's nowhere."

I could toss his carcass all over the galaxy if I wanted to. That's why I was boss. I pulled and he came yelling.

"Moon, moon, moon."

"There isn't any," I said, and dropped him hard beside me.

"Did you jink me while I was gone?"

Scratched my backside. "Forgot."

"Well, for the love—"

"Go on back to that rock where you were before. I want to try that again."

He looked at me as if I had asked him to give up breathing. "You want me to go back to nowhere?"

"Yeah."

He didn't like it, but he went, stomping all the way.

I turned my back to him and talked to myself to get it all clear and down pat.

"Let's see, what was I thinking about before? Oh, yeah, gold and that thing down there in my mind. Hinky called it an archetype. It doesn't look like one. Not that I know exactly what they look like."

The thing was still there, down deep. Fishing it up a ways wasn't too difficult, because it wanted to come. Slippery as grease, it wriggled out of the abyss and stared me in the face.

"Oops," said Hinx and disappeared.

Just me and the asteroid again.

"You there?" I called. "Is that place somewhere?"

"Nope, and I still don't like it. Pull me in before I take a fit."

"What are we doing wrong?" I said when he was back beside me.

He started to answer and then changed his mind. His head went up and his nose twitched.

"Rider coming."

He was right, and somebody had a lot of nerve butting into our territory. Whoever it was, he obviously had no manners.

A scowl on my face, I turned and watched a blank patch of space.

The biggest jak I ever saw came riding out of a window of ink. In slow motion he appeared, and before he settled into the solidity of D-3, I had a couple of seconds to look him over. He was huge and his baggy duds did nothing to hide the muscle packing his bones.

The best clothes anywhere were the skins of lanion pods. They could be found all over, and just about everyone wore them. Only the pods that hadn't ripened were unusable, and those could be recognized by their gray color. You simply broke off a ripe one that was bigger than yourself, stepped on the end so the insides popped out and then you hauled the skin over your head, fit it to your body and ripped off the excess. The skin would settle around you in a few seconds. It wore well and it was soft and shiny and smelled pleasant. Lanion pods came in all colors. I usually chose green or yellow. The big jak coming out of D-2 was wearing black. He had chosen a pod that was way too big for him, which meant he didn't like tight clothes.

Anyhow, his legs were stiffed out and his toes pointed straight at the sky, and he rode loose and easy as if he thought he owned everything. His mount was a grizzled old giant with rolling eyes and irritated ears. One glance at the pair and you knew they were made for each other. This duo was ugly as sin and tougher than stone, a couple of lonesome bums who would blow you down if you got in their way and cuss you when you complained.

That mount had a sense of humor, came climbing down empty space as if it were a steep trail. His four legs prowled for clods and he didn't give a damn when he found none. Hair as long as my arm hung from his body, thick and curly stuff that would have afforded any rider a generous grip, but this mount's rider hung on by nothing but the seat of his pants. Big Jak always rode that way, as I found out later, but that day he had good reason to travel freestyle. One hand was full of a big hat, the other held on to a body.

"Couple of showoffs," Hinx whispered to me. "That jak is full of ham and that mount is the sorriest—" He shut up when that mount landed solid and showered him with asteroid dirt.

It was done purposely, sure as certain. Just as certain, they had heard Hinx. In D-3 they were a spook and a dragon, and I started wondering if I ought to get lost in a hurry.

The big jak gent had skinny yellow eyes long gone in ice. He sat on the gray giant like a monument and stared down his long nose, and all the while his eyes tried to freeze me. "What's your name?"

"Don't have one. My mount here calls me Lone."

"All right, Lone, you'll come along with me now."

"Don't reckon," I said.

"Reckon you will."

"Don't see why you haul down on a pair of innocent strangers."

He didn't smile because he didn't know how. Lines showed in his forehead and his slitted mouth grew more invisible. Plainly, he wasn't accustomed to getting back in kind. "I say I was hauling down on you?"

"Can't swear you did."

"Tone counts more than words," growled Hinx.

The big gray mount lifted a hind leg and did something no self-respecting animal would be caught dead doing in public. What's more, he took his time about it. After a long minute, he gave a satisfied snort. Looking at Hinx and with a grin on his face, he said lazily, "Howdy, pup."

Right then I knew the pack of us were off and running in a bitter feud. Four rubbing four the wrong way could only mean a square-off.

Big Jak shifted his thighs. His face slammed together in a second and his eyes were deep and solemn. "Need a little assistance is why I interrupted you."

He ignored the mounts. I had the feeling he was ignoring me, too. If there had been any wind I'd have known he was talking to it. I should have headed in the other direction at a fast clip. What he was actually doing was taking me by the nose and leading me to a deep well, and as soon as he got good and ready he intended to kick me in it.

"Picked up this fellow in limbo and aim to take him to a safe place for a good rest," he said. Jerking his head toward the jak slung over his shoulder, he added, "He's bad scrambled and might send my mount off course if I keep traveling by myself. Could use you two as steadiers."

I walked around him in order to get a look at the other jak's face. "He must be pretty good if he can do anything while he's unconscious. Don't look to me like he can wiggle."

One corner of Big Jak's mouth drooped. "You arguing without all the facts?"

"Never did that and don't plan to now. Certainly I'll lend a hand. We'll put our mounts side by side and I'll help hold—"

"Get behind me," he said gruffly. "Hold on with jink, that's all."

Why he didn't just plain say, "Eat dust and founder," and get it done with, I didn't know, because that's what he had in mind.

11

I could have kicked that gray mount in the tail for sticking it in our faces. From my humiliating position, I could get a good look at the unconscious fellow, and I felt sorry for him. He was small and thin and poor-colored and beat-looking. He had a funny metal hat on his head. Of course he was crazy. Jaks in their right minds never wasted time fooling around with machinery. That was for children who hadn't developed their brain power.

Away the four of us went into D-2, and then I didn't see anything at all with my eyes; just with my mind.

Chapter II

Felt some alarm. I didn't like heat, and we were approaching a hot world. Recollected Big Jak's deep tan and figured this planet coming up was his birthplace. All my figuring that day was dead wrong.

Nobody lived on that world, nor had anyone ever. It was made up of endless deserts and bluffs, rough winds and a wicked red sun that boiled away for thirty hours at a clip before dropping out of sight like a speeding fireball.

We grounded in six inches of dust that billowed and clung to whatever it touched. My alarm mounted as I looked at Big Jak. He had dumped his shield. I knew this right away because a shield created a mist around a traveler and Big Jak didn't have any. Since he wasn't wearing one, I couldn't either unless I wanted to betray weakness, so I let my comfort drift away and began using the stuff of the planet.

The air seemed to have no moisture in it at all. I felt as if someone had shoved me into a furnace. Sweat popped out all over me and in ten seconds I was swaying like a drunk and gasping for air.

Big Jak didn't turn around to see if I was still alive after that dilly of a welcome from nature, just sat like a statue and stared across the red ground.

Thought I: It isn't possible that this gent—

Again I was wrong. Though it was unbelievable that anybody would travel three yards on this planet without skipping through D-2, Big Jak behaved as if ground-riding was just naturally the thing to do. His heels nudged the gray and the two of them began moving over the sand.

I couldn't complain and I couldn't retreat, so there weren't a whole lot of alternatives open to me. I did the in-between, followed that gray across the desert and ignored the soft whines coming from Hinx, and at the same time I wondered what in the hell I thought I was up to.

The big maverick was an assuming sort, never once looked over his shoulder to see if we were keeping up. That ought to have told me all I needed to know. Big Jak was a reader of people.

"He's flipped," Hinx gasped.

An hour later he said it again. By then, both of us were in bad shape. Dried sweat was caked on me in layers and I slumped like a hunk of dying meat. Hinx didn't even bother to pant. Now and then he shuddered and took in air.

It required plenty of squinting on my part to see what lay ahead of us, and it wasn't all that attractive. The horizon was on fire, looked as if the sun had unloaded its guts with one big flaming cough. A series of ridges ran like flowing lava from right to left all the way across my line of vision without ever coming to an end.

"He's aiming to climb those rocks," I said.

Hinx came to a trembling halt. A pool of sweat had formed beneath my thighs and I slid around for a while and then fell on the ground. I lay there blowing at the sky and trying to blink away blindness.

"That fella hates us," I croaked. "He wants to kill us."

Hinx licked my face with a tongue so dry it hurt.

"Let's get out of here," I said, and reached for the hair on his neck. "We'll recuperate somewhere and forget we ever met that gent."

A voice spoke behind me. "We're about there. Appreciate your coming with me. Would've had a tough time of it alone."

I couldn't make him out. He was one black spot among thousands swarming past my eyes. Misery made me helpless and feeling that way made me mad. I grabbed hold of Hinx and swung aboard. Back in my mind a hard clot of anger grew against

14

the big bruiser ahead. He'd about done me in and no doubt he had a reason for doing it, but his reason included no concern for me.

Hinx managed to keep going until we reached the foothills. He staggered a few yards up an incline before space fell away and we were looking down into a shaded arroyo. One side of its U shape was lower than the rest and ended in a sparkling little pool of water.

I got off Hinx, walked nonchalantly to the pool and fell in.

It took me a long time of soaking before I decided I was going to live.

"Rested up?" said Big Jak. He was a weird bird, sat looking out at the desert as if it were a road home.

"Wasn't that tired." It was dumb of me to be that much of a liar, since anyone with two eyes could have told how low I felt, but I couldn't help it. I was too stubborn to admit weakness.

Big Jak wasn't human. He had filled his hat with water for Volcano, his mount, but so far he hadn't had a drink. Didn't look hot or tired. The other jak was stretched out in the shade and he looked like a corpse, except that he wasn't dead, because every now and then he groaned.

I lay on the ground with my head on Hinx's side. I could tell by the way he breathed that he was comfortable.

"I expect you're looking for Doubleluck, the same as everybody in the galaxy," said Big Jak.

I didn't like his tone. Or his expression, either. Not that he could have helped that. He was as sinister as anybody I'd seen in a long time, reminded me of a vark, which was a rangy four-legged thing with gray hide and teeth as long as fingers. All a vark did was sit around smiling. After you had watched one for a while, you made tracks away from it. The sight of the teeth and the yellow eyes gleaming above them made your bones ache. As a matter of fact, I heard a vark could draw the marrow out of a jak just by sitting and smiling at him. It didn't bite and suck bones, it simply sat and smiled, and by and by the jak was stone-cold hypnotized and then the power in the vark reached across space and drained his stuff like water sipped up a reed.

Right then I had the feeling the jak sitting there on the ground looking at me wasn't a human at all but a vark in disguise.

"What does that mean?" I said. "You saying there's no such place?"

"Oh, no, it's there, all right. I been there often, but not because it's all that interesting."

Making sure there was no trace of a sneer on my face, I said, "Is that a fact?"

"Know it like I know the back of my hand." Big Jak looked exactly like a vark as he said it.

To myself, I said, Then how come you're not the most famous jak in the kingdom?

Quick as a wink, I lost my sneaking admiration for him. A good liar had a special talent but a poor one was just plain trash.

I looked up and caught a funny expression on his face. For a second I had the feeling he was getting a big kick out of something.

"What you going to do with this fella?" I asked.

He didn't give his groaning companion a glance. "I'll keep an eye on him. Soon as he's in good shape, we'll take a trip."

"Where to?"

"Glory."

"Huh?"

His face went cold. "Where you from?"

"Around."

He lay down and lowered his hat so I couldn't see his eyes, and then he jabbed his chin into his chest so I couldn't see his mouth. Crossing his ankles and supporting himself on his elbows, he sank into silence.

So did I. Dug my head deeper into Hinx's side and wished nobody was there so I could take a nap. It was a lot cooler in the shade than I had anticipated, and there was something satisfying about being comfortable while a few yards away the desert and sky were mixing a vat of brimstone. Worst place I was ever in. A few more minutes and I'd take my mount and go the hell someplace else.

Big Jak spoke so suddenly I jumped.

"Maybe you think I'm pulling your leg when I say I know the whereabouts of Doubleluck. Be the biggest mistake you ever made."

He kept his face in his chest and went on talking, and I naturally listened.

"One thing people don't take into consideration is attitude. Think everybody is the same. Can't imagine a jak finding Doubleluck and not screaming it to the mountaintops. Such a jak could make himself a fortune, since finding it would make him the owner. He could set up a gate and charge admission to tourists. For a fact, most jaks would do it that way."

"How come you didn't?" I said.

"Too much trouble." With that, he lay down flat on the ground, pulled his hat all the way over his face and made as if he were about to go to sleep.

The thing of it was, what he had said made sense in a way. Attitude had a lot of influence on a person's behavior. This jak beside me certainly wasn't the type to pitch himself into the public limelight; in fact, he would probably hate that sort of thing. Besides, he was no youngster. You could tell if a jak was an adolescent and you could tell if he was old, but one thing you couldn't guess was the age of a jak who was in between. I didn't know how old this one was. Could be thirty, could be a hundred and thirty. If he had been riding for more than a hundred years, why, it wouldn't sound so out of the head to say he might have found Doubleluck.

I forgot that the galaxy was saturated with the remains of dead jaks who had hunted all their lives for the planet of gold. Oblivious to reality, I went on talking to myself. What my silent yakking boiled down to was that I wanted to believe what Big Jak said, but in order to do that I had to smooth out the snags in his logic. Many talents had I.

"Why are you telling me all this?" I said.

He jumped a little, as if I had dragged him from a doze. Lazily shoving his hat onto his forehead, he looked straight at me.

"Been looking for a partner, somebody who isn't afraid of showing off to the public."

I swallowed hard and tried not to seem nervous. "This fella on the ground going to be that partner?"

"Him? Naw, he's addled." Big Jak lay down and covered his face with his hat and began to snore.

I wanted to kick him, wanted to get up and pace around, but I lay and fidgeted and tried to keep my stomach below my throat. All of a sudden I was a mess of nerves.

Big Jak stopped snoring and started to talk again. "Feel like telling you where that planet is."

A big lump in my chest dropped to the bottom of my guts.

"You lent a hand when I was in need," he said. "Maybe you're the partner for me. Maybe I ought to let you go take a look at the planet of gold. Of course, you'd have to keep your lips sealed."

He shoved up his hat and stared at me. "You know the Bounding Winter system?"

"Is that where it is?" There wasn't a sound in the universe except my beating heart. I was suddenly crouched on my hands and knees and wasn't paying any attention to anything but the pulse in my head, in my throat, in my whole eager body. Should have noticed how keenly Big Jak was watching me, should have seen how his body was stiffed out while he waited to hear something from me.

"I said, do you know it?"

"All I need is a direction and I can find anything."

He heard it. Relaxing, he said in a drawl, "Don't know, maybe I can't trust you. Probably can. Probably ought to go along with you, though. Recollect a traveler has to stake a claim before he can own a piece of property, and Doubleluck is certainly that. What do you think?"

"Wh—what do— A claim?"

"Yes. At the detention circle on planet One in the Bounding Winter system."

"What do I have to do?"

"Swear to your right as a citizen to hunt for the treasure planet. Then you get detention."

"What's that?"

"Permission to own Doubleluck after you find it."

18

I scrambled erect. "Just point the way. I'll go stake that claim and then I'll head for the planet."

"Whoa. Settle down. Sailing off half-cocked will get you nowhere. In the first place, I've decided to go along with you, not that I don't trust you to keep your mouth shut, but I want to make sure no one follows you after you stake that claim. Secrecy is important. Another thing, I'm thirsty."

He climbed to his feet and ambled off in the direction of the lake.

"Jump aboard and let's scram," said Hinx to me.

"What you talking about? I ain't going anywhere without him."

My mount stood over me and looked down. "Come on, hurry up before he comes back."

"Damn it, didn't you hear him?"

"I did, and a worse job of conning I never heard. Why, he ain't even slick about it."

"You're one stupid mount. That fella's taking us to Doubleluck."

"You think anyone is that crazy?"

"The galaxy's full of crazy people."

He cocked his head and looked at me from the corner of his eye. "You sure you don't mean greedy?"

"Make some sense. If he's conning me, why is he willing to take us to Bounding Winter to stake a claim?"

"Don't know. Am positive he's a liar with no reason to do you a favor. You're just an ignorant little gal and he's taking advantage of you."

"Nobody takes advantage of me and I'm not ignorant."

"I think it has something to do with that fella on the ground." Came the sound of feet stepping among rocks, and Hinx lowered his voice to a whisper. "Our time is running out. Make up your mind."

"Done made it up. We're going after Doubleluck with that big jak."

Chapter III

A Ridge Runner was a jak or a mount who came from the Ridge Cluster. I was one. Hinx was another. I didn't learn what it really meant to be a Ridge Runner until I followed Big Jak to the Bounding Winter system.

The Ridge Cluster was a place where people abandoned babies they didn't want. Every planet in the Cluster was nonhostile and infant jaks and mounts could survive on them simply by crawling about and chomping on whatever grew. Nothing there could harm them.

I didn't know where I came from before I was dumped in the Cluster. In fact, I didn't recall too much about my infancy. I recollected sitting up one day and taking a good look around. There were other children and tiny mounts all over the place. The planet was a good one, with plenty of nourishing roots and fruits and water puddles. I took care of Hinx and he took care of me and together we grew to be five years old or so, after which we looked up one night and saw a diamond winking down at us.

We couldn't bear looking at the diamond. It seemed to be calling to us and getting impatient because we didn't answer. We spent a month or so yakking and bawling about it, and then one night I crawled onto Hinky's back and screamed some baby-talk cusswords, and the next thing I knew I was in D-2 with him under me. We almost got stuck in limbo, which is a place that's neither here nor there. It's between D-2 and D-3 and is no place for a live thing to find himself caught in. Sometimes travelers got sick or fainted while they were in D-2, and their concentration was interrupted. They started to disperse; that is, their atoms began to separate, and unless another traveler came along and rode them out of limbo they were goners.

But back to Bounding Winter and Big Jak. It wasn't difficult to see how the system got its name. The eight planets had been snowed in some time shortly after their birth and a traveler approaching them got the impression that he was leaping from one deep snowbank to another. Pretty. Something about untouched places stimulated a responding chord in a jak. Eight little snowballs, and you got an itch to dive down into each one and leave your mark.

I didn't have time to really jink any of the planets, as Big Jak was riding hard and fast toward the one nearest to the sun; not that it was all that near, about 150 million miles. It surprised me that people lived on it, since it was as snowbound as the rest.

No, it wasn't. First I jinked heat, then people. Near the equator of that planet was a big patch of livable land, and this was where they were. There was also plant life in the patch. I jinked inside a huge purple shield of atmosphere and found everybody sitting in a garden, or sitting on the things in it. Big flowers served as seats. I had seen people use tree stumps that way, but I'd never seen them sitting or lounging on flowers. For some reason they looked lazy as hell.

Didn't see the practical point of that overgrown purple shield, since there was plenty of air, but I saw the esthetic reason for it. It was the right and final touch on the garden, put a dreamy aura to everything and everyone in it. It was so down-to-nature that I expected, any second, to jink someone walking around with no clothes on. There were plenty of nudist planets and I wondered if this might be one, but it wasn't.

I grounded beside Big Jak, about a hundred yards short of that purple shield. It wasn't cold or snowy where we landed; there was plenty of good ground between us and the white slopes.

A funny thing sat in front of us, a thing I'd never seen before and for a second I didn't believe my

21

eyes. I looked again and became certain of what it was. The thing was an artifact.

Felt disgusted. Didn't have any desire to do business with grown people who stooped to making things with their hands.

Big Jak swung off Volcano and waited for me to dismount. He took me by the arm. "This artifact is a hitching post and you have to take one of these ropes hanging on it and tie up your mount."

"What you mean?" I said.

"Well, wasn't it plain?"

"Not exactly."

His yellow eyes were too narrow for my liking and I also didn't want his hand on my arm. He weighed a ton and I had to hold on to the hitching post to stand up.

"You ought to know by now that you have to do what the natives do," he said. "It's the code of the galaxy. When you land in stranger territory, you abide by stranger rules."

"Still not sure I know what you mean."

Hinx told me. "What he wants you to do is tie me to this damned thing and then you and him's going inside where those people are."

"Oh, I can't go anywhere without my mount," I said to Big Jak.

His eyes went narrower than before. "Can if it's worth it."

"Can't. Besides, I don't see you tying your mount. You're going to take him in there with you."

"He and I have been together so long we can't part."

"That way with me, too," I said. Felt as if my knees were going to bend fifteen ways. Afraid he was going to insist, which he did.

"The only way we can get that claim staked is if we go in there. If you're going to be my partner, you'd better get one thing straight. I'm boss. You'll do as I say or we part company right here and now."

"Want to obey. Want to share Doubleluck with you. The thing is, if I split up with Hinx, I'll pass out on you. Happens every time someone divides us. Really don't see why he has to be tied."

"I don't see why, either, only they don't allow no

22

young mounts in there. Probably because youngsters got poor manners."

"Ca—ca—can't leave him."

"Okay. Go on, get out of here and ride. Don't want you."

He was one mean jak. Wouldn't budge an inch, didn't care if I was limp as a vine from worrying. He stood there glaring until I finally gave in and looped a rope around Hinky's neck and tied it to the post.

We took three steps away from that post and my head filled with fog. I looked around at Hinx. He grew shadowy, seemed to recede into the distance. I didn't know why I responded that way whenever somebody separated us. It might have been fear. Without Hinx I couldn't go anywhere, and if I couldn't travel I might as well have been dead. Whatever caused it, I couldn't stop it. Big Jak kept urging me along, and pretty soon the fog in my head got darker and the next thing I knew the lights went completely out.

I woke up flat on the ground inside that purple shield with a bunch of people bending over me and that son of a hound named Big Jak saying, "I got you a Ridge Runner. Do your duty and be sharp about it because she's a cunning pest."

I lay there scared to death. I hadn't done much jinking before, as I'd been too excited and greedy, but now I jinked like crazy, figuratively tore up one side and down the other of that star system. Learned a little that way but picked up more information by listening to the conversation going on above me.

Of the eight planets in the system, only numbers One and Two were used by jaks. The planet we were on, number One was occupied by custodians. Young people lived on number Two.

I had been betrayed. That was the first thing. No, it was the second. The first thing was that I'd been stupid. I never knew a jak had to become a citizen of the galaxy, never heard of the law that said folks had to swear to their names and birthplaces, and I never imagined that Ridge Runners were the only people who didn't know about the law and Bounding Winter.

An infant—a jak or mount less than twenty years

23

—from the Ridge Cluster was a drain on society because he or she survived by panhandling. Having had no training or discipline, Runners usually chose the easy way in whatever they did. Jaks who gave handouts to beggars had that much less to feed themselves, and the number of travelers who were in space simply hunting for a food planet made the whole thing impractical. Also impractical was the idea of rounding up all the orphans in the Cluster. There were too many planets and most jaks were so busy hunting for Doubleluck that they didn't want to be tied up with anything else.

The custodians of Bounding Winter seldom stayed long. Usually a traveler had to wear himself out before he would settle down to something useful, which was why all the people on planet One were so old. After they tired of the job, they wandered off and someone else drifted in to take over.

Bounding Winter was the place where homeless children were dumped when they got in the way. The custodians melded their minds and created a field of force around planet Two. No adolescent could break through that field, which meant that once he was dumped on the planet he was stuck there until the caretakers let him out.

As for the caretakers, I never saw so many creaking old bags and geezers in my life, and every one of them was bent over me and scowling as if I was diseased.

"She's about fourteen, I think," said Big Jak, and finally shut his mouth.

"Her mount tied so she can't pull him?" somebody said, and got an affirmative from that son of a skunk who had kicked me into the well. "We'll confine the two of them on the detention planet until they're twenty, and then we'll set them free. Hope they don't go insane like some do."

That did it. An old bag reached down to take hold of me and I kicked her in the belly. Like a snake I rolled and scrambled onto my hands and knees while wrinkled paws grabbed for me from every direction. I bucked with my feet. Cussing like a grounded mount, I got the hell out of there at top speed.

24

The arm of Big Jak shot out like a rope and his fist closed on my collar. I kept going. Nearly choked for a second and then was glad my lanion pod was just about worn out because it ripped away in his hand and the big liar went flying onto his bucket. The last thing I saw before plunging through the purple shield was Volcano heading for his partner at a businesslike lope.

Figured I was a goner. Confident as anyone, I still suspected I was no match for an adult when it came to traveling. On top of that, Big Jak had his mount to hand while mine was a hundred yards away and tethered to boot. As long as Hinx had that link with this planet, I couldn't pull him or take him anywhere. My pursuer could skip through as little as a hundred yards of distance, so he would likely be beside Hinx before I got there.

"Hinx, the farthest ever, hear?" I yelled as I split.

"Sure do," he yelled back.

"I mean the farthest danged system we ever skipped to. In the meantime, chew that rope."

It was a good thing he had strong teeth and it was a good thing that hound's issue behind me took three extra seconds getting on his feet and climbing aboard Volcano. I jinked him coming like a ghost astraddle a lightning bolt. Hinx had the rope in his jaws and was giving a big yank. At the same time I was in the middle of the air and sailing for his broad back.

We took the fence post with us. Hinx pulled so hard he tore it out of the ground. I concentrated on clawing across the galaxy to a beckoning light clear up at the tip from where we started. I had been there before and knew right away that Hinx had the same target in mind. As soon as we touched onto the nearest planet, we would take off again toward another star way back in the opposite direction. Maybe some fancy leapfrogging would save us. We'd ride, sweat and hope. There was always the possibility that Big Jak would lose our trail. That is, if he dropped dead or lost his mind. Jinking us to our destination would be easy for him.

We touched down on a world and I shouted, "Hold and wait for my signal. We'll jink him coming before we move. I don't want him crossing our path and shoving us into limbo."

Waited, waited, waited. That fella didn't come.

Strangest thing ever, but Big Jak didn't seem to be out there. What made the waiting more scary was that the hunk of planet under us was a swamp with crawling uglies everywhere and hardly any light in the sky to show us where to put our feet. I shivered and clung to Hinx and tried to make my teeth stop chattering. Any kind of enemy was a bad thing, but Big Jak was the worst kind I could have made. He was a type who didn't quit anything he started.

"Where is he?" Hinx whispered.

"Quiet. Jink your head off."

We jinked ourselves blind while every second I expected a spook and a dragon to come roaring down on us. It never happened.

"What kind of trick is he pulling?" said Hinx. A long time had gone by.

"Can't figure it."

"You think he got stuck in limbo?"

"Him? Not a chance."

"You think he decided to let us go?"

"Not a chance."

Hinx let out his breath in a slow, cautious rush. Sitting back on his tail and looking bewildered, he said, "Well, where is he?"

It took us a while to relax, but we finally made it. It looked as if we had lost Big Jak on our first jump, and though I could scarcely believe it, I had to admit it was true. Our worries were over. The galaxy was too big for us to ever meet him again by accident, and it wasn't in my plans to meet him on purpose.

Spent some time skipping star systems until we found a planet with some orchards. Stuffed ourselves with fruit, went wading in a creek, made mud pies, I got a suntan and Hinx was bitten on the tail by a bug, lay on weeds as round as my arm and watched the first evening stars wake up. It was then that I remembered what my mount and I had been doing just before we ran into all our trouble.

"You recollect that nowhere place you were in a

while back?" I said to Hinx. He was being a pillow for me and his big lean side felt good.

"Recollect. Didn't like it."

"Want to go there after sunup. Never ran into anything like that before and need to know what it was all about."

"I go wherever you go," said my mount, and we went to sleep.

Chapter IV

"Oops," said Hinx and disappeared.

Just me and the asteroid again.

"You there?" I called. "Is it still nowhere?"

"It's D-3, so you did better this time, but I call it nowhere."

"Look around and I'll jink what you see."

He groaned in disappointment. "It's another asteroid, is all."

"Wrong. Look again."

"Well, it's a bit odd for an asteroid. You think maybe it could be a moon?"

"What's the matter with your jink? Of course it's a moon. And look over your shoulder." I took another good jink of the big brown and white ball hanging over his head. It was a planet, and it had no business being there. Neither did that moon Hinx was on.

"What the heck?" said my mount.

"Time to move," I told him. I pulled him back to me, and we rode across a desert of vacuum and planted ourselves on that big brown and white ball that wasn't supposed to be there.

Hinx looked around and snorted. "Just another ordinary planet. What I can't figure—"

"Shut up and jink."

In front of us was a creek. It was choked with weeds and rotten growths, and it trickled sluggishly and sent a foul odor into the air. Thought I, with an odd thrill, What is it about that stinking water?

Beyond the creek reared a stark and barren mountain. Dreary and wind-lashed, it was a blunt finger poking into the ugly sky. Thought I: What is it about that mountain?

Such pitiful grass I'd seen before, but only on sick worlds where the air had been ruined by poisonous chemicals. Something about that grass . . .

I couldn't see the lake on the other side of the mountain but I could jink it down to its sludge bottom. It was half-filled with sediment that never stayed still but drifted with every motion of the water. Above the surface, fumes rose and swirled. I knew that lake.

There were holes in the hills around us, looked like a huge animal had gone around clawing out chunks. Those hills were as familiar to me as my own body.

Thunderstruck, I stared at a hill that formed the horizon to my right. It wasn't really a hill but a layer of dirt covering—what was that thing under the dirt? The word "city" flashed into my mind. I had never heard that word before but I understood it. A city was a great complexity of artifacts. It was made up of buildings where people lived, worked, ate and slept. It had streets, vehicles and a million other odd things that people put to use.

"Little jak, do you think what I think?" said Hinx.

With my face lifted toward the sky of that little gutted planet, I closed off the top part of my big brain and let the floods of racial memory pour out. It was all there in my mind like imprints in sand.

"The archetypes of my beginning," I said. "This is the place."

"Our beginning." Hinx's voice cracked. He hid his nose in my armpit and snuffled like the dog who had fathered him millions of years ago.

Something was the matter with my throat. "Thought you mounts came from the Bowkow Point," I howled.

"Thought jaks came from the Ridge Cluster," he howled back.

There were four artificial satellites in the planet's sky. Each one emitted electronic signals and created a field of interference between them. This interference wasn't exactly a mind-muffler to a jak. Rather, his perceptive probes approached and then slid around the outside of the field without his being aware that he had encountered anything. Each time he came near this star system, his mind was blinded to the one planet and its moon. As for his sense of sight, it was of practically no use to him when he was traveling.

Hinx and I had accidentally parked close to the planet, spent a deal of time on that nearby asteroid, and a portion of my perceptive sense had leaked through the field, a thing that couldn't have happened very often.

Anyhow, those artifacts sailing along in the sky were primitive and old and beat-up, and I hated them because they had done such a good job.

"We been gypped," said Hinx. "This planet is Doubleluck, and we been cheated."

He was right. For thousands of years jaks had hunted for the lost planet and its moon. Legend said the circumference of Doubleluck was about 24,000 miles, and that fact fit. Another fact—Doubleluck was old and tired. Another—jaks used to call themselves men, and this planet was their birthplace. Jakalowar—he who races with the stars. Men who followed suns left everything behind, even their name.

I touched the satellites with my mind. The hard lump in my throat tried to choke me. "Don't care what this dump is," I yelled. "Want the streets lined with gold the way they're supposed to be. Want to feel diamonds falling on my head like rain. Want rainbows to climb and clouds to ride on. Want to swim in lakes of perfume. Want Doubleluck to be the way the legend says it is. Want to be the most famous jak in the galaxy."

Sobbing into my armpit, Hinx whispered, "If this is the place, we've been cheated out of our souls."

"Has to be it. It's the only hidden planet I ever heard of. Biggest lie since time started. No gold or rainbows, just a smelly pile of ashes. Don't give a damn if jaks were born here. I'm ashamed of men. They were stupid. They used artifacts. I don't care about nothing anymore. Want to die."

Hinx gave a sudden scream of pure terror.

Was so shocked I couldn't do anything right. Naturally wanted to see what was what, that was in-

30

stinctual, only I should have jinked instead of using my eyes.

A big thick rope came whistling out of nowhere and looped itself around Hinky's neck. The end of that rope came into view and it was tied to a rock the size of a small meteor. The rock plunked onto the ground and Hinx was sealed solid to that planet. Out of a window of ink came a rider, and I didn't need a second look to know who it was.

Didn't wait around to take a second look. Lit out like a flustered bat and plunged into the stinking creek, sank to my knees and fell forward, hauled myself out and went legging it toward the hills.

I heard the thunder of four heavy feet behind me and swerved to the right just as a rope slashed past my head. Swerved again and the rope dropped ahead of me. Kicked it and the loop went around a tree-stump sticking out of a rock. I kept running and a few seconds later I heard that big son of a skunk reach the end of the rope and get hauled off Volcano's back. I heard him land, heard him cussing, was tempted to laugh because he couldn't skip after me when he had no way of guessing which way I would go.

My stupidity was showing again. Worked so hard at running that I forgot to look up and then when I finally did I saw him sitting there ahead of me and waiting until I came within range of his rope. Swerved and did the same every twenty yards. Way behind me, Hinx was yelling and cheering me on.

Which way to run? About fagged out, I decided on the buried city, sped toward the muddy mound covering it and jinked as I went. Sensed a hole in the mud and jumped in. And away I went. Thought for a moment I was going to drop clear to the other side of the planet, but then I hit something and was knocked out cold.

When I woke up, I knew I'd almost killed myself. Felt broken all over. Side of my head was wet and squashy.

Didn't care about any of it, didn't care if I died. Nothing interesting to live for anymore. I had gone on breathing all my life just so I could beat everybody else to Doubleluck, but my dream of fame had turned out to be a big sewer. I was ruined. Without a dream I couldn't keep going.

My head started spinning and I figured I was about to take the final trip every mortal takes when he's all done with living. Before I could decide whether or not I truly wanted to take the trip, I went out cold again.

This time when I woke up, it was with irritation that I wasn't dead. I was sore as a boil all over. Being alive was bad enough but when it hurt it was intolerable.

Everything around me was dust. I had entered the roof of a building and had fallen through to the basement. Some of the structure had kept its shape, though it was ancient, but the molecules had decayed, and when I came flying at it, the whole thing caved in.

I lay hating every second of my existence. "Stupid" was the best description of my ancestors, and no one would enjoy being the offspring of idiots. Not only had those people lived on one planet all their lives, they also lived in one place; like in this building. They tore up their world, made a smelly outhouse of it, and they saw to it that nobody could ever live on it again.

My eyes were red with grief, my belly was full of aching, my mind was only mean. "Hinx," I bellowed.

From far off came his blubbering reply. "Lone, sweet doll, little gal, you ain't dead like I figured. Should have known nothing could get the best of you."

I tossed and groaned some more. I could tell he was still tied to that rock, because I put a finger of force on him and tugged a bit. He didn't budge. If I pulled him hard he'd turn inside out and croak.

I touched the sore place on the side of my head. Felt squashy. Sensing it made me dizzy.

"Little sweetheart, tell me you're all right," Hinx yelled, and I answered under my breath.

"Go to hell. Everyone and everything, go to hell."

A patch of light showed far over my head. As I

blinked up at it, a dark shape blocked it out and a deep voice called down to me.

"Any time you're ready to get out of there, say the word and I'll toss down a rope."

Cunning, as usual, I said, "Need my mount to move. Hurt bad."

"You can talk, so you aren't too far gone. Wouldn't care either way, but when you come out of that hole you're coming on a rope. No room down there for a mount, anyway."

"Then don't aim to come," I said.

"That will solve my problem. Hope you don't change your mind." With that, Big Jak went away.

Talked to myself for a long time while I lay suffering. Would hate to die without getting even with him for ruining my life. It was his fault that Doubleluck turned out to be such a disappointment. I decided not to kill myself until I had tied him up in knots.

"Hey, up there," I yelled.

"What you want?"

"Throw me a rope."

The thing came hurtling at me. It landed about ten feet away and I had to crawl to reach it. Pulled it around my back and under my arms and tied it across my chest.

"You ready?" he called and without waiting to hear one way or another, he started pulling.

I hated high places. Shouldn't have looked down but I did and vertigo took hold of me. It got worse as I went higher. Stomach turned over and I threw up. My head finally came out of the hole, followed by the rest of me. Big Jak held his arm up in the air and I dangled like a leaf while he looked me over.

"Phew," he said.

I'd been ready and I felt happy as a bug when I let go with a roundhouse swing aimed straight at his mouth. Figured it would startle him enough to let go of the rope, which is what happened. My fist smacked his fat hole and his fingers opened. I lit on my feet and took off. Covered about ten yards before my head started whirling and I keeled over like dead meat.

Came to with Hinx licking my face. I looked up at the sky and immediately knew we were no longer on Doubleluck. Big Jak had ridden us out while I was unconscious.

"Where we at?" I whispered in Hinky's ear.

"Don't know. He shoved me into limbo right off and pulled me all the way while I was in a thousand pieces."

"You mean we're lost?"

He licked my ear in a soothing manner. "Reckon. He's mad at me now. I bit him."

"I got in the first lick. Expect to get some more before this is over."

"He'll probably take us to Bounding Winter."

"Not this time," I said. "We know about Doubleluck and now I realize he wants its whereabouts kept a secret."

"Then what's he going to do with us?"

"Kill us, maybe."

It was a lonesome planet we were on. Trees, short grass and ravines were about all I could see from where I lay convalescing. I was too sick to jink. Air jumped into the ravines and sneaked out murmuring and chuckling, and it took about five minutes of listening to it before I was spooked. There wasn't enough sunlight, either. Thin clouds skated everywhere and cut out most of the shine. The low breezes were rare and clammy.

For three or four days I lounged around recuperating from my head injury. There were six of us in the group, four people and two mounts: Hinx and Volcano, myself, Big Jak, the fellow who wore the funny metal hat on his head and an old geezer who lay with his face to the sky. That last one never shut his mouth; prayed continually.

After the third day, I wasn't allowed to get close to Hinx. He stayed on one side of the camp and I stayed on the other. Tied to a tree, my mount sat all day watching me. Once in a while Big Jak took him for a walk. I thought it was too bad Hinx wasn't one of those wild mounts who liked to chew up riders. He could have made a scramble of Big Jak. He stood about six feet high, weighed close to 1500 pounds, was black all over and had a mighty set of teeth. But he wouldn't really hurt anybody. He was like me, kept all his savagery in his mind and reasoned it out of his system because he wanted to be civilized.

The fellow with the funny hat was named Shaper. Shaper was born with something wrong in his head and never learned how to travel. This had embarrassed his parents so they dumped him in Bounding Winter. At the age of twelve, Shaper had been adopted by a loco traveler who'd skipped straightaway to a food planet and stopped long enough to stock up. Shaper wandered away to look at some rocks and when he returned to the orchard the traveler had gone. Either the fellow had forgotten his new son or had changed his mind about keeping him.

Shaper stayed on that planet for ten years. Fiddled around with things no decent jak would have wasted his time on. He built huge fires and burned whatever he could find, mostly rocks and chunks of lava. Eventually he began shaping the hot things and from there he went on to making metal hats.

One day another traveler picked him up and returned him to Bounding Winter. The custodians didn't want him because he was too old, so they asked him where he wanted to go. Shaper chose to live on a planet that was almost solid iron. He asked if he could have a mount and from somewhere they hauled in an old animal who was willing and whom no one else wanted. They stayed on the iron planet for five years and the old mount died. Not long after that, Big Jak picked Shaper up. This was the end of the story, at least it was all I could get out of either of them.

Shaper was cross-eyed and a giggler, but he was a quiet person, usually, and ordinarily I wouldn't have minded his company, but there was a certain side to his character that made him nearly impossible to tolerate. If you expected him to respond to your remarks, you had to accompany them with a kick to his rear, otherwise he wouldn't acknowledge your existence.

35

There was nothing wrong with his vision. It was simply that he had a brain like nobody else in the galaxy. Scrambled, I called it.

"Everything is funny, don't you see that?" he said to me once. He was rubbing his rear and looking at me from two directions.

"I don't."

"You would if you defined 'funny' the way I do, or if you liked laughing more than you liked crying."

"What you talking about?" I said.

"I don't think you're old enough to understand."

"Don't talk down to me, you gotch-eyed landlubber. Old enough to understand all there is and then some."

He wouldn't discuss Big Jak. I kicked his behind until I couldn't stand it anymore and gave up. It was plain that he regarded Big Jak as an idol, followed so close he tromped on Jak's heels and sometimes earned a kick in the pants that was unrelated to conversation.

I got so tired of listening to the old geezer—the other member of our party—moan and pray that I began to complain at the top of my lungs.

"Brought him here from limbo and am keeping him as a lesson to you," Big Jak told me.

"What can I learn from him driving me nuts?"

"If you don't find out then you're dumber than Shaper."

"No one's dumber than Shaper. But why is the old guy praying all the time? What's the matter with him?"

"He's dying, is all."

That set me back on my heels. I walked over to the old fellow and looked down at him. He must have been three hundred. All he wore was a piece of limp bark over his belly, and it looked older than he. He hadn't a hair on his head and his face was more creased than a dry creek bed. His body was bony and wasted, his teeth were rotten and his tongue was blue. Big wild eyes so alive they scared me rolled around in black sockets, and no matter how they tried they never focused on anything.

"Come on, Sonny, come on, Sonny, come on, Sonny,

we're almost there," he said in a high screech, and his skinny rump pumped as if it gripped a mount. "Almost there, I can practically see it, couple more short skips and we'll touch down on that ball of glory. Doubleluck, I'm comin', don't go away!"

"Why, he thinks he's traveling," I said in alarm, and behind me Big Jak answered.

"That's right. He's going out with his boots on."

"Dang you, that's cruel. Why don't you tell him the truth, that Doubleluck is nothing but a stinking hole?"

"You tell him."

Did. Knelt down and shook the old jak until he shut up.

"You don't want to grieve over that place, mister. Done found it and it isn't worth a' broken seashell. Whole legend is a big lie. Ain't no gold nor diamonds—"

Two skinny hands shot around my throat and the old guy tried to throttle me.

Big Jak pried his fingers loose, laid him back down on the ground and said in a loud voice, "I think it's in sight, old codger. Take a good look. Do you see it out there in the black? It's big and the glitter of it is enough to knock your eyes out. Think if you give that no-good mount under you a hard enough kick you'll land on your head on a pile of gold."

His words did the trick. The old jak stopped crying and started screeching again. "Come on, Sonny, come on, Sonny, come on. . . ."

I was disgusted enough to kick him but didn't because he was down and out. Knew I wouldn't be in a hurry the next time someone needed a favor. If the old nut wanted to croak believing a lie, that was his business. One thing I aimed to do was be around when he died. Never saw death happen before and was curious about it.

That night Big Jak piled up some sticks and built a fire in the middle of camp. We sat around it and after a while I lay down and dozed. Enjoyed looking at the flames, even though they were very much like an artifact. Big Jak entertained us by telling a story.

The story went something like this:

Once upon a time there were some people called

Nomads who liked to wander. Fiddlefoots, every one of them, and they were unhappy when they couldn't go any place at all that they felt like visiting or exploring.

One day a Nomad was standing on a big rock looking at the sky when a lightning bolt came down and hit him on the head. His brain wasn't damaged, in fact, it worked better than ever, and he found himself thinking things no Nomad had ever thought before. Right away he went back to his tribe and gathered a few of his most trusted and intelligent friends into his living circle and told them what had happened. He talked about all the strange ideas that had come to him. Some of his friends laughed and regarded what he said as a joke. Others were not so certain as to how they should respond. Maybe these had also felt some of the effects of the lightning bolt.

The ones who laughed went away, but the others stayed. Before the conversation was concluded, the Nomad's friends were convinced that he spoke the truth. They knew he was a prophet, knew it would be wise to listen to him. Unfortunately, they weren't wise. They went away and wasted their time wandering. The Nomad was left to handle the situation by himself. He went to his children and told them what he had learned.

The place where the Nomads lived was an island. When the fog wasn't too thick, they could sometimes see other faraway islands, but the fact was that a pit lay between their world and those distant places and there wasn't any way for them to get across it. The day would come when all the Nomads grew itchy for greener pastures. They would discover that the well of emptiness encircling their island was bottomless and impassable. They would realize that there were no more new places to visit. What was going to happen to them when they found this out? It was in the fiddlefoot's nature to wander, and fences were so offensive to him that if they weren't soon removed he might simply curl up and die.

The Nomad's children were young but they believed and understood their father. Not just one or two fiddlefoots were involved here. It was the entire species. The family discussed the problem for a long time and finally came to a decision. They would find a jewel and hide it and tell everyone of its existence but not of its whereabouts.

The family began their search and eventually they came upon a crystal ball in a place where they had once lived. They set up No Trespassing signs all around the ball, after which they went out into the world and told people to hunt for it because all knowledge would be theirs if they found it. Realizing that the signs might be disregarded by a few people, the family chose one of its members to stand watch over the crystal ball. No one must be allowed to trespass, because the virtue of the plan was in the hunting and not in the finding. Life was the purpose of it all. Nothing else mattered as long as the species didn't die like caged animals.

The first Watcher grew old and turned the job over to his son. And so it went, down through the ages. Many of the Nomads came to realize the enigma of the bottomless pit around their world, but it didn't sicken them because they were obsessed with finding the crystal ball and becoming omniscient. They never stopped looking for it, and they survived. Occasionally, some hardy but foolish soul would chuck everything and try to make it over to that other island beyond the fog. The death cries of such were heard all over the world. No one ever succeeded in making that journey. The pit was too deep, too fearsome, too unknown.

To this day a Watcher stands guard beside the crystal ball. A descendant of that ancient Nomad, this new fellow is the worst kind of fiddlefoot and is busting his gut to try for that new frontier across the bottomless pit. Soon he will chuck everything and make his try. And woe to the Nomad who tries to get ahead of him.

That was the story Big Jak told us. I thought it was pretty good. Fell asleep thinking about it.

The next morning I began drifting around to hunt for something that might help me escape from the planet. There wasn't much to find. It was a poor world I was on. Without Hinx I was on my own, and walking was hard work.

Did find one thing interesting, and I stuck to it longer than I either planned or wanted to. On the other side of a low ridge lay a culvert and I slid down the slope and walked along the bottom. Found a strange-looking object at a bend in the trail. Prettiest thing I ever saw. It was a strip of glittering blue substance that looked like ice. Not more than half an inch thick, this strip reached halfway up the embankment, and I fell for it as soon as I saw it.

Instead of giving it a quick jink, or at least feeling it with a finger or toe, I dropped right down astraddle of it and laid a good section of my tongue on it. I had already seen how clean it looked, also I knew it was cold because it gave off an icy aura. Anyhow, I started to take a big lap and found myself stuck fast. Whatever the blue slab was, it had no relation to ice. It wasn't even cold. My tongue felt as if it lay on a dry burr.

There was only so much twisting I could do without damaging my tongue, and before long I hunkered soremouthed and exhausted over the alien strip that held me prisoner. No matter what I did, I stayed fastened as securely as ever.

I got to wondering how thick the top layer of a human tongue was. If I yanked free, I might lose too much meat. On the other hand, I didn't want to stay there forever. Tried yanking and quickly gave up that idea. It hurt too much.

I tried yelling, learned how necessary a tongue was for a healthy bellow, and then I grabbed some tough grass and tried rubbing that against the spots where my flesh and the slab made contact. All I got out of the effort was a dirty mouth.

By the time Big Jak came up behind me and spoke, I was desperate.

"What you doing there?" he said, and I leaped with fright and then tried to howl as pain stabbed through my tongue.

"Damn it," I said, but nobody could have understood it.

"Every time I turn around, you're up to something unusual," said Big Jak. He stayed behind me so I couldn't see him.

"Get me loose," I yelled.

"Can't figure out what you're saying. Sounds as if you don't want to be bothered. Suit yourself. I don't want to interfere with your pleasure."

"You son of a skunk, get your bucket back here and get me off this thing."

"One thing I ought to tell you, though. I think that's a sucker, and if I was you I wouldn't hang around it too long. It'll take the water out of you pretty damn quick. Of course, you need water to get away from it. You have to pour it all over your tongue and it'll come free right away. Reckon you got a water pouch with you, although I don't see one anywhere around."

Mostly I wanted to be free at that moment so I could kill him.

"Remember one time I seen a fella after a sucker got done with him. Looked like a mummy. You ever see a mummy? They got some on a place called Gelsenar, found 'em in a hole in the ground. They're all shrunk and dried out. Time did that to 'em. Their fluid evaporated. Makes us people sound like puddles, don't it? I mean, we just give off juice like . . . oh, well, no need me crippling the subject. I'll just leave you to your fun."

"Damnit," I yelled.

"You shouldn't have your tail stuck up so high. The sun will burn that lanion skin away and then you're going to get a sunburn. But it don't matter to me what you do, except I can't figure out why you didn't just lay down beside that sucker if you thought you couldn't survive without a lick. Well, so long."

"Damn it."

He sat down on the incline beside me. I could see one of his hands. I longed to bite it.

"You learn anything from that little story I told last night?"

I said the same thing I had been saying all along.

"That story was a parable and anyone didn't understand it was a dumbbell, which naturally you aren't. I know you learned from it, know you're mulling it over in your mind, trust you bear no hard feelings toward me in case there was something I could have done for you but neglected to do."

He went away then. Yes, he really did. Left me with my tongue stuck solid, and no matter how I yammered he didn't come back to get me out of my fix.

Nothing for me to do but crouch over the slab and wait for it to drain me of my body fluids. Toward evening I became too tired to crouch anymore. Lay all the way down on that sucker and relaxed. With one cheek flat on the blue slab and my tongue twisted nearly out of its socket, I quit worrying and got ready to die. Felt completely dried out. In a few more hours there wouldn't be an ounce of juice left in me.

Learned something when the sun went down. The blue slab was really called a sucker, and it would have been difficult to find a better name for the thing. Humans were a curious lot and a sucker was a human who relied on half his brain instead of the whole organ. Anyone who stuck his tongue on a blue chunk just because it looked like ice was a sucker.

The moment the sun dropped behind the horizon, the blue slab let me go. It was a plant and at sundown it quit its daily activities and went to sleep. I didn't know what other activities it engaged in besides luring in suckers, and I never found out since that was the last time I ever went near one.

"Come on, Sonny, come on, Sonny, come on. . . ."

The old jak hadn't shut his mouth for days, but the second I walked back into camp, he shut it.

The sudden silence startled me so that I stumbled. A big cool drink and sadistic revenge had been on my mind. I'd been wondering what would be the worst thing I could do for all concerned, but the abrupt quiet in the camp drove anything and everything from my head.

That old jak looked odd as he lay on the ground. His body was splayed out like a limp poke and his eyes were round moons fastened on the sky. Again I stumbled and this time I fell. On my hands and knees, I started crawling toward him.

"Hold on, jak," I said. "Don't do it. I didn't mean what I said before. Don't want to see you die. Can't stand thinking on it. Nobody ought to croak. Ain't civilized."

I didn't realize I was yelling until someone took me by the collar and lifted me off the ground. "Stop him, don't let him do it," I screeched, and big gouts of water broke from my eyes.

"Shut up and let him go in peace," Big Jak said in my ear.

"No, no, no—" A hand clamped over my mouth.

Nothing but eyes and horror now, I watched the old jak. He was about to die and I was learning a lesson. Hadn't wanted to believe death existed, wanted to be a million light-years from that spot, couldn't move because Big Jak held me fast.

The old fella made no sound, but every fiber of his body became active. Aboard an imaginary mount, he lay on the ground and rode like an eager child and his hips and shoulders gouged shallow pits in the dirt. His mouth wide in a silent howl, he kept it up, kept on going, rode, rode, endlessly rode right there on the ground, and all at once he wasn't lying on the ground anymore but hovered a foot above it, and then he was two feet above it, and still he rode like that eager youngster until it seemed as if his jerks and spasms would cause him to fly to pieces. And so he did, but how gradually this was accomplished. He rode his nowhere mount and he rose higher into the air and his body became misty and changed from flesh color to a faded blue. He grew more misty and spread out in space until he was fifteen feet wide, then twenty, then fifty, and he wasn't blue any longer but a sparkling silver. The silver particles began to scatter. He no longer resembled a solid mortal. Now he was a cloudy traveler who was about to skip to D-2.

Thousands of little twinkling bits of light were all that was left of the old jak, and in a few moments these too flew away straight toward the stars.

Chapter V

Shaper looked at me and the mountains at the same time. "Don't want to talk about star-hopping. It's a game I never indulged in. Matter of fact, you won't be indulging in it anymore, either. Big Jak aims to keep you here."

I ran around him and kicked his rear. "Say that again."

"You're dangerous to humanity."

"What kind of talk is that?" I yelled. I turned and looked across the clearing. "What's he putting all those little trees together for? Is he making a box? What's going to end up inside that box? And if you say me I'll kick your behind off. He can't do this. Kidnapping is against the law."

"What law?"

"There's law everywhere."

"But not here," said Shaper. "I wish you wouldn't get so emotional. That never helps."

"You're wrong, as usual. It does help. It'll help me kill you and that lying skunk."

"Unfortunately, you never learned any culture. Any lowlife can cuss and threaten, but they always end up in a ditch somewhere."

"I already been there and didn't like it." I turned away from him and marched across the clearing. As I went, I watched Big Jak from the corner of my eye. His back stayed toward me and I began to breathe easier.

Volcano was flat on his back, snoring up a storm, his belly to the sun. He got my foot in his ribs.

"Up, dang you," I said, and when he rolled over I slid into place.

I took a grab at his mind.

Sleepily, he said, "Who's that?"

"What's the difference? Now we meld."

"We do?"

Again I grabbed for his mind. Once I had it, I'd take him a far piece. Hinx would just have to wait here until I had a chance to pick him up.

"Oh, Big Jak, look here and see what the little gal is up to," called Shaper in a high voice.

Kicking Volcano in the sides, I yanked his head hair and grasped his mind like it was a chunk of D-3. At least I thought I had done the grasping. The next thing I knew that big mount dropped his rump and bucked hard. I went flying, not in heavy air but through a hollow hole of D-2. He was a very practiced animal, did what he did with very little effort. I went a short distance all by myself. In a frenzy I swarmed back into 3, found myself about fifteen feet above a tree, after which I did what came naturally. I dropped like a rock.

Hinx comforted me by licking my face.

"You were going to run out on me," he said.

I sat up. "Yeah."

"Why don't you go talk it over with Big Jak? Maybe he isn't as unreasonable as we think."

"Did you ever hear of a mount as mean as that gray?"

"Once in a while. I guess he bruised your feelings by not cooperating."

"No, he didn't bruise my feelings." I looked at the tree Hinx was tied to. It wasn't much of a tree, young and kind of spindly. The rope on my mount's neck was a thick vine. He had been chewing at one spot on it for as long as we'd been on this planet but I couldn't see any teeth marks unless I squinted.

"Remember Bounding Winter?" I said, and he rolled his eyes. "Remember that thing called a fence that you dragged out of the ground as we skipped?"

Turning his belly to the sun, Hinx stretched out to his full length. "I feel a pain in the neck coming on."

"From now on we play things crafty. I'm going to

loosen the roots of that tree. Might take a long time doing it. A sharp rock ought to help and I'll cover up my digging signs so that big outlaw won't catch on."

"You realize what shape we'll be in if the tree stays in the ground when we skip?"

"I'd rather be dead than stuck in this place forever. Figure you would be, too."

He wasn't quick to agree. In fact, he never said anything at all and that irritated me. I wandered away to wash off in the creek, which was so shallow it was beginning to stink.

For the first time in my life I felt like an orphan. What was more, I was an orphan with brutal caretakers. Shaper was too dumb not to be brutal. He could have helped me get away but his mind was filled with admiration for Big Jak. I knew without a doubt that he wasn't being admired back. Jak didn't care a bean for Shaper, was simply using the poor fool, but how and why I didn't know.

"You ought to see to your bruises," a voice said behind me.

I didn't turn around, just kept washing my feet in the creek.

"There's a plant looks a bit like a sucker growing over yonder. It's yellow instead of blue, and if you were to bare your hide and lay it on that plant it would suck out the ruptured blood. It's called a vampire stick."

"Don't have any bruises," I said.

"Your backside and belly must be purple, and the vampire stick is what you need."

Turned my head and gave him a long look. It was frustrating to be full of venom and not have any fangs handy. I didn't allow my anger to show; matched his calm. That was one of the things I admired about him. No matter what butchery he was up to, he wore a lean and riotless face.

I sat looking at him and wondered if I could sneak up on him in the dark some night and brain him with a rock. It didn't seem possible, since he seemed to be alert and alive in every part of his body and was probably that way even when asleep. He had one foot propped on a stump and a hand hung over his knee. It was a big hand and brown as a nut.

"Suit yourself," he said. "Keep your bruises and your bullheadedness. Right here you'll stay until you learn—"

"Lie to Shaper but you needn't waste your breath on me. You don't care what I learn or don't learn."

He didn't look at me, just came over and sat down beside me and stuck his feet in the creek. "Know you don't trust me."

I didn't say anything and a long time went by before he spoke again.

"Lone is no fit name for anyone. Think I'll call you Jade. Will that be all right?"

I didn't answer. What a dumb name.

"I'm a loner myself, except that sometimes I get fed up with it and wish I had a partner; someone who doesn't talk too much or complain about the weather. Never did have a friend to ride with. Sometimes I wish I had. Maybe I'd have learned how to be sociable."

He pulled his feet out of the water and examined them. "Never went back on my word, except when it was necessary. It was necessary for me to keep you away from Doubleluck and after that story I told you, you know why. Took you to Bounding Winter because that was the first idea popped into my head. People are going to die by the hordes, once the secret of Doubleluck is out. That's my guess. Don't want them to find out yet because I've discovered something that might save them."

I didn't know what he was talking about. I really didn't. Later I realized the full extent of what he was saying, but right then I was in the dark and sulking. Wanted him to go away. Didn't want to listen to him, as everything he said sounded earnest and true. He had a way of talking that always lured me in and left me dangling in confusion.

"The world is insane, you know that?" he said. "By 'world' I mean the galaxy. It's insane because it's full of jaks who have no sense. You take those men who started the whole thing on Doubleluck; they had com-

47

mon sense because they were stuck on that world. Couldn't go anywhere, so they created a small insanity, which was better than the big one we have. Doubt if any of those men committed suicide because they couldn't cross an ocean. You take jaks, they evolved toward hedonism; wanted the easy way all the time. Didn't like responsibility and didn't stop to think it was sheerly a lazy way of thinking. Nowadays, if jaks can't go where they want to go, they get sick. Like you, for instance. I'm keeping you here and you're getting to look more peaked every day. Worrying about you. I built a box as a lesson to you. Want you to imagine having to live in that box. Would scatter your mind, for certain. Only you don't have to live in it. You can have this whole planet. Or any other empty one that you choose."

He got up and went away and I was left to wonder and worry. What had he been talking about?

I went off to watch Shaper play with his artifacts. That maniac had dug a great pile of dirt. A big piece of curved tree bark lay propped on two rocks, one end lower than the other. The reason why the creek was so low was because Shaper was draining it for his games. He had got hold of a long tube plant, stuck an end of it in the creek, sucked the other end for a while and then the creek water began running up through the tube plant into the curved piece of bark. It ran down the bark into a hole in the ground, along with piles of dirt. Every once in a while, Shaper scooped out the stuff at the bottom of the hole and washed it all over again.

He had a big fire going and had built a box of rocks in the middle of the flames. After the heavy dirt had cooked a long time, it got hard and Shaper would dump it out on the ground and pound it with stones. Hats were what he was making. They were strewn all over the place, about two dozen of them. What he did was finish a hat, examine it, cuss a while, throw it away and begin making another one.

"You're one crazy man," I said, after I kicked his rear.

"So is a vark," he said with a grin. "Say, gal, what kind of a mount is that Hinx?"

48

"What you mean?"

"He cranky?"

"No."

"Good and obedient?"

"Good enough for me. What's it any of your business?"

Again he grinned. "Need him, is why."

This time I kicked him for pleasure. "I don't think that was exactly plain, but don't matter. You can't ride him. You can't ride any mount."

"That's because of celestial static. With the right kind of hat, I'll ride. Why do you think I'm working so hard? Think I like staying in one place all the time? I'm a jak, as much as anyone. Been going nuts all my life, but that's about to end. I'm going to glory."

"What's celestial static?"

"Don't know, except that it's there and it interferes with my jink so bad I can't skip. Matter of fact, it's the reason why no jak can skip across the— Oh, well, never mind that, it's off the subject. Only I was wondering if you taught that mount of yours to buck strangers."

Now it was my turn to grin. "Hope you don't try to find out by skipping him. Be too bad if you got a good foothold in limbo, because I'd be stuck here, unable to help you, and I have the idea Big Jak would only sit on his lumps and shake his head in sorrow. Shows you what kind of friends you have."

Wandered away, picked up a hat from the ground, laughed in contempt, jammed the thing onto my head, yelled at Shaper to look at me, danced around and made faces at him, finally got tired and tried to pull the hat off my head, felt the rough sides dig into the meat above my ears. . . .

Couldn't get it off. The hat was stuck on my head. Started screaming because every bit of jink I owned was gone, like it had never existed.

No matter what I did and no matter how many times I tried to get it off, the hat seemed to be on my head to stay. It wasn't funny, and I didn't hear anyone laughing. At first, Big Jak watched me with a thunderstruck look on his face, but after a while he wandered away and I didn't see him again for hours.

Shaper tried to help me. Once in a while, when I cried, he cried, too. Looking at his silly, solemn face, I knew he was probably the only human friend I had in the world, which wasn't saying much, as he never changed his manner for anybody, was sympathetic or critical or serious-sweet toward all, depending on his internal whim.

"You're one strange jak now," he said to me. "Nothing is leaking from your head. What I mean is—"

"Shut your mouth."

"Yes, I guess you already know your head is empty. There's nothing in you now to approach. If I were to meet you somewhere for the first time I'd swear you were just wearing human clothes. It's a good thing I already know you, otherwise I'd get away from you and stay away."

At the moment I was lying on my back glaring at the sky and waiting for the sun to dry my soggy face. "You have a rotten nerve. You're the reason I'm lying here wishing for death." I moved my hand, grasped Hinx's nose. He wasn't tied up now. There was no need for it. No communication between us was possible. About all Hinx did these days was crawl around on his belly and whine. Whenever I wanted to find him, I looked for big scraped paths in the dirt.

"That mount is going to go out of his mind if he doesn't open up to someone," said Shaper.

Squeezing my mount's nose, I said, "Leave him be."

"He can't understand what happened unless somebody tells him, but no one can do that if he won't open his mind, at least for a few seconds. What I can't figure out is why he still hangs around you."

"Loves me, that's why. Doesn't care if I'm not broadcasting jak personality. He knows what I am."

For hours on end I would lie with my head on the side of my mount and try to talk to him. I could think, talk with my mouth and dream, but there was no jink in me. The thoughts or intents of others could be conveyed to me only by voice or action or facial expression. I was a closed circuit where reality was concerned. I still felt pretty much the same, except for the sensation that a piece of meat in my head had

50

gone stone-cold asleep. Though I nudged that piece continually, I remained what I was. And I was no jak.

I spoke aloud to Hinx, and he whimpered. His belly heaved, he raised his head, licked my neck, stared at me with stricken eyes and once more subsided to doze, dream and stay miserable along with me.

Big Jak. I hated him more than I hated Shaper. He was the real reason why I had turned into two-thirds of a whole. It was his fault that I had a bloody neck and an aching skull. The metal hat wasn't too heavy. Thankfully, it was one of the thin ones. The sample on my crown weighed about three pounds, was little more than a slice of bent metal. But jagged. A lump inside pressed against the top of my head, and as time went by, the feel of that lump almost sent me out of my mind. What hurt now were the sides of the hat above my ears where the thing gripped hard and held me prisoner. Those sides were charred and irregular. I had cuts running all around my skull because I'd shoved and pulled in the beginning, so frantic was I to get the hat off.

The only comfortable position I could find was lying on my back with my neck propped on Hinx's side.

Big Jak finally got around to trying to get the hat from my head. "Don't think it's possible," he said at last.

"I guessed you'd say that."

"Try jinking a star."

"Can't even jink my mount, and he's right here."

"See if you can make a snake out of your jink. Dip it toward the ground and then curl it upward."

I howled. "Don't have a bit of jink. Can't find it to curl it."

"Quit crying."

"Trade places with me and see if you smile."

"No need looking at me like that. All I ever did to you was wonder how you got born."

"Same as you and everybody got born. My folks found me under a lanion pod. Didn't like the looks of me, I guess, so to the Ridge Cluster I went, but they were better with me than you. They didn't try to kill me."

"What I think," he said, "is that you have to stop

51

pulling on that hat. Those cuts over your ears look pretty deep."

"Maybe they'll fester and then my head will drop off, and since all I care about is getting rid of the hat . . ."

He went away and didn't come back. That evening I watched him over the campfire. Think he would have gone nuts if he couldn't build a fire every day of his life.

For the first time, I realized how seldom jaks looked at each other with their eyes. That was the only kind of sight I had, at the moment, so I used it to examine my kidnapper. Without jink, I was able to see every bit of what showed, but nothing of what was hidden. It was strange to discover how much Big Jak existed on his outside. I had jinked him before but hadn't gotten much of anything other than a sensation of deep water with a slow-moving surface. That was what Big Jak had meant to me before. Now, with my eyes and my mutilated perception, I saw a very odd person.

He weighed in the neighborhood of three hundred pounds and stood eight feet tall, which made him a bit bigger than most adults. Kind of long and lanky in build, though he had big bones, he walked in a sleepy way with his hands held slightly out from his sides, as if he were getting ready to choke something. Maybe he always had the feeling that an enemy was coming at him.

His black lanion skin matched his hair, which had no wave or curl and grew wild and shiny. Though I couldn't see much of his body, I knew the hair on his head was the only place he had any, other than over his eyes. No jak had hair anywhere else on him. Big Jak's face was as smooth as mine, but mine didn't resemble a mean bird's, as his did. His yellow eyes, bushy brows, wild hair, cruel jaw, drooping nose and high cheekbones made his an interesting, forbidding appearance. His hands held an attraction for me. Bony and brown, they reminded me of powerful animals. I could imagine how warm and fatal they would feel as they took me by the throat.

And then there was Shaper. Seen with my new

eyes, he had scarcely any personality. Viewed with jink, he was a foolish, skitterish person who kept a little hunk of his self buried under a rock. The rock in Shaper was easy to see with jink, and the seer naturally opted to peek under it to see what he was hiding. Didn't know if anyone had ever succeeded. I failed, both with and without jink. To the naked eye, Shaper was a well-built jak, nearly as tall as our big-skunk acquaintance. Shaper's hair was soft and sandy in color. It didn't fly wild, but lay on his shoulders without protest.

I was amazed to discover how pretty his face was. All his features were straight and gentle. That was fine. All well and good. But then Shaper had eyes, too, and this was where he dropped out of the human race. His eyes were big and blazing blue and so crossed . . . well, looking at people's eyes was a normal pastime, and every so often you flicked a glance at each one. Shaper was nobody to do that with, because when you did, each of your own eyes matched his, and you stood there being as crossed as he. Every time I did it, I got mad.

It took me about a week to accept my situation. After that, there were no more tears, only regret, despair and flashes of panic.

"Nobody will ever interfere with my life again," I said that night. We sat by the fire, the three of us. Hinx crouched behind me and Volcano hunched behind Big Jak. The mounts eyed each other with hatred. As for us humans, we looked at the ground, the dark sky, empty space, anywhere but at each other.

I continued. "I'm a crippled jak. Like Shaper, only worse off. At least he can communicate with mounts. I can't do that, can't do much of anything, which means I won't stay around where people are. The way I see it, this hat is going to be on my head all my life."

Hinx stuck his nose against my back and I shivered. I was cold and no campfire would ever warm me up.

"You two can do whatever you like with me, but I'll ask one last favor. Take me to Earth and leave me. Of all the worlds in the galaxy, I belong on that one.

Inferior jaks lived there and I feel like I want to go back to the starting place."

I didn't care if they took me to Earth or dropped me in a bottomless pit. I simply knew I was in their way and that they couldn't go on about their business until they disposed of me. The planet Earth was the first place that popped into my mind.

"I don't know about leaving you all alone," said Shaper.

"All of us have always been alone. If one place was dangerous or a disappointment, we skipped to another. I can move from place to place on Earth by walking or running. What's the difference? There's little that's dangerous in that stinkhole, and now that I've no jink, any place will be a disappointment."

"Hmmm. Big Jak, what do you think?"

"Don't ask him," I said. "I just want you both to do as I asked and draw this thing out no further. I'm tired and want to go home."

"What about your mount?" said Shaper.

Big Jak spoke. "You know how naive mounts are, always believing anything a jak tells them, and how willing they are to pair off with anyone. Her mount has more brains than most. He won't trust you or me. At least I got that much out of him. He says he won't part with her."

"He can't stay with me," I said.

"He says he will."

"Tell him to go to hell. It's a mount's nature to be one with a jak. I can't give him anything."

Hinx went with me, after all. They tied him to a tree and he yanked so hard the vine broke. They tied him again and this time he pulled the tree out of the ground. Big Jak lassoed him. He came charging and Big Jak let go of the vine and ran, but not before he got bitten on the rear. Like a burr that couldn't be picked off, Hinx tagged along with me, and I was glad of it, though I felt sorry for him.

"Maybe I'll come back one day and see if he's changed his mind," said Big Jak.

The yellow sun of Earth beat on our heads. The gray mountains stretched around us, and a chill wind swept over the ground and froze my soul. I had ridden Hinx while Big Jak shared his pocket of atmosphere with us and pulled us through space. For me, the trip had been big and blank.

Now, straddling my mount, I blinked at the sky and wondered if I were going to bawl.

"Good-bye," I said.

"I'm sorry, girl."

"Your secret about this old dump is safe. That's all you wanted, and now you have it."

"There are lots of things I want, but I won't harm a child to get them."

"I hope I never see you again."

He held out his hand. I let it hang in the air without taking it. After a while, he dropped it. "This is proof that the human race went wrong somewhere," he said. "There isn't a handful of jaks in the galaxy knows how to cut that hat off your head. We have nothing but our appetites. Some day we'll pay for our stupidity."

I kicked Hinx in the side and we turned and walked away. "Don't come back," I said over my shoulder. "We don't need you. From now on, we're by ourselves. We're Earthmen and this is our property. Don't trespass."

Chapter VI

That night I lay on a sandy beach by an ocean and counted stars. By and by, Hinx crawled close to me. Huddled against his big body, I patted his face, whispered to him, told him all my regrets. I had more fear for him than for myself, felt I could take anything fate had to offer. As for my mount, I wasn't so sure. Nature was a thing that couldn't be changed. It was a one-track road that had no detours or forks. If Hinx went out of his mind, I'd have to put him out of his misery, and if I did that I'd be compelled to do the same to myself.

Big Jak had taken us to a semitropical zone, which was all to the good, since I hadn't enough sense to get in out of the rain. No jak really had that kind of intelligence. It was easier to skip elsewhere than to stay in an unpleasant situation.

The roar of the surf got on my nerves, but I didn't travel inland because there were too many trees to close me in. The openness of the beach had more appeal. Hinx and I went hungry until a fish flopped onto the sand and got stuck there. I had never eaten fish before, but I did that day. So did Hinx, and he liked it no more than I.

We tried the trees. And found fruit. And an odd rock sticking out of the dirt. It was shiny and smooth and rectangular, too smooth for my liking. It had to be an artifact. To one side of it was a hole in the ground, about five feet deep. At the bottom was another shiny block.

I didn't know much about Earth, despite the fact that I had jinked it before. Things far away, like space debris, were easy to read, at least where general descriptions were concerned. A jak could tell how far away a heavenly body was, could come close to knowing its exact mean temperature and the position of its satellites, et cetera. Grounded, a jak could penetrate only several miles of a world. The sky was something else. That was truly jak territory.

So, even if I'd had jink at that moment, I couldn't have said what lay on the other side of the planet. I had no jink, however, and couldn't read around the nearest tree.

Constantly looking around to see if Hinx was following me made for a strained neck, so I stopped doing it. Like me, he was on his own. We were together but separated, the same as ordinary men and dogs had been long ago. I would come to know why those early people and their canine friends had chosen to be with one another. Now it didn't matter. Nothing would warm the cold lump of fear in my mind. There was no real companionship for me. I loved Hinx and liked looking at him, but I couldn't talk to him, and that was that.

The moon was a yellow gourd in a black field. It was so bright and lonesome, sailing up there at night. Every evening I looked at it until I began shivering, every night I prayed for it to disappear, always I commanded the lights in the sky to take me away. Hinx watched the stars, too. At first, he did nothing but whine. Night after night he slept, dreamed, grew more restless. He took to licking my face until I woke up and patted him back to sleep. He lost weight. I stuffed him with fruit and nuts, made him eat every fish that foundered on the shore or brained itself on rocks. A stone jetty stuck out into the ocean, and I sat on it for hours and hauled in crabs, which I fed to my mount. None of it did any good. He grew thinner and lost his enthusiasm for life.

"Here's where we part company," I said one morning. I'd had enough of watching him die before my eyes. "You made up your mind to croak. Do it by yourself. Good-bye. And one last word to you: I'm ashamed of you for giving up so easily. We only been here a month."

He lay on the sand and watched me go.

"Good-bye," I said again. He didn't move. I marched into the trees and kept marching. He didn't come after me. It was dark in the woods, the kind of dark that seeped into the soul because you knew you had nothing and no one in all the universe but yourself. I wanted to run back to my mount, throw my arms around his neck and bawl my eyes out. Instead, I made myself walk deeper into the woods. What I was walking away from was surrender. My life was all I had. I wouldn't let it go down the drain with Hinx.

There was no sun in the woods, no sky, no space stretching on all sides of me. I felt hemmed in by a circle of ghosts. What would I do with my life, and what was it worth to me?

That night I built a fire, as Big Jak had always done. He had seemed to do it because he liked it, but my reason was to keep away the ghosts. Maybe that had been Big Jak's real reason, too.

Sitting with my back against a tree, I stared at the flames and thought about my ancestors. They had wanted to travel to far places so badly that their bodies gradually altered to accommodate them. Their desire must have been fierce. Or maybe it was simply the presence of the stars overhead. If a place existed, it had to be explored by those who knew of it.

Again I asked the question: What will I do with my life?

In the morning, I walked farther inland. The jungle had encroached upon everything, so I made slow time. Standing on a hill, I could see the ocean, so blue and sparkling in the distance that it looked like a huge jewel. The sky was pale in comparison to that great slab of water.

I made myself a house. It was such a disgusting idea and so unlike anything I wanted to do, and that was why I did it. I wanted to be like an Earthman, otherwise I would die.

My house was built in an open field. It was made with small logs and mud. The first time it rained, the whole house fell down. Next time, I scooped out trenches and laid heavier logs for a base.

After the house was done, I couldn't go in it. I slept

in trees or on the ground beside a fire, but I couldn't make myself walk into my house.

The leaves of the roof dried out and crumbled, blew away in the wind. The sun baked the mud, made it crack, but the house stood. One day I went inside and built a fire in the middle of the dirt floor. Smoke drove me out. I took down a wall and put it up again but left a small opening in a corner. Most of the smoke from my new fire drifted through the doorway. This made me think of drafts and wind pressure. I made a coned wall of stones and mud that reached from floor to ceiling. Clearing away a section of roof above the cone, I built a fire on the floor, inside the cone. The smoke went up it and out through the roof.

Again I slept outside. The next day, I gathered grass and scattered it on the floor of my house. In one corner I made a bed of straw.

Still, I slept outside. I was afraid to go in the thing I'd built. In the morning, I found a small, furry animal nesting in my bed. I chased it out and built a fire in front of the doorway.

It rained hard that night. A chill breeze swept from the ocean and froze my bones. In a tree, I hunched and shivered, finally climbed down and went in my house. It was dry and warm and I fell asleep thinking of Hinx. I would never go back to the beach. I didn't want to look at his bones. Normally, he would have died in space. Some jak would have sent him off to the stars in a billion particles, and Hinx would have died happy and traveling. Now he rotted on an alien shore like a chunk of meat, with nobody to mark his grave. I would die likewise. An Earthman was I, and a dog was Hinx, and we would return to the dust that bore us.

The hardest lesson I ever learned was that men and jaks had the same personality. Under the skin, we were two of a kind. My reaction, when I finally and reluctantly realized the truth, was probably similar to that of a twentieth-century man when he dug up an artifact that proved to him the Cro-Magnon was as intelligent as he.

How could twentieth-century man be as bright as

I? He had been moldering in the ground for two million years, he had been a landlubber, his miserable spaceships rattled to the edge of the solar system and fell apart, he made artifacts to kill his own kind, he cried his way to eternity and blamed God for every bit of it.

All these things I learned, some later, but some when I found another shiny stone that led down into a buried building. Twentieth-century man was long gone, but his relics were in the building. Some generation of my ancestors had built a museum and dedicated it to their forefathers.

Looking at the man and woman in the glass room scared me. Their eyes stared into me as if they knew I was there and hated me. They were so strange. I was more interested in the woman. Nobody would ever have doubted her gender, even if she had been heavily clothed.

Jak women had breasts but they were nonexistent in comparison with this woman's. A jak chest was almost the same, male or female, and the rest of their bodies was similarly proportioned. Half the time we didn't know what we were talking to, unless we used jink, and I don't think many did that. The issue wasn't an issue. It was irrelevant. As for love and sex, I knew nothing about it, had never known and never wondered. I thought everybody was found under a lanion pod.

The man and woman encased in glass had body hair, especially the man. And how small and dainty they were. Already, at fourteen, I was much larger and stronger than they were. I had come from such people and I didn't look much like them. These two stood like statues with their sides touching and their hands entwined. Unity was the impression they created. My forebears hadn't sailed off in every direction, one by one. They had gone two by two. I didn't think they would have approved of jaks.

Since I wasn't an adult, I couldn't compare our skulls, but I was curious to know if the jak brain was larger than the human brain. Surely the ability to jink made a difference somewhere in our bodies, and most likely it was in the head.

Here were the preserved bodies of two little people without whom I might never have existed. They hadn't been stupid. They could read and write, while I could do neither. Never had I heard of a jak who kept records of anything. Whatever we knew resided in our heads and our posterity learned by word of mouth or by experience. At that moment, I couldn't have said which was the better way.

Man loved art. To me, this was incomprehensible. Why paint images on canvas? Such an endeavor consumed time and the painter necessarily remained stationary. Why carve things in stone or rock? Why make indelible comments such as these? Was it for the same reason that the scattering of footprints on the moon were encased in glass, like a shrine, and inscribed with man's writing? Man had stepped on the moon, he had made pictures and statues, he had thrown machinery into the sky around his world. Always he spoke through the medium of his peculiar artifacts. Always he had something clasped in his hand. He seemed to say, "God forgot to include something when he made me. Maybe this thing I hold is it."

I regretted that I couldn't read. The history of my forebears was in that underground museum. There was a map showing how Earth looked in those early days, and there were others that pointed out how the planet's geography had been altered by stress. One odd thing I learned was that man had been very exact about giving names to different land masses. The museum itself was buried in a piece called Texas. All the peninsulas south of the border had broken off and either drifted or crumbled to sink in the ocean. Now the land of Earth was a single chunk and formed an apron for the North Pole. Water and islands made up the lower half of the sphere. The equatorial water along the world's shore line was warm but it was cold several miles out and frozen solid where it approached the South Pole.

The map of the world, as it was now, caught and held my interest. I knew about earthquakes and supposed those had much to do with the continental shifts. Asia hadn't moved from its former position.

Australia and South America occupied what had once been the North Pacific Ocean. Africa was situated between North America and Europe. The shiftings must have occurred more than a million years after the twentieth-century. Why later man placed such significance upon that century wasn't clear to me until I took a good look at the metal capsule in the back of the glass-walled room. Twentieth-century man was the beginning of the Jakalowar: "He who races with the stars." Man, in that tiny capsule, had tumbled and revolved far beyond the boundaries of his world. He had drifted in and out of clouds of space debris, viewed his sun through the vacuum of the outer limits, spied beckoning suns with an unfettered eye.

What did it matter to me? I was Jakalowar and no relative of that hairy little man and woman. I could have broken them both in two with my bare hands. Had the iron hat not been on my head, I could have skipped to galaxy's edge with no more than a thought. To the man and woman, I would have been a god.

I went back to my house, lay on my bed of straw and thought about what I had seen. My soul soured overnight. Maybe I never should have looked at the artifacts in the underground building. They symbolized fences, and these were intolerable to jaks.

Morning came, I awoke and knew I was sick. I opened my eyes and realized I couldn't move. Lethargy was a cumbersome weight that pressed me into the straw. I tried to eat some fruit. The thought sickened me. Sweat was a clammy gown on my skin. I was human, but I was a jak human. I couldn't go back to the past, didn't want to go back, only wanted to go forward with the freedom of eternity stretching out around me.

Even that first day I lost weight. Sickness invaded my mind. Whatever had afflicted Hinx had now attacked me, and it wasn't physical disease. Jaks simply didn't get sick that way, otherwise, there wouldn't have been any jaks anywhere. The survival of the fittest had been our way for so long that it had become a self-evident truth. My illness was of the mind or spirit. Though the temperature outside my house was very warm, I felt cold. Fever made me tremble.

Crawling about to gather the necessaries, I built a fire in my makeshift stove. Toward noon, I fell asleep. It was dark when I woke up. The house was thick with smoke. Wishing I hadn't come to consciousness, I crawled outside and coughed until my lungs cleared.

In the morning, I forced myself to enter the smoke-filled house and examine the chimney. Somehow, leaves and twigs had gotten jammed into a wad in it and the smoke couldn't get through. I poked with a stick until the wad loosened. It fell into the flames to burn.

Again I lay on my straw mattress and slept. It was night when I sat up in a smoky house. This time I cussed. Once more I slept outside on the ground, once more I examined the chimney at dawn and found the same thing. A wad of leaves and twigs blocked the flue.

At that point, I was too sick to wonder or care. I hadn't eaten in more than two days, coma seemed more attractive than reality, and I was too weak to struggle.

How I climbed a tree, I didn't know, but I managed to haul myself into a great brute that had a roomy crevice in the top of its trunk. This hole made as good a grave as any, so I settled into it. Didn't intend to rot on the ground where scavengers could make meals of me. The crevice was comfortable, made me feel as if I ought to shed some tears or hold some kind of funeral service, like man had done in his time. We flying humans—we hadn't any superstitions —had left all that behind us. We did have subconsciouses, though, and mine was more in command that day than was my other part.

I lay reliving the good days I'd had with Hinx. We'd skipped all over the place, eaten when we'd felt like it, gone swimming in clear lakes, lain under blue suns. Hinx. My friend. We needed nothing and no one but each other.

I saw him that night, except he was more ghost than mount. My crazy mind made hash of reality. Hinx came riding like a living chunk of snow, and how very fancy he was in his white coat. Everything about him was different. His fur was curly; in fact, it looked like little white flowers pinned all over him. Instead of big ears, he had little ones that stuck up like arrows. His body was much too delicate. Ordinarily, Hinx was built like a boulder, big rippling muscles and power evident in every line of him. Now he was a dandy. His chest was small, while his rear was downright miniature. Stuck to his little hind was a ball of fluff. His legs were long and thin, his paws were undersized, and I could have sworn he had lacquer on his nails. The face of Hinx was usually big, blunt and friendly, but this day he had a sharp, cruel visage with two green sparkling eyes.

So instead of a black powerhouse of loving kindness, my mount was a little white stinker.

In my feverish state, I mourned. Hinx was carrying a rider and it wasn't me. It was a funny-looking little dude who might have stepped out of that glass room in the underground museum.

I was so mad at my dream that I woke up. There I lay with my belly to the sky and with the rain soaking into me like I was a desert. Lord, god, didn't it ever do anything on Earth but leak water?

My second thought was of Hinx. Peace settled in my soul. I wasn't going to die, had changed my mind and decided to live. I'd loved Hinx, had taken care of him the best I could, and he'd had it better than a lot of mounts. Now he was dead, so I'd best forget him. First thing in the morning, I'd go back to the beach, bawl my head off and bury him in the ground.

Did I have any loving thoughts for Earth? I didn't know, only knew that the rain hit me in the face, the wind touched me, the tree made secretive sounds and somewhere inside of me a voice said, "No matter how far or how fast you run, there's a string between you and this planet. The string is in your mind. If you had never seen the place, the bond wouldn't exist, but you have seen it and you'll never cut the tie. Everything has a nest."

Sun in my face, I stretched, sat up, grabbed a big yellow fruit hanging nearby and gobbled it down. Ate six of them, belched, climbed to the ground. My lanion pod had disintegrated. All that was left was a yard or so, and this I tucked between my legs and then tied the edges around my waist.

Hinx wasn't on the beach. His corpse lay nowhere that I could see. There were no tracks leading from where I'd last seen him, but, then, there wouldn't be because of the long arm of the surf. It was possible the tide had washed his body out to sea.

I sat on the sand for a long time. My last link with my own kind was gone. It didn't matter how I felt about it. Wishes never did anything but give a person a bellyache. The hat on my head weighed a ton. Didn't know if I could stand it much longer. The cuts on my scalp were long healed, but I had a perpetual bruise on top and at the back. The weight never changed. It was always too heavy. Also, it drove me out of the sun unless I wore a crown of leaves over it. Now I sat and considered my grief and bad luck and what I could do about them.

Went back to the underground museum and spent the day with my ancestors. There were some machines that I sat on and tried to ride. They were too old, and, besides, I didn't know how to make them work. The most interesting one was a big cylindrical thing with a pointed nose. Its outside looked as if it had first been chewed by teeth and then set fire to. Man had built proud types of machines that aimed toward the sky with stubborn gall. Maybe this one had gone farther into space than any. I didn't wonder that men had turned into jaks. A vehicle like this one couldn't have skipped through D-2, and D-3 was full of obstacles. Just plain air could gang up on an invader and become as solid as a wall. The yearning in man's soul for distance had showed him how to go around obstacles.

The man and woman in the sealed room did nothing but stare holes through me, so I finally left the place.

I was walking through the woods, heading for my miserable house, when there came a flash of light to my left. A huge tree fell. It tried to hit me square and only reflex and fright got me out of its way. After my nerves settled, I took a look at it to see why it had fallen without giving any warning. Funniest break I ever saw. About a foot and a half of stump was left in the ground, and it had a clean, angled surface. There were no splintered parts at all, just that smooth white slope of wood, like something had whacked it off in a split second.

The idea of going back to the house made me yawn. There was nothing in it for me to retrieve, so I took off inland just as I was, half-naked, and sore in foot, head and heart.

In the afternoon I stopped at a waterfall and took a swim in the pool below the gushing foam. Made the mistake of dunking my head. The hat filled with water and weighted me down, the current tipped up my feet and I floundered for a good two minutes before getting my face out for air. As an Earthman I would have made a good vark. Muddy and exhausted, I had a rest on the bank, after which I hunted for food. My guts were giving me trouble because of all the fruit I'd been eating. Found a field of yellow corn, built a fire in a hole in the ground and had a dozen or so charred ears, following which I lay moaning and groaning until I fell asleep. Woke up with a big furry long-toothed beast sniffing my feet. Later I learned it was a bear. Right then I didn't care what it was. The thing had brains. As soon as I opened my eyes it hightailed it away a few yards, sat down and looked me over. That it was carnivorous was obvious. It had tall, tapered ears, very long neck and short body. Its legs were slender, its paws small and long-toed.

I figured fast. If it were bright enough, it would soon realize how helpless I was. It would have no instinctive fear of humans, never having seen any.

My figuring was partly accurate. The bear let out a roar and galloped straight at me. I couldn't outrun it so I stood my ground, grabbed up a corn stalk and waited for the enemy. Just before it got close enough to leap, it veered sharply. I managed to swat its tail, which made it roar and hurry that much faster to get away from me.

I didn't believe what I saw when I turned around. Coming at me through the grass was a bunch of snakes. Big ones. Fat ones. They were all the same species, not that I knew or cared which species they were. Grayish-pink, they had dark spots, small heads and tapered tails. I hated their eyes. They were fixed on me, about twenty pairs.

Surely I was crazy or dreaming. That many snakes couldn't live in one nest, couldn't all decide to take a stroll in my direction, not at the same time. Blinking my eyes didn't help. The snakes didn't go away. They made no noise as they came like drunken ropes through the corn, their heads seeking safe ground as if that were the only body they possessed. Wherever the heads went, the rest followed.

A snake hater from way back, I did some more fast figuring. If I made no sound, they might not spot me. On the other hand, these were Earth snakes and I didn't know how much like other snakes they were. Not that any species was ever like another.

All this was mental gibberish. It was my way of telling myself that my goose wasn't cooked. Except that it seemed like it might be. Behind me, the bear screamed and I looked that way long enough to see that the snakes were there too, and a batch of them had the bear down on the ground and were trying to love him to death.

I backed up. There was nowhere to go. The bear kept screaming. Whirling, I ran straight toward him, went as fast as I'd ever run before, sped up his writhing body like it was a hill, stepped on snake and fur alike, shoved my belly forward so that a flashing snake head went behind me instead of snatching me with its teeth. I sealed my arms to my sides so I would be a smaller target. Down the other side of the mound of wriggling bodies I ran like hell, leaped up and down like a bug, whether I saw anything or not. There were snakes in the grass but they wouldn't catch me standing still. One was balanced on its tail, directly in my path. It looked like a skinny tree, except for its head that arched at a gorgeous angle, with the hideous eyes in it alert and waiting for me to come and get squeezed to a pulp.

To heck with its head and teeth. It might not have any of the latter, but it had that deadly tail and that was the part which was going to clobber me if I didn't watch out. I mustn't swerve and I could never build up enough speed to evade the tail, once it started to strike.

I hit the snake with my shoulder, low and hard. If it hadn't been balanced so cutely on its most murderous part, it could have snagged me with no trouble. Like a mound of rocks, it started to fall when I knocked it off its tail, and in the meantime I was past it and cantering off into the sweet distance. I kept running; the bear continued to yell. It took me a long time to get beyond the sound of a creature dying in a terrible way.

Not much did I like Earth, right then. The place was a battleground. Maybe everything in it was a predator, which meant that everything in it was also a prey.

Something was following me. I sensed it a few days later. My decision to walk around the world was part of my plan to stay alive. At first, it seemed I was my worst enemy. The sickness that always hit grounded jaks couldn't kill me as long as I had a destination. Animals were enemies, of course, but my ego assured me that my better brain would help me win in any contest with them. Now I wasn't sure. Whatever or whoever followed me was damned clever. There was no losing it, not for more than a few hours. I crossed a stream, it picked up my trail later on the other side. I climbed a mountain, it did likewise. I holed up in a cave or a tree, it hung back out of sight and waited until I moved on.

Got on my nerves. In a way, the stress was a welcome one. Anybody who was being stalked by an unseen thing had to concentrate on that problem and wasn't likely to grieve about not being able to skip to the outer reaches of the sky.

My feet were calloused, but not enough, so I bound them with leaves, renewed the paddings two or three times a day. Felt comfortable as long as my feet didn't hurt, that is, with the exception of my head. Fifty times a day I told myself the hat was part of my body and that it really didn't bother me.

My hunter had to sleep. So did I, but I didn't. Traveled two days and a night, hoping to lose him. Failure. He picked up my trail because I overslept the second night.

Tried to trap him in a gully, so I could at least get a look at him. I hid in high grass on a hill, watched that gully until my eyes blurred. He didn't go in it, chose the harder way, climbed another hill and closed in behind me. Heard him coming and rolled into the gully and almost broke my back.

Set another trap for him. Piled some rocks on the low branches of a tree beside a path I intended to take. A stiff wind would have sent the rocks tumbling down. A vine had already been anchored on the other side of the path. About three inches above the ground, it stretched around the tree trunk and was fastened to the branches that held the rocks. A nudge on that vine would get my stalker a few bumps on his head. He wouldn't be damaged much but he might be discouraged from following me.

Later, I circled back to see what had happened. Nothing. The rocks still lay on the branches, and my shadow was still on my trail. He had used the path but hadn't touched the vine. A high stepper with good sense. More than I?

There was no use my trying to out-think him unless I wanted to spend a lot more than a few minutes at planning. That didn't seem like a good idea. I had to stay on the move.

Dreamed of Hinx again that night. He was still white and the fancy dude on his back gave me the shivers. There was something wrong with that jak. I tried to get closer in my dream, so I could see what it was that was so peculiar about him, but he kept fading back, back, how slow he made Hinx go backward, until the pair of them was a shiny sliver of silver. The sliver was parked straight up in the sky above the tree where I slept. I never moved, it never moved.

Maybe I snored. Something woke me up. My eyes popped open and my gaze was fixed on the shiny silver patch that shouldn't have been there. When I blinked my eyes, it was gone.

I saw them in another dream. This time they did calisthenics in the sky. In and out of D-2 they ducked like beautiful birds, and I couldn't help admiring them, though I disliked that jak who had stolen Hinx and turned him into a snowy dandy.

Chapter VII

They came after me in earnest the next day, the two of them, and this time I wasn't dreaming, or even groggy.

I had already made sure of my territory. There was a barren field ahead of me, but it wasn't too spacious. Plenty of trees were spread out around it, so I could dart into them without having to run in the open too long. It wouldn't be bright of me to be caught with no protection, and I wasn't stupid.

Across the field I started at a slow lope. Knew full well where my enemy would come from. I meant the strange jak, the fancy dude, the weird character who had been dogging my footsteps almost since the day I'd come to Earth. That jak meant to kill me before he went home, wherever his home was. He had tried to suffocate me by blocking the chimney of my house, and when that didn't work, he had sent a tree crashing down on me. Now he was fixing to try something else. He would come from the sky of D-2, maybe right over my head or maybe in front of me.

I looked up and there he sat, a hundred yards ahead of me. His white mount had taken a sedate stance on its delicate legs, and it had its head tilted at a perfect horizontal angle, its nose pointed right at me. The jak had a shiny thing in one hand. This, too, was pointed at me.

Leaping like a rabbit, I changed position, about four yards. A hole appeared in the ground where I'd been standing. Scared me out of my wits. The hole was deep and clean. I knew what I'd have looked like had I been standing still when the flash of light came: like the trunk of tree that had nearly fallen on me a while back. I would have been sliced in a neat, clean, two-part package.

The jak was using an artifact and it was dangerous. I plunged into the woods and ran. Trees fell behind me, holes were dug in the ground to my right. I leaped ahead, faded to the left, ran around a tree and doubled back onto my previous course. I was probably a dead jak, and I knew it. Not a chance had I of evading for long somebody who had good jink.

He didn't have good jink. I practically crept past his nose. He sat between two trees, turning his head neither left nor right. Upright on his mount, he stared straight ahead. He was trying to feel me.

I got behind him, lifted a rock and let the white mount have it on the rear end. Startled and sore, the mount shot into D-2. I was alone in the woods. But not for long. Back into the field I ran. And came to a dead stop.

In the middle of the field stood the sorriest looking black mount I'd ever seen in my life. He had lost about three hundred pounds and was nothing but a bag of bones. Filthy from head to toe, he was the best thing I'd seen in a long time.

"Hinky," I whispered, and ran, jerky-legged, toward him. "Honey," I said, laying a hand on his nose.

His eyes were clear, thank god. There was no more sickness in him. As I touched him, he shivered all over, ducked his head, licked my feet. Gingerly I climbed onto his back. He couldn't understand a word I said, but if we didn't get out of that field in a hurry we'd both be dead. I told him so, and at the same time I nudged him with a leg. His head came up to my waiting hands. I gripped his ears, pulled harder on the right one. He got the message. Turning in a flash, he leaped toward the trees.

We slept in a cave that night. Stuffed full of potatoes and corn, Hinx lay on his side while I rested with my head on his ribs, and together we thought of our adventures since we had separated. Neither of us needed any more understanding of what had happened. He had gone his own way to find his destiny, just as I had gone mine. Now he was back and we were alive and healthy. There was no communication between us other than that of touch and whatever emotion our voices conveyed. It had to be enough.

I told him about the jak who had been chasing me. Evidently I'd had two pursuers, Hinx on the ground and the jak in the sky. The jak had poor jink, but he was better off than I, who had none at all. Chances were, he'd catch me sooner or later, but now that I had Hinx, he'd have a tougher time of it. Hinx could run fifty miles an hour, when he had to, and if the white mount tried to match that ground speed, we would be long gone.

Hinx woke me up in the middle of the night. He was prowling around the cave, growling under his breath and pausing now and then to stare through the opening into the darkness. Leaping onto his back, I guided him outside. We hugged the cave wall, circled to the right, came all the way around the back of the cave and entered the forest just left of the entrance. Hinx could see better than I, but not nearly well enough. We made poor time, practically walked the whole distance until dawn. Toward morning, we smelled smoke. And food. And coffee.

Hinx and I lay in a patch of weeds and watched the jak who sat by a campfire. Our guts were giving us hell. The smells that fellow made drove us nearly to yelling. He had his back to us, and if he hadn't been so big I'd have thought it was the fancy dude with the white mount. I hadn't tasted coffee for a long time. Usually, the only time a jak drank it was when he could find a little hot spring to dump it in. No self-respecting jak would cook it in an artifact. Except for the one who sat by the campfire. Not only was he boiling coffee over the fire, he had roasted fish and potatoes and beside him sat a can full of beans and another little can of hot sugar.

Hinx whined, stuck his nose in my neck. Hell, I did the same thing to him. Against the ground, my skinny belly crawled, complained, turned in flip flops. My mouth was dry and watery at the same time.

I hated that jak. Or maybe he was a man. Was this possible? Of course not. There weren't any men. But

72

there weren't any jaks here either. Earth had No Trespassing signs all around it. No jak who found Doubleluck would be sitting by a fire cooking breakfast. That is, no jak but . . .

"Damn," I said.

My mount looked at me as if I'd lost my mind. I had spoken in a loud voice, and Hinx got ready to crawl back into the woods.

"Damn." I jumped up and looked about me. Yep. There was a mount in the bushes near the fire. Flat on his back, belly to the sky, an animal was snoozing, and he was the biggest, ugliest animal I had ever laid eyes on.

"Come on, Hinky," I said. I didn't look to see if he followed me, just walked into the firelight and stood with my hands on my hips.

"Wondered when you'd finally use your brain and figure it was me."

"You knew it was us out there?"

Big Jak leaned against a rock and swilled coffee from a jug. "You forgot a lot about jink already. Should know it's hard not to jink somebody as close as you and that mount."

"What you doing here?"

"My planet, too. Belongs to everybody. Can go and come as I please. Where are your clothes, gal? You'll catch your death."

The smell of sugar was driving me nuts. "I'm not pleased to see you."

"That's what I call rationalizing. If you want to be stubborn, go ahead, but you'll not eat a bite unless you bow and say, 'Good morning, sir.' "

Bowed. "Good morning, sir." Reached for the sugar and found Hinky's head in the can. Reached for the potatoes, found Hinky's head in the pile. Reached for the fish—same old story. My mount was ahead of me all the way. I fought for a place beside every can, and he shared everything with me.

"Take it slow," said Big Jak.

"My manners are as good as yours." I ate like it was going out of style.

"Sure. You're as good or better at everything as anybody is, I reckon. That's why you're an outcast with no jink. Is why your mount looks like he has one foot in the grave."

I was eating too fast. In a minute I'd throw up. The coffee poured inside me in a steady stream. Felt like heaven.

"You can't hurt my feelings," I said.

"I'm beginning to believe it. Why I came here, well, my conscience was bothering me about you."

Not for a treasure would I have sneered, nor would I have allowed anything else I was feeling to show on my face. Lounging against the rock, he had his knees drawn up and the coffee jug was propped on them so I couldn't see all of his ugly face. His yellow eyes were gleaming slits against a face shadowed by the breaking dawn. Looked like a specter, he did, with his black wild hair and his fierce cheekbones. He had picked up a neat new lanion skin. His feet were bound with fine leaves. His big hands held on to the jug, and he regarded me over it as if I were a curious specimen of fauna.

"That sounds humane of you," I said politely. "Only you're such a big liar I suspect you ain't humane in any way. Hinx and I don't care. We're getting along. You'd be surprised how easy a jak reverts. We're human, after all. Hinx is mostly dog now and I'm mostly man. Or woman. It don't matter. I'm of Earth."

"Do dogs and women keep looking over their shoulders all the time?"

"Why not? With no jink we don't see so good in the dark. Yellow eyes, you know. They shine at night. It's funny how all dangerous animals always seem to have yellow eyes. How come you're trying to kill me?"

He swilled coffee. Yes, he did. Then he picked up a fish, a big one, and bit it in half. Chewed the bones like they were corn. Crack, crunch, snap. Sounded like rocks hitting together in the still morning. I flinched, looked over my shoulder.

He swallowed the tidbit of a foot-long fish, rubbed his mouth with his palm, cleaned his teeth with his tongue. "Been asking around. Mostly at Bounding Winter. Old jaks know a lot, since they've had experience. They tell me a young jak in your situation is bound to go nuts inside of thirty days. How long you been here?"

"Two, three months, and you know it. It's too bad I'm so nuts."

"They also told me a mount will revert faster than that and start eating any meat he finds under his nose."

For a second, I thought my stomach would turn all the way over. "In that case, I'm a mirage and you're really talking to yourself. Hinx reverted and ate me and I'm not even here."

"You trying to tell me you and that mangy black mount are unique?"

"You're changing the subject, though I don't see why you care one way or the other. You came back here to kill me, so you aren't concerned with my health or the mental state of my mount. I've been trying to figure out how you did it."

"Hmmm."

"That Volcano is so big, I don't see how you could make him look white and puny. And you're anything but a fancy dude. But you have the right face."

"Interesting, you mean?"

"Not by a hair."

"Brainy looking?"

"Ha ha."

"Friendly?"

"Like a snake, which reminds me, how'd you get 'em all in that field at once? It was all I could do to get away. It was a waste of time. You're an adult and I'm not. Could save yourself some effort. Just break my neck and leave me to the buzzards. Only I want to know if you'll do something. Want you to take my mount away with you. He's innocent of all the crimes I'm supposed to have committed. You could take him to a mount planet, one where they're all crazy, and that way nobody would pay any attention to what he tells them."

"What you trying to say?"

"You already understand. You don't have to kill him too."

He took his time about guzzling some more coffee.

"Think I've had enough. Think it's time you got up and got out of here. My hospitality doesn't extend to crazy jaks. Take your mount and leave my camp."

I didn't think I believed my ears. "Y—you—won't reconsider?"

"Not today or tomorrow."

I stood up. "Never did anything to you except accidentally cross your path. There ought to be wishing wells or good fairies. I'd have mine skewer you and hang you in the sun for a thousand years. Come on, Hinx, we're not welcome here, besides which, the air smells terrible. Think the place is full of skunks."

My mount and I marched away. As I passed the fire, I did a good deed. Kicked the coffee can over, knocked the pots of food over, and as I passed a certain thicket I kicked a certain mount in the belly. Looked over my shoulder just once before I headed into the woods. Big Jak hadn't moved a hair. All his stuff being junked hadn't bothered him at all. The yelps of his mount might never have reached his ears, so immovable was he. All he did was sit against the rock, slowly swill what was left of his coffee, and stare at nothing.

"You lied about everything," I yelled. "You could have gotten this hat off my head if you'd wanted to. You just like the idea of me suffering and dying. You ain't a jak. You're a devil."

Hinx beside me, I ran, ran, ran. Sweat streaked my chest, the chill wind burned my face, my legs became chunks of stone, but still I ran, and my thudding heart beat a message of despair.

"Leave me alone," I yelled.

It was a new dawn. My sleep had been interrupted a dozen times by a white specter who rode overhead in the sky and took potshots at Hinx and me with a shiny artifact that poured out bright light.

Maybe it had been a dream. There were no holes in the ground around us, Hinx and I hadn't been sliced to pieces, the sun was up, the sky was otherwise empty. So was my stomach. Right then, I considered life to be a dreary routine. Being a jak was better than being a man. Finding food was easier for the former.

76

My mount and I had to walk for our breakfast and on Earth it was an elusive meal, if not nonexistent. I normally weighed about one hundred eighty and needed plenty of calories to maintain the bulk. Calories on Earth were usually neither here nor there. I had dropped fifty pounds or so, while poor Hinx was getting scrawnier by the minute. For the first time I seriously worried about starvation. Eating two or three times in one day and then fasting for half a week wasn't good for me or my mount. Neither was getting killed by Big Jak good for us. We couldn't hole up too long in any one place, which meant a shortage of food, as I couldn't carry much and couldn't always depend on finding a supply at the next stop. If I'd had the time, I could have planned a strategy for stopping the enemy. But I had no time, really had nothing at all.

Sneaked back to the campfire, but Big Jak was gone. He wasn't a litterer, had taken away everything that wouldn't rot. There was no use my trying to hide from him, and I knew it as I looked at the pile of dead ashes he had left behind. He was a full-grown jak with perfect jink, and if he wanted to know where I was, all he had to do was open an eye in his mind and he would see me.

"Come on, Hinx," I said. "No use hiding in the bushes. When he decides to come for us, we'll be two bright spots on a dim cloud."

Made myself a spear out of a tree branch. It weighed about four pounds, was ten feet from its wicked point to its grooved-out handle. Practice made me expert at throwing it and sticking it into soft masses. I aimed to get me a jak before I died.

What I got was the ear of a mount. It was a white little animal with a dead-eyed rider and neither of them looked a thing like Volcano or Big Jak. Hinx and I were minding our own business, raiding a peach orchard. He was on the ground, flat on his back, while I was up in a tree tossing peaches into his open mouth. He even chewed the pits, that's how strong his teeth were. All of a sudden, he closed his jaws and growled. A humming sound came from over my head, up in the sky, beyond the upper tree branches.

At first I couldn't see what made the sound, but it didn't matter. The spear was in my hand in a second, my legs were braced and ready, my back was arched, and my arm was back and letting go at the same time a rider broke into view from D-2. My aim wasn't exactly bad. It was just that I overestimated the size of mount and rider. Had it been Big Jak and Volcano, the spear probably would have taken a chunk of the mount's neck and the entire belly of the rider.

The little white mount took the spear in his ear, right at its base where there was enough meat to grab it and hold it solid. He screamed and bucked and disappeared into D-2. An ordinary jak would have hit the ground in D-3 and his mount would have been lost in limbo. This rider wasn't ordinary. He was a thing, didn't cry out in those few seconds that he hovered in the air over me, didn't look alarmed, didn't even look alive, but he stayed on that mount as if he were glued to it, and away they both went, a hurt animal and a rider who gave me the creeps every time I thought of him.

"Don't like to admit some things," I said to Hinx, later. "I knew all along it wasn't Big Jak after us. But he's a skunk, all right, left us to be gotten rid of by this other fellow. He has peculiar friends."

We had two days respite, spent them eating and swimming. My lanion skin was about done for. It was just a piece of material tied around my hips, and even this was shredding and tattering. I looked like hell. My yellow hair grew like a waterfall, I was covered with scratches and burned to the color of copper by the sun. But I felt pretty good. Hinx had put on a couple of pounds and his coat was getting shiny. We ate lots of carrots to keep our teeth clean. If people had only left us alone, we might have been happy. I wanted to give the planet a thorough examination, discover all I could about men, see if I could find the missing links between them and jaks. Instead, Hinx and I spent our waking hours watching the sky.

Another good spear beside me, I sat on the bank of a river and watched Hinx bathe. He'd buck to get his hind quarters clean and rear and duck his head to take care of the front parts. He even gargled.

Felt sad as I watched him. He needed more than my company, had a right to grow up and find a mount he could love. I didn't know anything about sex, couldn't have cared less and would have laughed and been horrified had I known of it then. But I knew about love because I'd never had any, other than what Hinx had given me. Jaks in love paired off with mounts in love. It had to be that way. Only sensible thing to do. I had heard that the only real horror jaks knew was when they were in love while their mounts hated each other. A jak and a jak might part, but a jak and his mount, never.

Anyhow, my 'Hinky was a fifteen-year-old stud, whatever that might be, and he was handsome and intelligent, and any day now he would hear the call of Cupid. Except that he also might get killed any day now, or I'd get killed and he would be stranded on Earth. I couldn't think of a worse tragedy.

"Hinky," I called. He was ducking his head and didn't hear me. "Hinky."

The ground to my right exploded. I hit the river. My leg hurt. I was dazed. As I surfaced, the water beside me became a hot geyser. About to be boiled alive, I sank and came up near the center of the river where Hinx had been swimming. He wasn't there now. Geysers shooting all around me, I went down deep and found my mount swimming like crazy toward the opposite shore. Close to the bank, we separated. Leaving him was the hardest thing I ever did, but the dead-eyed jak had found us, and he wanted me, and Hinx would be taken out with me if we were together. Underwater, I swam back to the shore where I had first entered the river, stuck my head out and looked around.

In the air, above the river's center, hovered a little white mount with a bandaged ear. On his back sat the dude in fancy clothes. They whirled and the dude spotted me. I was holding myself up by pushing against the river bottom with my hands, and if I hadn't stuck my leg out of the water to take a look at it, I might have had enough strength to dive again. And the time in which to do it. My leg looked so chewed up it shocked me into taking a second look.

By then, it was too late to do anything but scoot up the bank on my back and wait for the dude to kill me with the artifact in his hand. The mount was about a dozen feet over me. He couldn't walk on air. What the pair did was drift in and out of D-2 so fast it looked like they were stationary. As soon as Dead Eye was satisfied that he had his target well sighted, he would kill me and then either take his mount away or settle it onto the ground.

Hinx came up out of the water behind them like a geyser himself. Black and dripping, he leaped high into the sky and sank his teeth into the white mount's rear. That damned Dead Eye wasn't human. While his mount screamed bloody murder and started whirling in circles, he turned in his seat and shot a piece of hair from Hinky's forelock.

I was on my feet and throwing rocks. Thank god Earth was a sloppy planet. I even had big chunks of mud at my disposal, and I heaved them one after another. Hinx never stopped coming up out of the water and chewing on the white mount, Dead Eye continued firing his weapon and lopping off pieces of black fur, my missiles made a filthy mess of the enemy, and . . .

Did I say before that Dead Eye wasn't human? How could anybody be involved in such a fracas and still jink a rider coming? Volcano just missed them. He and Big Jak roared out of D-2 like a single, whistling monster, big as life and twice as deadly. Volcano had his teeth bared, Big Jak had one fist ready for a powerful swing. The fist missed but the teeth connected. The little white mount lost his tail and a bit of meat, while that damned Dead Eye lost nothing, not even his cool. Took his mount and scrammed in a flash. One second they were there, the next they were gone into D-2.

Sat down hard in the mud. Looked at Hinx. My eyes misted. Would have killed myself if one tear squeezed out. Big Jak and Volcano lit beside me.

"Every time I see you, you're doing something strange."

"That's because I'm unique."

"You have an ugly leg there."

"If you don't like it, look at the other one."

Hinx crawled onto the grass, lay down beside me. I put my hand on his head. Instead of screaming, like I wanted, I laughed. Hinx cried for me, big sobs that should have cracked him in sections.

"That mount of yours hysterical?" said Big Jak. He was tending to Volcano, smoothing his fur, patting his ears, making sure the animal wasn't injured.

"He'll shape up," I said.

"Hate to say it, but think you'll lose that leg."

"You mean it'll just rot off?"

"Well, no, think it ought to be cut off. It's burned too bad."

"Anybody tries to do that, I'll kill 'em."

"You don't want to live with only one leg?"

"Nope."

"Then you'll die."

"So be it," I said. It made me mad, but I knew what was going to happen, and it did. I fainted dead away.

Chapter VIII

Shaper's hats lay all over the place. Every so often he came over to me and gave me a double stare with his nutty eyes.

"Where's Big Jak?" I asked.

"He isn't the kind to linger and watch a little gal die."

"He's the kind, just like he's a liar. Could fix me up if he wanted to."

One of Shaper's eyes looked west, the other glanced elsewhere. "Shouldn't endow jaks with omnipotence, even if they do seem to have it."

"What you mean? You saying he ain't a liar?"

"Maybe, but one thing he ain't is a medicine man."

"Then who laid me here and stuck my leg in this mud hole?"

Grinning like a simpleton, Shaper scratched his head. "I'm a medicine man."

"All you believe in is iron."

"Plenty of it in that mud. How's your leg feel?"

"Don't know. It's numb."

"I'm sorry you're going to die." He started to walk away.

"Hey," I yelled, and he turned back. "Where's Hinx? How come we're here?"

"Your mount got taken away by Big Jak, so he'd eat. All he wanted to do was lay beside you and howl. As for why you're here, well, Big Jak says you been marked for a target by the Dreens, and since you're wounded and dying you ought to have some peace."

"What's that target part mean? What's a Dreen?"

"Haven't the slightest idea." This time Shaper made it away from me. He went back to his fire and his hats.

I gripped the one that decorated my own head. I groaned and cussed but it did no good. I didn't know if I was glad or sorry about having been taken from Earth. What was the difference in graves?

The wind on this planet was still as spooky as ever, crept across the ground and leaped on me like a million cold demons. My sore leg was submerged in freezing, stinking mud. As I cussed and suffered, I considered that jaks hadn't climbed the evolutionary ladder but had, instead, descended it. No doctors, no compassion, no intelligence. Only jaks in trouble would ever realize this, which meant jaks would probably never change, not as a species. People like me would go down into the final hole, complaining, while spectators either ran away, like Big Jak, or clucked and gave useless sympathy, like Shaper.

"He could get this hat off my head," I yelled at my fool of a companion.

"Doubt it, but wouldn't do you any good. Don't know of a place where there would be a body knew how to heal you."

"Ain't you ever heard of herbs?"

"Not any that could restore meat."

"Frogs do that by themselves."

He came over and looked down at me. "I could get that hat off you. Could burn it off."

"Along with the head inside it."

"Right. You remember one time I told you laughing was better than crying? This is what I meant. A stupid frog can grow himself a whole new leg. You can't." Shaper showed his teeth. "Ha ha. Hear me laugh? I do it all the time."

"I know. It keeps you insane."

"Yes," he said, seriously. "First time I go sane, I'll turn this galaxy upside down."

I started yelling, kept it up until my throat couldn't make any more sounds. After a while it felt better so I yelled again. Pretty soon I couldn't even whisper, couldn't breathe hard. That was fine with me. Had no desire to die noisily, not when there were people around. Had I been alone I'd have gladly screamed bloody murder all the way to Hell.

"You're young and healthy," said Big Jak. Night had come and he had one of his infernal fires going. Hinx lay beside me.

"If you happened to be old and sick, you'd go quicker," he added.

"And that way it would be easier on you. It's too bad I'm croaking in a messy manner."

"Figure if Shaper held you down, I could get rid of that leg with a sharp piece of metal."

"He made me a promise."

Drooping eyes regarded me with no feeling. "Hate to argue with a suicide. Believe in freedom of all kinds. But there's such a thing as Unrecorded Law. Can call it Legend, if you like. Applies to fools, animals and children."

"Don't touch me, jak. It's my right to keep what I own."

In the morning I was burning up with fever. Couldn't see straight. Was aware of Shaper and Big Jak standing over me and saying things. No doubt they were fixing to take off my leg. I didn't care if they chopped me in fifty pieces. Way back in my mind, despair and anger vied. I wanted to live but if these two crippled me I'd give them back in kind if it took the rest of my life.

Some time toward noon, Big Jak came walking toward me with an artifact in his hand.

"Maybe you're omnipotent, after all. She said you were." That was Shaper talking.

"Mind your own business."

"You're a little late, I think. Fever's got the best of her. You should have used that thing yesterday."

Big Jak knelt beside me and stuck the artifact under my nose so I'd see it. It was a bent bar of metal with a handle on each end. The metal was dull silver and looked soft enough to make a dent in it with a finger. It was harder than anything I'd ever touched. I had seen the thing before, on a planet called Earth, in a glass-walled room where a man and woman stood petrified by time and death.

"I swore to my father never to use any of those machines," Big Jak said to me. "Am breaking my promise. Listen hard. If you don't hear me, I'm wasting my time. This artifact is going to fit over your hat. I'm going to twist these handles so the bent bar will grip that metal. After that, I'm going to push this button on the right handle. The molecules across the top of your hat will die. Once they're dead, any kind of pressure can crumble that section like it was dust."

"I'd like to have that thing when you're done with it," said Shaper.

"It goes back where it came from."

Again Big Jak spoke to me. "Listen, gal. Soon as the hat comes off, I want you to take your mount and skip farther than ever you went before."

"Just a damned minute," said Shaper.

"Shut up." To me, Big Jak said, "Go somewhere that might have people who can heal your leg."

Shaper was blubbering. "You're a traitor. Mustn't guide anybody to glory. She knows there ain't anyone here who can heal her. She'll do it, she'll skip all the way out, and you said we'd be the first. And it won't work, anyhow. Won't be any people anywhere who can help her."

"Then no harm will have been done," growled Big Jak. "She'll be dead and the thrill of being the first to make it over will still be waiting for you."

"It's the principle—"

"Who has any use for your principles?" Shaper shut up and Big Jak put the artifact on top of my hat. I could feel the handles tightening on the metal above my ears. Hoping it would kill me, I shut my eyes so I wouldn't see him press the button. A second later, death flitted across the hair on top of my skull. It was a touch of such awesome coldness that the fever in my blood fled away for an instant. The jak with the scythe stood beside me, grinning as he got ready to lop off my soul. My hair crawled. I opened my mouth to bellow.

The cold went away in a hurry. Big Jak unscrewed the artifact, raised a hand and brought it down on top of the hat. My iron jail collapsed and fell away from me.

"Call your mount," he said.

Hinx was beside me, but I knew what Big Jak meant. For me there was another language now, and it was as if I'd never lost it.

"Hinky," I said.

"At your beck and call. Welcome back."

"You want to help me one last time?"

"Yes."

"You might be left in limbo."

"I'll try not to be."

Big Jak lifted me out of the mud and onto my mount's back. "Save yourself," he said, and it was a lot of years before I realized he was giving me the chance to do what he had wanted to do all his life. "Reach far with your mind. Go there. Find people who haven't spent the last million years looking for fun."

"Good luck, honey," cried Shaper.

I grabbed the hair on Hinx's neck.

"Remember," said Big Jak. "Farther than the farthest you ever went."

I was dippy with fever. Somebody to help me? I'd been practically everywhere, but never had I heard of any really good medicine men. Farther than ever? It would have to be that, if I expected to find things I'd never seen before.

"Hinx, do you see it?" I croaked.

"Sure do. Where's it at?"

"Don't know. Let's skip."

We traveled. Behind us, on a planet uncounted light-years away, a jak named Shaper stood and cried, while another jak followed us with his mind until . . .

Ahead of me, out of the fog of D-2, came a band of riders, about twenty of them, and at first I thought the fever in me made one rider seem like so many. That's how alike those fellows looked, and each one was Dead Eye, and each sat astraddle a little white mount.

So I didn't get to go to glory that day. Dead Eye and his friends encircled me and pushed me through limbo all the way back to the planet I had left a few moments before.

Shaper was already running across the clearing. Maybe he thought he could hide in the woods.

Eight riders cut him off and sat around him in a circle so he couldn't move. The rest took care of Big Jak and me.

I might be sick, but my jink was all there, and I figured to put it to good use. It took me about three seconds to realize something terrible had happened to my jink. It had a range of about twenty feet. Above that height, I couldn't feel a thing.

Two riders had galloped to opposite ends of the clearing, stopped, faced each other. Their arms were in the air and the artifacts in their hands released rays of pink light. The rays met above the clearing and stopped our jink dead. Nobody in the group was able to skip through the light.

Eight little riders leaped from their mounts and beat the hell out of Big Jak. After they had finally gotten him flat on the ground, everybody stopped moving and looked at one of the Dead Eyes. This one seemed more like the Dead Eye I knew. He sat on his mount, as unblinking as a snake, and took in the scene like he was smelling a bad smell.

"Leave their mounts here on this world. They'll go nowhere by themselves."

"May we kill the male jaks?" said a little rider in a sweet voice.

"The only time we've ever been ordered to kill was when they sent me after the girl," said Dead Eye. "Now they've changed their minds. As for these two males, our orders were specific. We're to leave them unharmed. And so we shall. On the planet of the varks." He gestured to the riders beside him. "Take them away."

Chapter IX

The insane asylum was a quiet place. Most of the
inmates cried, but they did it softly, politely, so that
rarely were any of the guards disturbed. I supposed
they were guards. Once in a while, someone went
berserk and ran around the room screaming, or tried
to brain himself against the walls, or climbed the
twenty-foot-high grill that kept us all from freedom.
The room was about two hundred by four hundred
feet, and the only sane exit was the door in the
metal grill. No inmate could use that exit until he had
been confined for thirty days.

There were a dozen insane exits from the room.
These were situated along one wall, depressions or
indentations deep enough to accommodate an upright
body.

All the inmates were voluntary commitments. For
thirty days they were locked up. If, at the end of this
period, they decided to leave the way they had entered, they were free to do so. The guards on the
other side of the grill unlocked the door and the jak
whose time was up was allowed to leave.

The choices were overwhelmingly for the insane
exits. About ten percent opted for the sane way out.
The rest surrendered to their emotions and took to the
indentations in the wall. As soon as a body fitted itself
inside one of these, a light went on, the wall behind
the jak opened and he was carried away on a moving
floor strip that transported him to an artifact called
the Lobot. This artifact performed surgery on his
head. Microscopically thin wires plunged into his

brain, snipped two nerves, withdrew, and his skull was sewed up. He was then taken to a recovery room. The operation took about fifteen minutes. Its effects lasted a lifetime. One of his sensory organs, a thing the size of a small pebble and situated just above the pituitary gland, no longer functioned. The Lobot was a maker of men. It disconnected the jink organ.

"I find your story incredible," said Arnet. It wasn't the first time he had expressed that opinion.

"That mean you don't believe me?" I said.

"Frankly, if it weren't for the way you talk and look, I wouldn't believe a word of it."

That was fair enough. If it weren't for the way he and the others talked and looked, I wouldn't have believed a bit of anything that had happened to me. Arnet was fifteen, and the reason we struck up an acquaintance was because we were the only two in the whole place who weren't out of our heads.

We generally occupied a corner in the back of the room. There was nothing to sit or lie on but the floor, but it was spongy and comfortable. Along the left wall were doors leading into places called bathrooms. Once in a while someone had to be dragged out of one of these. They were popular spots and when a nut decided to lock the door and never come out, the others became impatient or downright hostile.

"Am worrying about my leg," I said.

"I've told you several times that you needn't. Beneath that bandage is a salve saturated with a dozen enzymes. Your wounded flesh has everything it requires to rebuild itself. Are you quite certain you've never been in a hospital before?"

"Told you there ain't any. Told you this planet is an atavism."

He laughed, and right away I liked him all over again. He was the most relaxed person I'd ever met. That is, on the outside. Inside, he had to be messed up, otherwise he wouldn't have committed himself to the asylum, once a year, every year.

"We're two different kinds of people," I said.

"But you're the atavism."

"Look at it this way. A bunch of people go walking

up a hill, and they're all in step except for one person."

"That doesn't mean he's the inferior one," Arnet said quickly.

"If he isn't, then everybody, and I mean everybody, is worse than inferior. It doesn't make sense that all people would act naturally and go the wrong way. If they were free and chose a certain path, and they felt their way along this path and used their intelligence as they walked, and then if it turned out later that the majority took one fork in the path while two or three took off onto another path, couldn't you say something interfered with the free thinking of those two or three?"

"Such as?" he said.

"Such as stubbornness, or something close to it."

"For an atavism, you have an annoying way of expressing yourself." Arnet said it as though he were offended, but his face was relaxed and his eyes remained friendly. He was a little fellow, much shorter than I and more on the slender side. In fact, he was almost delicately built. His hair was dark, curly and cropped short. His features were small and regular. I'd never seen eyes the color of his. They were vivid gray with flecks of blue in them. Another thing different about him was his teeth. They were very small and the third pair in front weren't sharp but were as flat and even as the others.

"You say this planet is called Gibraltar. What's it mean?"

"Invincible," he said.

"Seems a waste of a word. Wouldn't anybody try to attack it, though I know plenty of jaks who'd like to find it. You sure it ain't called Doubleluck?"

"Yes, I'm sure."

"One thing you're wrong about is that your people are men. They ain't. They're jaks. Men were our ancestors and they had no jink organ in their brains."

I didn't regret saying it, as I was always one who never saw purpose in keeping silent about facts. But tears squeezed out of Arnet's eyes and dribbled down his cheeks. Happened every time I said "jink," or it happened whenever he even thought on the subject

Jink was the reason these eighty people were in the

asylum. It wasn't my reason for being there. I was in it because it was where I woke up, and I still didn't know half of what was happening. But the inmates, other than Arnet, were insane because they couldn't handle their jink. Nobody on Gibraltar skipped, other than the Dreens, who were law enforcers. It seemed that the galaxy was overrun by lawless heathens called jaks who unfortunately were cousins to men. The latter were citizens of Gibraltar. Men were civilized, jaks were depraved. Also unfortunate was the fact that there were a hell of a lot more jaks than men. Not wanting to be contaminated, men stayed on Gibraltar and waited for the day when jaks committed suicide. It was bound to happen, and soon. Afterwards, the galaxy would be wide open for civilization.

"I come here every year to test myself," said Arnet. "Only during periods of depression do I feel unable to handle the situation."

"What situation?"

He fingered the sweat on his brow. It was on his upper lip, too. "I'm not positive I can explain. Jink isn't a particularly good thing to possess, but we mustn't alter our genes because of Emancipation Day."

"What's that?"

"When all the jaks commit suicide."

Snorting in disgust, I said, "Don't tell me more, because I see what you're driving at. You have jink but you can't use it and it makes you crazy but your posterity will need it when they get the whole galaxy to run around in after a hundred billion jaks jump off a cliff."

Arnet clamped his little teeth together. "I have periods of depression, yes. About every six months. They occur because I'm not perfect. My mind is stronger than my body, though. I'll win."

"That's the most peculiar argument I ever heard. Why don't you admit it's your mind that longs to skip? Only time your body experiences longing is when you're hungry. But never mind. If you're right about this being a mind-over-matter thing, what are these other people doing here?"

"They gave in. They're a tiny minority, believe me."

"Any of them just here for a visit, like you?"

"No. I think I'm probably the only man who does that."

"So you're unique, too. That makes a pair of us."

He looked at me and gave a faint smile. "Yes, I believe you're unique. We men are familiar with the nature of jaks. A jak couldn't survive a week on Gibraltar. His mind would be destroyed."

"You believe I'm a jak?"

"If you looked in a mirror in one of the bathrooms, you wouldn't ask me such a question."

"Afraid of them. Accidentally saw my hand and it scared me half to death. Didn't know things besides water could cast reflections."

A thing I marveled at was that the big room remained so clean. Eighty-one jaks confined within a comparable area would have made a garbage pile of it inside of twenty-four hours. Here, even a berserker picked up after himself. One fellow kept tearing off his fancy clothes and stomping up and down on them. Then he would run around the room, only he always put his clothes back on first. Another fellow fingerpainted on the walls with his food. Three times a day the guards brought each of us a meal on a tray. The painter would choose the brightest item on his tray, say, tomato soup, and with it he drew images on the walls. But he always cleaned his messes when he calmed down.

I didn't take Arnet's word for the situation, not the least syllable, that is, until I had no other choice. From the time I first opened my eyes and found myself in the asylum, I had been busy jinking. It was the weirdest experience I could remember. There simply wasn't another place like this in the galaxy. Every time I touched something with my mental fingers, I withdrew in shock, sometimes mild, stronger at other times.

A jak naturally disliked artifacts. The jaks on Gibraltar had hardly anything else to live with. Everywhere I turned I ran into something in an unnatural state. The entire planet seemed to be artificial. I didn't believe it.

"I recollect a big fellow saying one time to me that Doubleluck—hey, did you ever hear of the place?"

"I don't think so," said Arnet. "What is it?"

"A lie, or a legend. Same thing. A city of gold. Supposed to be the most beautiful place in all the universe."

"You must be speaking of El Dorado."

"You been there?"

He smiled. "I've never been anywhere. But El Dorado isn't real, which means no one has been there, nor will they ever. It's a vision that was born in the minds of men."

"Which men?"

He looked startled. "That's very odd. The men of Gibraltar created the legend of El Dorado. The city of gold, the place of beauty."

"Jaks been hunting it for a thousand years. You suppose that long ago somebody from this world decided to join my people and got around to telling them about the legend?"

"Nobody has ever left Gibraltar permanently, and nobody ever leaves it temporarily except for the Dreens."

"Look here, I'm no Dreen."

Shaking his head, Arnet looked away. "I hope your mind remains stable. You'll never leave Gibraltar."

"Someone going to keep one of those fancy gray rays over my head all the time so I can't jink?"

"No," he said.

"You have mounts on this world who know how to skip."

"Yes."

"That's all I need."

He sighed and gave me a long, earnest stare. "Only the Dreens command mounts on this world. It had to be that way, has to be that way now."

"What kind of mounts?"

"Highly bred, perfect blood lines, extremely intelligent. Not one weak mount is permitted to grow to adulthood. Their obedience is flawless."

"Meaning they're so ornery or narrow-minded they won't move for anyone but a Dreen?"

"If you wish to put it that way."

"Now tell me, what's a Dreen?"

"Morons. They serve us, and they love doing it. That's all they want to do."

I didn't say anything, leaned back against the wall and watched the guards on the other side of the barred exit. There were two of them, seated on opposite sides of a table, and they looked enough like Dead Eye to be his brothers. Small and natty, they seemed purposeful even when they were just sitting and quietly talking. They wore tight-fitting black uniforms and high black boots. On the shirt pocket of each was a small white marking, a circle with a jagged slash running through it. Eternity and violence? Is that what the Dreens represented? Did they intend to blast it all wide open? I looked at Arnet. One thing he didn't look was stupid. I must be wrong. The jaks on Gibraltar couldn't be breeding a mess of war.

"You don't seem upset," Arnet said. "Doesn't the thought of never leaving here bother you?"

"I'm not considering it."

"But you must."

"Why?"

"Are all jaks like you?" he asked.

"Don't know. Never met all of them."

The number of people in the asylum never changed. As soon as someone chose a cubicle and got transferred to the Lobot, the barred door opened and another person was admitted. The new entries were generally quiet and introspective, and it was only with the passage of two or three days that they became erratic and belligerent. Arnet said that, on the outside, it was easy to pick out future candidates for the asylum. A man or woman about to crack up refused to leave the streets and go indoors. He or she walked, walked, walked, talked to everyone they met, got their friends to bring them food, slept in doorways or gutters, yelled at Dreens who tried to get them to move on or go home. Sometimes they popped up in the middle of a crowd and agitated for the abolishment of the skipping prohibition. All invalids behaved the same way, said and did the same things, and by and by they went to the registration building and applied for admittance to an asylum. They never had to wait, as there was always an opening somewhere.

Everybody took notice of me. In fact, I was so interesting that a few inmates neglected to go to the Lobot. This made me curious about the guards' reactions. Did they care which choice an inmate made? I stopped wondering. Trying to read a Dreen was impossible. They reminded me of Shaper with his little piece of self hidden under a rock. But Shaper was an angel compared to Dreens. That is, he was pretty obvious, while they had nothing showing. A Dreen was a blank slate. They were exactly like the few jak idiots I'd met. An idiot's mind was always going around and meeting itself. There was no further action and, therefore, nothing more for an examiner to read.

The mirror in the bathroom showed me one disheveled human being. Shocked me. In the presence of jaks, I'd have thought nothing of my appearance. But the folks beyond the bathroom door weren't neighbors, were actually very distant kin and strangers to boot, and some humorless fellow had dumped me into the middle of everyone, looking like a rat.

Staring at myself made me blush. Nothing covering me but a ragged tatter of lanion skin. About ninety-nine percent of me was visible to the naked eye.

The blush went away and a scowl took its place. Pushed my face close to the mirror and stared me square in the eye. My mind clicked away. I had been in a hospital, because that was where they fixed my leg. Maybe I had been at a few other places. So why hadn't they put some clothes on me? And who was responsible? Who decided to drop me naked among a group of my fancy relatives? Had their purpose been to rock some insane jaks? Did someone care that people were losing their minds and giving up an important part of themselves? Who had brought me to this world? Dreens? Who had taken me to a hospital? Dreens? Who had brought me here? Dreens ? Who cared about insane jaks? Dreens? Or—who was trying to embarrass me?

Grinned at myself in the mirror. Turned on a water faucet, wet my hands and pushed the hair back from my face. Sucked in my belly, shoved my chest out, stretched my good leg. Compared to the citizens of Gibraltar, I was one big, muscular, yellow-haired, black-eyed—hmmm, and my skin looked good, too.

95

Imagine some silly little Dead Eye trying to shame Galactic Jade?

For the first time, I appreciated Big Jak. He had given me a name. I would have been hard put to think up one for myself. Another thing he had taught me: When in the sticks, one behaved like the other hillbillies.

"Why are you always watching me?" I asked Arnet.

"You've been here two weeks. Why haven't you lost your mind?"

"How long you been here?"

"Three weeks. I leave in seven days."

There was one woman who had been watching me pretty closely for the last several days. Think maybe she thought I had a bad smell, as her nose was always wrinkled whenever her eyes were on me. She finally came up to me in the bathroom and spoke. I was to learn that such places were meeting grounds. If you wanted to talk in secret with someone, you met them in a bathroom. They were spots where you could find plenty of water and seats to sit on. The water was for washing or drinking, the seats were for getting rid of excess food and fluid in your innards. Very sanitary. But confining. If you wanted to use bathrooms, you couldn't do much skipping.

Anyway, the woman came up to me when I was playing in the sink, and she said to me, "You're from out there. Tell me what it's like."

"Big."

"Is that all?" She had a pale face and round eyes. Her uniform of the day was the same as the other inmates, a long, shiny, softly colored loose-fitting gown. It was too large around her shoulders. Probably she had lost a deal of weight during her confinement.

"It's there," I said. "It's free. Use your imagination. It's not at all like this planet. There, everything is real. I've seen worlds made of nothing but red gas, seen worlds of solid black rock, or they're balls of yellow water. Best ones are green, with lots of flowers. The sight does something to your body. Think color speaks to the human soul. People are incurable conversationalists. Their minds have to talk to quality. If there ain't any to talk to, the mind turns like a worm and talks to itself."

She went away without asking me anything else, and that afternoon she took the trip to the Lobot. Maybe she'd had her fill of a one-way conversation.

"My father used to do this," said Arnet. "I mean, he tested his mental stability by occasionally admitting himself to an asylum where he could be close to the Lobot."

"Like standing behind a tree, knowing the jak with the scythe is standing on the other side."

"Jak with the scythe?"

"Death."

"Oh, no, it's nothing like that." Later, he said, "Why do you suppose we speak the same language?"

"Your people probably copied it from mine, then when yours came to Gibraltar they decided not to change it."

He wasn't offended. Never did I see Arnet take offense at anything. It would have been better for him if he'd let it all out and not bottled it up. Everything made him mad. Why didn't he enjoy it?

He left the asylum a week later, and I thought that would be the last I'd ever see of him. One week after that, it was my turn to go. Not that I thought the Dreen guards would let me out. They fooled me. The day came when they motioned me over to the barred exit. Not speaking, they opened the door. Didn't seem like they hated me or felt anything for me.

Didn't know what I expected to be waiting for me outside. Expected something in the form of trouble, though. Arnet hadn't believed my story about Dead Eye trying to kill me. Violence was supposedly as unpopular on Gibraltar as it was in the rest of the galaxy. No use my arguing with him, so I hadn't. But neither had he been shot at and wounded by a burning ray.

Arnet had been relieved when he'd left the nut house, seemed to experience a little sense of emancipation. Not so with me. Inside the asylum or outside on the bronze street, to my mind that world was a jail. If you made an artifact, you instinctively wanted to hang around it. Make over a planet with your mind and hands and you were almost morally obligated to live on it. The secret of freedom was to never make anything. Artifacts were vocal comments. So, don't talk so much.

Had known, five seconds after I woke on Gibraltar, that I was stuck to it, at least for the time being. A jak and a mount were never separated, no matter how much distance lay between them. I had a mount. Could toss his butt all over creation. That is, if he weren't tied down. Hinx was tied down. Not by a vine, or anything like it. He and Volcano were back on that planet of the gruesome wind. Sitting on two hills were two artifacts, the noses of which pointed to the sky. Out of the noses poured rays of gray light that stopped the mounts' jinks dead. Stopped mine dead, too. Couldn't reach Hinx. Stuck to Gibraltar was I until I could get my hands on one of the little white mounts the Dreens rode.

There was another planet I was interested in, but I couldn't find it with my long-reaching antennae. Never having been there and never having discussed its whereabouts with anyone, I had no way of homing in on the planet of the varks. Felt sorry for Shaper. Felt something else for Big Jak. It was annoyance. Varks wouldn't do a thing to him. He was invincible to everything but his own bile. The varks would spit him out like a rotten seed.

Was surprised the Dreen guards in the asylum hadn't shoved me in one of the wall exits so I'd be carted off to the jink killer. Felt a little puzzled by the fact that nothing bad was happening to me. Though my leg was still bandaged, it pained me none at all, felt like new. The wrapping was supposed to fall off by itself. The inside lining was stuck to my flesh and the enzymes, whatever they happened to be, that were smeared on the lining were supposed to work until the skin on my leg was healed enough to discard the lining.

At any rate, I felt no sense of freedom as I stepped onto the street of Gibraltar. The place was insane and so were its inhabitants. It was populated by people with perfectly good jink who never used it. Couldn't imagine anyone being satisfied with somebody else's description of a place when all he had to do was open his eyes and he would see it for himself. The galaxy was out there, wide open and roaring, but nobody here had ever looked at it, except for the Dreens.

Arnet was outside, waiting for me. "I'm the only friend you have," he said, smiling a little.

"Where we going?"

"To an orphanage. I hope you don't mind. As a minor, you're subject to juvenile law."

"I don't see why, since I'm not a citizen."

"Everyone on Gibraltar is a citizen."

"And 'citizen' means 'prisoner.'"

"Being a jak, you would naturally think so. Don't be offended, but I have some advice for you. Try to think of Gibraltar as your lifelong home."

"Right now am thinking about your top government official. Want to talk to him. I don't belong here and wish to leave."

Arnet shook his head. "We have no government. Everyone here rules himself. We're all equal."

"In that case, you should have named the place Heaven."

Chapter X

It was called the Union, and it was the largest building of all, so high it seemed to have no roof, shining like pale gold in the sunlight. It wasn't gold but a thin coat of bronze. Arnet had already told me his father came here every Novet, or the first day of the five days of the week, which were named after Gibraltar's moons: Novet, Rija, Quare, Ander and Shian.

In the planet's upper strata, a metal mesh orbited. It was kept in position and motion by mutual gravitational systems, one within the mesh itself, the other deep in Gibraltar's body. The mesh had many purposes. It locked out undesirable solar rays, scooped in light and distributed it evenly so that the planet was in perpetual daylight, did the same thing with heat so that the citizens enjoyed a constant temperature of seventy-five degrees. The mesh also served as an oxygenator, air cleaner and weather maker (when some city's populace decided it wanted a little rain or a hotter sun, etc.).

Arnet and I trailing behind him, Cedron walked into Union's main entrance, stepped into an elevator and rode to the twenty-sixth floor. We saw no one as we walked down a long corridor. Cedron pushed through a door marked Employment, and stopped at the first desk.

There were a hundred desks in the room and beside each was a three-foot-high computer. The noise was deafening, came not from the computers but from the hundred-odd men and women who worked at typewriters, fed cards into the computers, shouted at each other, scraped chairs or wandered around. The place looked frantically busy, but Arnet had told me the people weren't doing anything except putting in their time at a job any single computer could accomplish more effectively. In fact, after everybody went home, the computers redid what had been done.

The man at the desk was young and annoyed-looking. "Yes?" he said to Cedron.

"I am applying for employment."

"What have you been doing?"

"Surgery?"

The man scowled, examined Cedron, noted the frayed sleeves of the blue gown.

"You must be quite a doctor," he said, laughing a little and waiting for Cedron to laugh with him. Cedron remained impassive, and the man lost his smile. "What's your name?"

Cedron handed him a card. The man accepted it, placed a finger on the first number near its top, punched the corresponding number on a computer beside him. He did the same with the remaining eight numbers. A blue card belched from a slot into his waiting hands.

"Why have you come here for a job?"

Cedron didn't answer.

"You odd ones with high intelligence, you don't follow rules. You don't read regulations. You think you can come in here looking like trash and take someone else's job." The man leaned forward. "You wouldn't be in this office if you weren't shaky in the cranium. What were you doing? Fooling around with the wrong woman?"

"I retired," said Cedron.

The man looked at the blue card. "At forty-five?"

"I can explain that though I was a surgeon, I'm no longer interested in the profession. I want a position writing for medical journals. I don't want to be a surgeon anymore. I believe I can write articles about operations."

"You can't do more than one thing. That's the rule."

"I don't intend to have more than one job," said Cedron.

"If you're a surgeon you can't be a writer."

"I'm not going to be a surgeon."

"You have to. You have a blue card." The man tapped the card to make his point. "You're classified. If you don't work, you don't eat. Once you're classified, that's it."

"You must forward my application exactly as I state it."

The man looked offended. "Please don't tell me my job. I have all the regulations memorized. Let me give you a little advice. I don't know what you're trying to pull, but I know it won't work."

"I'm applying for a job as a writer."

"You're a surgeon."

"I am to be reported as—"

"You don't have to get smart."

"My name is Cedron. I live at—"

"Okay. I'm doing it. You're going to get kicked right out of this building." The man rammed another card into his typewriter and began pecking carefully. "You know, I never could figure out why they let you guys handle those jobs. You screw-happy nuts can't have much time to cut out guts when you're all the time cutting out our wives." He threw the card at Cedron. "Upstairs, two-seven-six-zero."

Cedron retrieved both cards and moved away. A fat woman at the next desk said, "Traitor."

Room two-seven-six-zero contained fifty desks, fifty computers and fifty noisy people. No one paid attention to Cedron, including the clerk beside whose desk he stopped. He placed the white card on the desk where she could see it. She gave it a quick glance and said, "Next clerk."

Cedron went to the next desk and laid down his card. "Next clerk," said the man, not looking up.

He received the same response from every clerk in the room. He went back to the first desk.

"I told you next clerk," said the girl.

"I went there. He said the same thing you did. All of them said the same thing."

She snatched the card and looked at it. "I don't know what to do with this," she said angrily. "Cam," she yelled at the nearest clerk, "what do you do with this?" She sailed the card through the air onto Cam's desk.

"Didn't know before, don't know now."

"You're in the wrong room," the girl said to Cedron.

"Where is the right one?"

"Look, mister . . . oh, hell, you goofballs are all the same." She scrambled from her chair and climbed onto her desk. "Shut up," she screamed, waving her arms. "Everybody quiet." Nobody was quiet, so she screamed again. The din died down. "This guy," she yelled, pointing at Cedron. "This white card," she yelled, pointing at Cam who held the card aloft. "Who knows what to do with it?"

"Shove it," cried a woman. Everyone laughed but Cedron's clerk.

"Knock it off. Come on, come on, cooperate. We have a job to do."

"I think it goes to Mr. Dock," someone called.

"Yeh, Dock gets it," said another. "I once saw some white cards on his desk."

By the time the woman clambered off her perch, Cedron had retrieved his card from Cam and was gone.

Dock flipped a switch on his intercom.

"Yes, sir?" said a voice.

"Get me a profile on Cedron, two-zero-four-nine-nine-six-eight." Dock turned off the machine and looked at his secretary. "Have him wait."

The secretary looked at Cedron, who stood beside Dock's desk. "You have to wait."

Thirty minutes later, Dock had the profile in his hand. Arnet and I stood in a corner and listened to him read it.

"Cedron, age forty-five, menta two-ten, classification Blue, qualified to practice the sciences of medicine, psychometry, psychotherapy. Employed on staff of Peace Clinic Three. Request for reclassification considered by Union Board and—"

Dock stopped and glanced up. "You're a qualified scientist."

Cedron was silent.

"Your interest profile shows no preference for creative writing."

"But I have such an interest," said Cedron.

"The world needs scientists."

"I believe it."

"Society benefits from talent," said Dock.

"It does."

"You owe it to your fellow men to perform where you excel."

Cedron was silent.

"What would happen if every scientist decided to change his profession?"

No comment.

"There is no opening in the technical-writing field," said Dock. "Or in any writing field."

"What does that mean?"

"The professions are full."

"What does that mean?"

"Your request for reclassification is denied."

Next day, Cedron went to work, and Arnet and I went along to watch. Nobody cared that we were there.

Peace Clinic III was big and busy. One architect had designed one building that was duplicated thousands of times. Nobody lived his life without entering one.

The clinic covered a ten-mile area, a massive succession of walls, windows and driveways. Patients did not park their vehicles near the buildings. Buses ejected passengers before the place was even in sight. The sidewalks were usually crowded.

Clinic services were free and citizens were urged to get their share. Witch doctors were available for non-believers, as were mediums and astrologers.

The clinic was eighty floors high. The first floor was a traffic-directing bureau. We went to General Surgery, eleventh floor.

The operating rooms were assembly lines. Patients were prepped and a tag was taped to each forehead. One at a time, they were loaded onto a metal strip that moved them past several relay stations. At the first stop they were anesthetized, at the second they were checked to determine their state of unconsciousness, at the third the anatomical area to be opened was cleansed, the fourth stop placed the patient under the surgeon's hands, and at the last stop his incision was closed and dressed by a person who passed him on to a recovery cubicle.

Cedron's working space was large enough to accommodate an assembly strip and four technicians. The room was a dazzling glare of steel and lights.

Someone threw Cedron a white smock, shoved him into place and hauled gloves on his hands. The metal strip in front of him began to slide.

He removed ten appendixes, three portions of liver, an ear, a lung with three inches of knife in it, a stone from an eye, four collapsed uteruses, three goiters and fifteen tumors. He didn't pass out.

Neither did I. I didn't know what I was supposed to have learned from all that. What I did learn was that, on Gibraltar, if you had a skill, you worked your ass off.

The reason Cedron wanted to change his line of work was that his present job was killing him. At forty-five, he looked two hundred. Had he been classified as a writer, he could have produced at his own pace, as creativity was, supposedly, possible only when inspiration was present, and inspiration was like a belly-ache in that you never knew its cause or when you'd have it.

The lifespan of the people here was one hundred, so Cedron's life was nearly half over.

It didn't take me long to learn how to recognize the dedicated citizen from the slacker. Cedron said I had it wrong, that the difference was actually between the skilled and unskilled. Whatever it was, those who worked looked like they had one foot in the grave, while the rest were lazy and had big appetites, like Otho, Cedron's brother. Otho lived with Cedron and Arnet.

Otho was an artist. He painted pictures that made no sense to me. Sometimes Cedron criticized the paintings, seriously, and always Otho seemed smug and annoyed. He taught Arnet how to paint, but either he taught better than he knew or Arnet had more talent because the boy's pictures were better than his uncle's. Cedron was like Arnet, skinny and thoughtful. Otho was fat and graceless and had no use for me. To him, I was always the poor relation. In fact, I was that to everyone I met on Gibraltar. Seldom did I have the feeling that people really believed I was from the galaxy. This included Arnet. Maybe he believed me with his mind, but not with his emotions. Only the Dreens accepted me for what I was, and this only in an unspoken way. The Dreens had little to say to anyone.

The orphanage where I spent the next few weeks was a big building on an empty boulevard. It reminded me of Bounding Winter because it was supervised by old people. They had been workers all their lives and, still dedicated, they spent their last years being useful.

I soon began referring to the people around me as gibs, and I dropped the capital from the word "dreen." None of them deserved more than jaks, as far as I was concerned. Anyhow, gib males were bigger than gib females, and both seemed proud of the fact, but males more than females. Everybody was expected to marry, and most lived up to the expectation, save for gibs like Cedron who had either buried a mate and were too tired to try again or who were that way to begin with.

A big strong female gib, no matter what or who, was disapproved of. This took me a long time to understand, and when I finally did I still didn't really understand. A tall girl was all right, as long as she wasn't overly strong. If she was muscular, she wasn't all right. Obviously, there weren't too many big strong girls. Genes had a way of copying themselves and if men continually married little weak women they weren't likely to produce big strong daughters. I think if gib men had found some way to reduce the menta or intelligence quotient of their women without affecting themselves, they would have done it and said it was for the good of the race.

The emphasis on gender was so intense that I found myself going around cross-eyed as I jinked people for this quality. After I realized why I was doing it, I stopped. It was unnatural for me and I'd never grow accustomed to it. A person was a person and gender was irrelevant to all but lovers and then only in a peculiar way. That is, lovers knew what they were. And it was still irrelevant. So it seemed that I knew more about sex than I had thought I did.

Orphans were second-class gibs, at least during their confinement. After they matured and moved into the general population, their heritage was forgiven them by all but prejudiced minority groups.

The orphanage had two wings. Boys lived in one, girls in the other. In the beginning, I starved, as I was expected to need no more food than a ninety-five pounder, which was the average weight of a fourteen-year-old girl gib. Maybe the supervisors thought I would shrink to normal size if I had normal rations. On the average of once a week, I raided the kitchen. At first, one old bag tried to send me back to the dormitory with empty hands. Eventually they tried it by the threes and fours, but never did I leave empty-handed, and never did I hit any of them. I simply ignored them. They, meanwhile, climbed up my back or tried to tie me up, and finally they learned how useless it was to interfere with a one-track mind, so they ended by standing stiff-assed and glaring at me like I had eight legs, which bothered me not at all. I got plenty to eat and nobody caved in my head.

Arnet was the only real friend I had. He went against the grain by loving me and I always had a fond affection for him, but one day I lost my mind and fell in love with a vark, and this marked the place where my life really began to change. Or maybe I was simply growing up.

The girls in the dorm changed their hair style from cropped-curly to long-shaggy. Like mine. The head supervisor, a horrid old gib named Alvis, bawled me out. The boys in the other wing copied the girls' hair style. Everyone went around bushy. Alvis took me aside and gave me a lecture. I didn't know what she was talking about.

"What is it you think I should do?" I said.

She screwed up her prune face, sneered with her scrawny shoulders. "You must conform."

"What'd I do?"

"I don't know."

"Well, me either," I said.

"Why should they emulate an uneducated freak like you?"

"Maybe they're bored."

"They don't care for you," she said. "You haven't a friend in the place."

"I actually think they like me. They're afraid to be seen being friendly to me."

"Why should they?"

"Because of horrid old gibs like you."

Her eyes got wet. Little blue buttons, they stabbed through me. "You've been talking to them about the galaxy. As if you know anything about it. They found you under a rotting cabbage. You're the first cabbage-head in the universe."

"I was found under a lanion pod."

Poor Alvis. She shrank, she fidgeted. She said what was on her mind because she couldn't help it. "What's it like out there?"

I went away without answering. First time somebody young asked me that question, I'd tell them. They might understand. But the girls never asked. They wanted to. That's why they grew their hair long. It was why they all began to talk like Ridge Runners. They believed. Inside of three months, I practically wrecked that orphanage, and I did absolutely nothing. The girls taught the boys and before long no one in the place had any culture.

I was transferred.

"My brother has more compassion than sense," Otho said to me. "Do you know where they were going to send you?"

"I'd appreciate it if you'd tell me who 'they' are. Sounds like an authority and I been looking for one so I can get gone from here. What I need is a mount. You know where I can get one?"

"You are living proof of the degeneration of our backward kinfolk. As an uneducated lout—"

"Where were they going to send me?" I said.

"To live with the Dreens."

"Damn. Wish they had."

"My dear girl—"

"As a puny little runt who can't paint—"

Otho laughed. He always did that when he was enraged.

"Actually, I think you're kind of brainy," I said. "You

know damn well you have no natural talent for painting. That's why you made it your profession. If you were good at it, your stuff would be in demand and you'd have to paint your ass off. As it is, you simply fart around, living off Cedron and pecking at him till he's bleeding and he doesn't even know it. He believes what 'they' told him. Art is more important than science. Creativity is treasure. Maybe it is, but you have none."

Otho's face was pale. I think he liked me, right then. Everybody needs an outlet for their emotions. "What makes you an expert?"

"Don't know. Am sure I read you right, and am sure this planet is upside down."

"You have to be educated. It's the law." He looked happy as he changed the subject.

"Think it isn't a good thing."

"Unavoidable, nevertheless. Do you know how children are trained?"

"Saw it in the orphanage. It gets done during sleep. They never got around to me."

"Machines," said Otho. "Those lovely things for which you have such fondness. And here, you'll be gotten around to."

"Know damn well I hate 'em."

"Of course. Continue to hate them. For now. The day will come when you won't be able to survive without them. You'll go running to the Lobot, though."

"Why do you call it that? It doesn't have a thing to do with lobes."

"Oh, go away," he said in an irritated voice. "No one can talk to you. Can't you do anything but ask questions? Who cares what they call it as long as it silences you?"

One day Arnet and I were kissing down by the well. This was a big noisy piece of machinery that brought water from underground and dumped it into the reservoir, a large concrete pool full of paddles, filters and other stuff.

"Isn't there any place quiet on this world?" I said.

"Our population is great. I've heard the dreens' property is relatively peaceful."

"Why do they have their own land?"

"It pleases them and us to have it that way."

"Tell me everything you know about them," I said.

"There isn't much to tell. A long time ago we men were all very intelligent. The first dreens were freaks with low mentas, too stupid to function like normals but not so stupid that they didn't have most of the drives other people had. They made good law officials because they didn't mind paper work or tracking down criminals. Not that there were ever too many of those."

"How do the dreens live?" I asked.

"In barracks. They like plain living."

"They breed a lot?"

"I don't imagine so."

"You mean you don't know?"

With a sigh, Arnet lay back on the stone-covered ground. "On an immense planet like ours there's room for everyone. We could handle a population of thirty billion if we had to."

"What I can't understand is how your people can know so little about each other."

"Don't be silly. And stop talking. Lie down and look at the sun."

"I would if I could. All I see is a glare and that metal net way up there."

He took my hand. "You could see it if you'd stop jinking."

"Is that the secret? If I quit jinking will I be able to see all the beautiful things you say are all around me?"

"Yes."

"That's proof of something I suspected."

"What?" he said.

"Never mind. Suppose you tell me how you can ignore a part of yourself."

Looking irritated, he sat up. He squeezed my hand hard but he wasn't strong enough to make me wince. I figured that any day now he would get annoyed enough to give me the brush off. I'd be sorry, but there would be nothing to do about it.

"One thing you should understand is that men have agoraphobia," he said.

"What is it?"

"Look it up in the dictionary."

110

"You know I can't read."

It was about a month later that I learned what the big word meant. One night I woke up and found my bed had grown steel fingers and was making my head a prisoner. I had my own room in Cedron's little house, and I took advantage of my privacy by wrecking the bed.

Otho gave me hell for it. "This property belongs to the state and now we have to pay for it."

"You mean Cedron has to pay."

"He'll have to go without some new medical equipment he needed."

"Why don't you go without new canvases? Damned things are all over the place as it is."

Otho called the dreens. On the kitchen wall was a copper panel dotted with colored buttons. Otho punched the red one and in a little while a dreen came to the door. Gibs recognized dreens by their uniforms. All I had to do was look at their faces and I knew them.

"How are you, Dead Eye?" I said.

"The bed will be replaced today. You will receive an education. It is the law."

That was the way they all talked. Of course, I'd heard them sing a different tune, but that had been in another time and place. On Gibraltar, the dreens were more like robots than people.

"What happens if I tear the new bed up, too?" I said.

Otho answered with a snarl. "I'll see you put into the asylum."

To the dreen, I said, "Can he do that?"

"Cedron is your guardian. Only he can change your place of residence."

"He wouldn't do it," I said. "He'd see his house in splinters first."

The dreen stared at me without batting an eye.

"Damn you," said Otho, through his teeth.

"I'll have to think about it," I said to the dreen.

He went out without a word. That afternoon I got a new bed.

Spent all the time I needed to think about how much I wanted to cost Cedron. Slept outside on a stony road for a few nights. Went to the zoo with Arnet and saw a vark in a cage. In another cage were two monkeys. One of the monkeys acted like a bird while the vark acted like a monkey.

"I hate those damned things," said Arnet.

"Monkeys?"

"No. Varks."

"How come?" I said.

"I don't know. A couple of books have been written about them, but we still know so little. They'll eat anything, they never seem to sleep, their mentas are at rock bottom yet they survive in almost any environment."

"Kind of ugly," I said. "Why does it act like a monkey?"

"What are you talking about?"

"Nothing that isn't obvious, but never mind."

"Let's go see the difers." He seemed anxious to get away from the vark's cage.

"Where'd all these animals come from?"

"The dreens bring them from other worlds."

"Any mounts in cages?"

He laughed. "No."

"You go on ahead. I'll catch up with you."

The rangy, four-legged thing with gray hide and long teeth, which was a vark, sat on a high bar inside the cage and picked fleas off itself. Next to it, in the other cage, one of the monkeys sat in a corner and smiled at me.

"Which of you is which?" I said. "I know a monkey when I see one, and you ain't one."

The monkey smiled and smiled.

"I feel like calling a dreen," I said.

The monkey quit smiling and let out a loud squawk, after which it raced around the cage, beat up the other one, swung like crazy on its bars and shivered like it was scared to death. In the next cage, the vark sat on its gray rear and smiled at me.

Disliked to admit it but I learned more from Otho than anyone else. He was the only gib I ever met who had no illusions, and since I annoyed him so much he always painted the blackest pictures possible whenever he explained anything to me. Unintentionally on his part, I got more of the truth that way.

"You think there's anything dangerous about this night-learning in bed?" I asked him.

He was a weird fellow, sat outside the front door with his easel in front of him and brush in one hand while he watched the sky and painted a cloud.

"By the way, that ain't how clouds look," I said. "If you want to see one, why don't you open your third eye and take a stare at the ones swarming above that net way up there? Of course, they're all just a bunch of shadows at that height. You ought to do a big white fluffy one in a purple sky. Recollect a planet I was on—"

"I'm a surrealist, besides which, art is all imagination," he said.

"Besides which, practically nobody knows what a cloud looks like, so you could give them a tree and they'd never know the difference. This world is messed up. But that machine in my bed—"

"It will probably do you no good," said Otho. "Rote learning. Preps you for conditioning. Tutors the subconscious, which is an idiot. But if you study the books by day, you learn all by yourself."

"Will it teach me to read?"

"That first of all."

"How does it work?"

"You get a lesson during deep sleep. After you wake, you take the same lesson yourself. It's very elementary in the beginning. You learn the alphabet, first the sounds and then the figures. The machine can show you pictures."

"Without me looking with my eyes?"

"Yes, dum-dum, without that. Now go away and smash something while I paint my clouds."

Next day: "Do you like varks?"

"Hate the damned things," said Otho. "There are exactly three zoos in the world, and each has a fine specimen of that ugly creature."

"Do you like dreens?"

"Hate the damned things."

"What's agoraphobia?"

113

"A dread of open spaces." Otho had been painting. Now he swung around in his chair and viewed me with little mean eyes. "You'll get it too."

"That why nobody around here will open their third eye?"

"What's it like out there?" he asked.

"Big. Like a hole with no bottom."

That evening I made the mistake of asking Cedron why the dreens hadn't put me in a zoo. He gave me a long lecture on the sanctity of human life. I asked him why the dreens had dragged me to Gibraltar in the first place. Cedron gave me a long lecture about something called samaritanism. It couldn't have applied to me, as I hadn't been lying wounded in a ditch when the dreens plucked me out of my big happy home. I'd been kidnapped. But no gib would believe it, not even Otho. He couldn't imagine anyone wanting me badly enough to steal me. As for Cedron, he never believed anything bad about anybody. He couldn't and live with Otho. Arnet thought I was the galaxy's biggest storyteller. So I had nobody to confide in.

A few nights later I was lying in my bed, looking out the window at the sky and wishing I could see the stars with my eyes. In a few minutes I planned to get up and sleep on the floor. Opening the window, I got back in bed. Began brooding about my problems.

Came a slight racket at the window and a thing flew in and settled onto the bureau.

"Figured you wouldn't mind some friendly company."

I sat up. "You escape from the zoo?"

"Nope."

"Never knew varks could talk and never knew they could fly."

"Now you do."

"You honest?" I said.

"What do you want to know?"

"If you're a friend or an enemy."

"Friend."

"What can you do for me?"

"Show you how to survive," said the vark.

114

Chapter XI

Valdar hadn't escaped from a zoo.

"Mind your own business," he always said whenever I asked him very personal questions.

"Would it be too personal to ask how you can fly when you have no wings?"

He was built oddly, seemed to have total control of his body temperature to such an extent that he could make himself into a jet-propelled missile. Inside, he was mostly tubes or pipes. With his mind he brought up his internal temperature, slowly or quickly, whichever he desired. Hot air moved through him, round and round, and when he was ready to fly, the air he released was so hot that it reacted against the air outside by shoving him forward at a rapid rate.

I thought he was lying about this, though I often saw him fly for short distances. His gray body became almost attractive when he heated up, turned pink and transparent-looking and somewhat boneless. It lengthened and slimmed down, his front legs went forward while his back legs stretched behind him, his head arched upward and away he went, soundlessly and as speedily as an arrow. One thing I had to admit was that during takeoff and in flight Valdar was as graceful as anything I'd ever seen. Another thing I admitted was that, on the ground, he was also uglier than anything I'd seen.

"I never heard of a vark ever being anything other than hideous," I said to him once. "How do you account for that?"

"Anybody who believes all hearsay is an idiot."

115

"You saying the tales people tell have no factual basis?"

"Could be, or couldn't be."

"Well, which is it?"

"Best way to find out is shut your mouth and observe."

"Am already learning by observing. For instance, we're talking jink language, but you're no mount. Though you're an animal, you aren't the kind I evolved with. We shouldn't be able to converse."

"There you go again, spouting hearsay. Who told you only mounts and jaks had intelligence?"

I thought I had him trapped somewhere. "When did you ever meet up with a jak?"

"Am talking to one right now."

"You must have met others, since you know our name."

"Met up with all kinds of creatures, dumb or bright, great or small."

He was too boastful and if he hadn't been so interesting I'd have gotten bored and thrown him out of my room or reported him to the zoo authorities.

The galaxy was his responsibility. That was what the vark said. All his life he had done his duty and he was sick of it. Wanted to be free. Wanted to be a common ordinary hedonist, like everybody and everything else in the galaxy, with the exception of the gibs and dreens.

"Want to do a lot of hypnotizing," he said to me.

"Who's going to be the subject?"

"Don't be naive."

"Go on and get yourself out of my room. Don't come back. Nobody takes control of my mind."

"Of all the dumb—"

"No use your going on. You're wasting your time."

I listened, but only because he was interesting. He had delusions of grandeur.

Hypnotizing was a way of life on Gibraltar, and the best way to counteract its effects was to do some of your own. Or his own. Valdar's. He said if I didn't listen to him I'd turn out to be a gib with less stability than Arnet, Cedron or Otho.

He was quite a storyteller.

116

Once upon a time there were three eagles. Brothers, they always flew together. One day they flew through a narrow crevice in a mountain and exited over a valley. A sudden earthquake knocked down rocks behind them and closed up the crevice. Overhead, the rocks were so solid that the eagles knew there was no way out in this direction. But ahead of them were three skinny cracks in a sheer wall of granite. Which one should they take to get out of the valley?

None of the three eagles opted to stay where they were. It was pretty enough and there were plenty of game and plant life, but the idea of being in such a small place was intolerable to eagle personalities. They wanted to escape and the only way to do it was through one of the cracks in the mountainside.

The three had an argument. Having already investigated, they knew what lay beyond the cracks. The first led straight to a handsome mountain lair which promised safety and an abundance of supplies. Only drawback to it was that it was a possible dead end. The rock walls around it were so high that even an eagle might not be able to fly above them.

The second crack led to everywhere. It wasn't exactly pitch-black beyond that second crack, as there were tantalizing lights blazing in the distance, but it was a wild and empty, scary and challenging entrance into mystery.

The third crack led into a valley that contained a microscope. This was a huge artifact that had the capacity for focusing upon the movements and behavior of things great and small. There were a number of other artifacts in this valley, and some of them were dangerous.

The three eagles had a fight and parted. Each chose a separate exit from the prison. One went to safety, settled down and had a family. Occasionally he went to check on his brother who had gone through the second crack. The first eagle was scornful at what he saw. His brother was foolish and wasteful, wandered like a loose feather, bred like an insect, didn't have a place he could call home, did nothing but chase after lights in the sky. The second brother had forgotten he had any siblings, went his own way and explored

117

his environment. He found that chasing lights was more entertaining than anything he could think of.

The third eagle? He put his eye to the microscope, first thing, and what he saw interested him so much that he didn't leave the valley of the artifacts for a long time. He saw his brothers on the slide, could follow their patterns and see what they did, and what they did was make mistakes. Or so the third eagle thought. He wasn't sure. But he was convinced that none of them should have split up. They were all eagles, destined to fly, and here on the one hand was his brother who did nothing but sit on his nest and seldom move out of it, and there on the other hand was his brother who sailed around like a mindless spore.

What to do? The third eagle spent an aeon thinking about it. He figured he was more stable than his brothers, more philosophical, more sensible. He also knew he had more power, what with the artifacts in his valley. Yet he hesitated. Finally he came to a decision. He would do nothing about his brothers' mistakes until a crisis arose.

"Didn't like that story and don't want you to tell me any more," I said to Valdar. "They make my head ache."

"That's because they're sitting on your reason. It wants to respond but you won't let it. You're now in a dilemma and I'm leaving you in it. Never believed in doing anything other than making people offers. Won't persuade. It's immoral."

"Why is it immoral?" I asked.

"Because this is an open-ended universe."

"You think I'm too ignorant to understand, but what you mean is that you might be wrong."

"Yes, I might be wrong."

Where did that pesky vark come from? A dozen times a day I asked myself the same question.

"About every two months or so I figure you ought to get sick. Like that sissy friend of yours. Arnet. You think maybe you could copy him when he takes to ailing?"

So where did he come from?

At night I slept with my head in the machine connected to my bed. In the morning I read whatever books the machine doled out to me. I also read the books Valdar gave me. He called them compensatories. I learned to read pretty well and my head was stuffed with all kinds of ideas. The books Valdar gave me were the better ones. My favorite was *The Three Musketeers*. Another good one was *Les Miserables*.

The dreens began coming to the house regularly, and Otho commented about it until we wanted to kill him.

"Do you suppose they like my art?" He said this at the supper table one night. Arnet didn't even look at him but Cedron grew thoughtful, looking as if he were genuinely considering the question.

"No, they don't like your art," I said. "They hate me is why they're coming around."

"Nonsense," said Otho. "They can't care enough about you to hate you."

Said Cedron, "Leave the child alone."

"This is no child. This is a creature."

Arnet laughed and Otho got mad and ate more than he usually did, which meant the rest of us didn't get enough.

"Your perfect society has rats in the granary," I said to Otho.

"You don't have to tell that to someone who already realizes it. I have talents nobody will ever know about because it would mean I'd be forced to work myself into the grave. Cedron here is a fool. He's killing himself and for what?"

"The future," said Cedron, calm, exhausted, not offended.

"Did you know Gibraltar is almost like the cities that existed two million years ago?" I said to no one in particular. "If you call that progress, we don't have anything more to say to each other."

"How do you know what cities were like two million years ago?" asked Arnet.

"Read about them, is how I know. Found some books in an old building."

"Where?"

"I forgot. But the old cities were like Gibraltar. The brainy people worked and everybody else sat on their duffs."

"The morons have to be supported," said Otho.

Arnet laughed.

"Expect the dreens hate more than just me," I said. "Expect they hate everybody who isn't one of them. What I'd like to know is why no one but me is curious about them? I'm beginning to think they're like the air or the cars in the streets. You're so used to them you don't see them."

"In a way, this is a perfect society," said Otho. "Someday our posterity will leave our world and until then we all work for the common good. Those who can't or won't are tolerated because the only alternative is to let them starve. As for the dreens, they enforce the law and we don't care what they do in their leisure time. It's irrelevant if they hate us."

Several months went by. I found myself soaking in culture, even reached the point where I made fun of the way Valdar talked.

"You sound like a hayseed. Can't you do better?"

"You sound like a snob. Can't you do better?"

He lived in the tree outside my bedroom window.

"If the dreens catch me they'll put me in the zoo. Or kill me. Kindly refrain from talking about me to your sissy boyfriend."

"Ain't a sissy. I mean *isn't*. He and I may get married when we're grown."

Valdar laughed like a hyena. "No punky little fella will ever suit you, gal. You've lost your mind."

"Never mind that. Why do I have to play sick all the time?"

Said Valdar, "That's personal, so butt out."

"There you go again, thinking I'm stupid."

"I'm counting on it," he said, and his ugly face was frozen with concern. "I want you to be ignorant of all that goes on around and above you. Let your curiosity get out of hand and I'll have a little dead friend to send to the stars."

"So you admit that we're friends?"

"Hate to admit it. Should have known better than to see you twice, much less more. You grow on a person."

"Which you aren't," I said. "You're a vark, and I wish you wouldn't talk like a jak. It mixes me up."

120

He was wrong. I wasn't ignorant. As long as I suffered periodic bouts of illness, the dreens were assured that I was like everybody else. Jaks who were fenced in became ill. So did gibs. Why didn't I? The one and only time I had suffered from space sickness (a longing for it) was when I had lived on Earth.

On the order of once a month, one or two dreens stopped by the house. They had all kinds of excuses for doing so. For instance, they complained about the way Cedron parked his car, or they were serving a summons and had come to the wrong address, or the curb needed repair and residents were duly notified. Things like this. Always did one of them come in our house and inquire about the health of its occupants. But why would they care if I was no different from other people? As long as I couldn't get my hands on a mount I was stuck solid to Gibraltar. Hmmm. Needed more thinking about.

Valdar bothered me. He said too many strange things. Take the remark of his about sending me to the stars if I died. That was something a jak would say, not a vark.

"Do you come from the planet of the varks?" I asked him one evening.

"What kind of question is that? It's like asking a jak if he comes from his birthplace."

"Do you know where the planet is?"

"See those lights in the sky. Well, one of them is it."

"Can I talk to you about something that's bothering me?"

"If you don't take too long and if you don't cry," he said.

"I could learn to hate you without a whole lot of trouble."

"Tell me your problem."

"I'm losing my jink."

He said, "Know all about it and have an answer for you. The reason is because you haven't been with a mount for a while. Jink is for people with mounts. Your power will ebb to a certain low and stop there. These gibs around here can't hardly feel anything at all."

121

"Will I lose it permanently?"

"Not unless your jink gland dries up."

I said, "The reason I asked you about the vark planet was because a pair of acquaintances of mine are stranded there."

"Friends?"

"I said acquaintances."

"Hate 'em, do you?"

"Butt out."

For a while I had a crush on Cedron. He was so sweet and gentle and so tired all the time. A super-patriot was he, but there was no government, only a world with nobody at the wheel. Or so Cedron thought. In my opinion there was a government on Gibraltar and it was made up of dreens.

"There is little violence on Gibraltar," Cedron said.

"I've noticed that," I said. "Jaks and gibs are about the same in that department. I think maybe gibs are more civilized. You're all planted together here, yet you tolerate each other. Jaks usually get away from each other rather than quarrel."

"What's it like out there?"

It would take a genius or a nut to think up something no one else had thought of. This I believed. Gibs knew little about anything because they had no old history to read. Valdar Vark had supplied me with a mountain of books, and from them I learned about money and the hypnotic and corruptive effect it had on the human soul. Once upon a time there lived a cave man. He looked into his viscera one day and realized he was a sissy. He had good reason. Nothing was certain but death. This was some deal. No matter how you sliced it, you, the cave man, must spend your life warding off eternity. To begin with, you lived on a rumbling world, which meant that eternity continually beckoned. It would, therefore, be natural for you to want to surround yourself with protective agents. At first, the cave represented these. So did a family represent them. Society wagged its finger and you saw it as another protection. You joined. Within society's framework stood a ladder and the surest safety lay on the top rungs. Money was the quickest way to get up there. Just exactly what was

122

on those top rungs of society's ladder? Power. With that, you needed no money in your pocket because it was on every side of you and at your immediate disposal.

Power was desired because of eternity. The black hole didn't have to be the total end. You could make your mark on history, stamp the imprint of your bootheel on the face of the future. Obtain power and there need be no end to your influence.

The gibs made money. They didn't keep it, didn't even hold it for a second. What they received were daily rations. They had homes, furniture, clothing, food, and they worked. My question: Where did the money go? Who collected it? Cedron would say it went into the common coffers to be distributed for building funds, et cetera. I didn't ask him who held the coffers, didn't ask him who did the distributing. Cedron, like most gibs I met, was innocent and naive. Stupid?

At the end of Gibraltar's production lines were benevolent ghosts who mysteriously dispensed every last farthing for the good of everyone.

In the words of some unknown and long-dead cynic, "Patriotism is the last resort of scoundrels." Feed the public bull and they'll lap till their tongues wear away.

I saw humanity as people who imagined they were drowning. Rarely, I came across someone who swore there was solid ground under his feet. This meant he wasn't climbing up someone's back.

"I have an idea," I said to Valdar. "Since you can fly, why don't you do a little spying on the dreen camp?"

"Am trying to go to sleep, in case you hadn't noticed."

He was up in his tree, while I was under it on the ground. Sprawled on a big limb, he looked like an empty sack of hair. Raising one paw, he peered down at me. "One thing I know is that artificial trees are not really fun to sleep in. This one smells like tar."

"Didn't you hear what I said?"

"Need to caution you about something. Don't go anywhere near the dreen camp."

"I don't even know where it is."

A loud snore was his response. Mad, I crawled back through the window and got into bed. Naturally I would do what he had warned me not to. Didn't I always, and wasn't that what he intended when he gave the warning?

Someone from Testing came by the next day and interviewed me. She was a severe little creature with suspicious eyes and a big prejudice against me.

"You must answer my questions to the best of your ability," she growled. We sat on two sides of the kitchen table. She had piled a stack of papers between us, perhaps as a protection in case I decided to attack her. I had looked at bugs in the same way that she looked at me.

"Why?" I asked.

"Because you wish to receive a high mark. Everybody does." She stared at me and made no move to write anything down, nor did she haul out her testing books. "Are you achievement oriented?" she said.

"Basically I'm a hedonist and see no purpose in wearing myself out."

"You don't wish to engage in meaningful work?"

"If it's meaningful to me."

She frowned. "What can you do?"

"Skip."

"I beg your pardon?"

Already I didn't like her. She was insecure, obviously. Her mind was one-track, which meant she was afraid of imagination. I tabbed her as strictly conservative.

"What I mean is I like to jump on a mount and hit D-2 fast," I said. "I'm attracted to darkness and bottomless pits and space so vast that the echoes of Nothing hit my ears and bounce and travel in all directions forever. I love hugeness, wideness, distance with hidden destinations."

"Stop," she said. "Don't tell me things like that. You're plainly disturbed."

"I don't feel so, but it's all right for you to believe it."

124

"Did you ever take a written test?"

"Not to my recollection."

"What do you want to do with your life?"

Said I, "Not plan it."

"I beg your pardon?"

"You keep saying that."

"Answer the question."

"Well, I care about today and don't worry about tomorrow. Unless I'm dead, it will come."

"What's it like out there?"

I never met a gib who didn't get around to asking me that, sooner or later. Practically everyone swore up and down I was simply a freakish native, and just as surely they contradicted themselves, as the tester did.

"Go find out for yourself," I said.

Gathering up her papers and getting away from me and the table, she paused. "I have authority and I intend to use it in your case. Morons can't be tested for work placement. They live on the public dole. While I won't call you a moron, I predict that you'll be utterly useless in any responsible position."

"I expect you're right."

"However, this isn't the end. You'll have to be analyzed. You may need medical treatment."

"My leg is healed," I said. "See. Look at it. Good as new."

"I'm talking about your head."

"You can't make a silk purse out of a sow's ear," I said. "I read that somewhere. What it means—"

"I know what it means and consider it applicable."

"Well, go on along now. Write your report and see how deep in trouble you can get me. You're that type. You'd be all right if you found yourself a mount and followed your nature. But that doesn't excuse your small soul."

I was classified as a moron and unfit for just about every kind of job.

"You're not as dumb as I thought," Otho said when the report came in the mail.

"And you could be brighter if you put a little effort into it," I said.

Arnet and I went to find the dreens.

Chapter XII

Arnet wanted to know if I loved him, and I told him that of course I did. Did I love his father? I said I did. Did I love Otho? Said I, "Never in a million years." Did I love the imaginary vark I was always talking about? I said I thought so, though that vark was very real and it wasn't my fault if he wished to remain unseen or if he had a chameleonlike ability to fade into any background. Yes, he lived in a tree outside my bedroom window; no, he hadn't come from a zoo. Where did he come from and did he love me? Answer—his origin was that of any vark's, and he didn't know the meaning of affection, being a beast. Wasn't the foregoing statement an evasion? Mounts were beasts and I'd always mentioned how they loved their riders.

"Mounts aren't beasts," I said at the top of my lungs. "You gibs have a distorted view of everything. Mounts are human."

"Meaning?" was Arnet's sarcastic remark.

"Meaning I don't know what, but they're human."

"I preferred your old way of talking."

"Are you sure that wasn't because it enabled you to feel condescending? Right away I can see you're offended. Remember, it wasn't my idea to become stuffed with education and culture."

Arnet was plagued with inferior feelings. His curiosity or fear led him to ask me if Valdar had ever watched me undress. How could I take such a query seriously? Gibs didn't trust—what? I didn't know, but they were careful never to expose breasts or groins to one another.

126

"There you go again," I said, getting annoyed. "How many times do I have to tell you—"

"Just answer the question," he yelled. He stopped on the road and glared at me.

Scratching my head, I thought for a minute. "Now that I recall, I don't really think so. Arnet, it honestly makes no difference to me or him. He thinks like a jak and jaks never go near one another unless they're in love. There's simply no appeal."

"That isn't normal, you know?" he said fiercely.

"It isn't gib."

"How do jaks fall in love?"

"You'll have to ask one who has experienced it."

"But you just said you loved that vark."

"Oh, sure, same as I love Cedron and you."

"My god, I don't want you to love me that way," he cried.

"How else can I be but earnest?"

"Shit."

We quarreled all the way to the first dreen outpost, which was about two hundred miles down the road. As I said, somewhere before, if a jak became tiresome his companion abandoned him. Arnet wasn't a jak, but tiresome he did become during that trip. I couldn't abandon him, having no mount, and I learned a lesson from my frustration. What I wanted to do was knock him down. Had he been a jak I would have done it. As it was, I couldn't. Arnet was already humiliated to the point of breaking, emotionally, so I chose not to add to his misery by flattening him on the road. But I wondered about the lesson. Did frustration always invite violence?

A field of green was the first thing I saw, and I felt as if I had arrived home. The green, green galaxy was my love. Anything resembling it couldn't be all bad. But it was.

Plenty of people had stopped to give us rides in their cars, mostly because they wanted to ogle me, and Arnet and I finally arrived in the land of the dreens. Later I realized that the many dreen outposts were what kept gibs sane. Had the dreens been able to prevent giving succor to the enemy, they surely would have accomplished it, but nature was something they couldn't completely fence off without revealing their obnoxious and egotistic souls, and so they shared with the gibs who frequently took walks around the property.

Could color establish rapport with brain or mind? Indeed, yes. Perhaps at some time in the far future the human brain would evolve beyond the need to stay in contact with the ancient home or first nest. Before there was a mind, there was environment. The music of the ancient origin soothed the savage breast. The music was color. It was also sound, texture, smell and taste. Strolling through the flowers was a necessity for all things Earthly. Put a man forever on a world of stony silence and he went mad. Take such a madman and heal him with the proper music.

Horrid thought: Suppose the gibs continued making an artifact of their world until it was totally devoid of natural environment? There would be innumerable clinics where broken minds must be nourished with images of forests, brooks, skies and animals. Sounds of bird twitterings, flowing water, rustling grass, combined with other sensory images, temporarily revived a dying psyche.

Such a world would be no home for me. Scent or taste wasn't enough. I knew only the whole meal would satisfy.

The fence in front of me was about ten feet high. Getting a firm grip on the links, I started climbing.

"We'll get booted out, whichever way we try to get in, but why not try the gate?" said Arnet. He stood on the metal shoulder of the road and made no move to join me.

"Why should I do that?" I said. "I'm in a hurry to get in and this is the quickest way."

He sighed, shook his head. Folding his arms, he made a wry face and looked at me from the corner of his eye. "You don't believe in propriety. I simply meant that those dreens over there by the guardhouse would be more polite if we asked permission."

Pausing in my climb, I said, "I thought they were never anything but nice."

"It's the principle."

"I know all about them. Just start climbing. We won't be chased out."

"Dreens never let gibs onto their property."

"They will if the gibs are in the company of Jade of the galaxy. Those fellows are crazy about me." I threw a leg over the top of the fence and sat there. "Come on."

It took him longer to get over. I was on the ground and walking away before he reached the top. There were three little white-uniformed figures standing beside a booth by a big gate, about a hundred yards away. They weren't looking my way at the moment, but they had clearly seen me.

Any second I expected them to come after Arnet and me, as we were heading toward a band of pretty white mounts. I didn't know whether I liked the looks of the mounts. They were all the same color, very much resembled the creature Dead Eye had ridden when he'd tried to kill me. Admittedly, they were handsome. Still, they were entirely different from the kind I was accustomed to. The dreens and their ideas of purity had made them breed out all coarse strains in their animals. Maybe they forgot that "coarse" didn't have to be all bad. I was certain these beasts weren't as intelligent, strong or courageous as their tougher relatives out in the galaxy.

Never did I find out if that assumption of mine was true. What I discovered was that the dreens' mounts were as thoroughly conditioned as gibs. They were located in a shallow green valley that had a cold stream of water, shade trees, fruit trees, nut and berry bushes and a small vegetable garden.

Arnet didn't want to go near the mounts. "They aren't why we came here."

"They're why I came."

"Don't you want to look at the growing things?"

"I'm up to my knees in grass. That's enough to suit me. Come on."

"They make my skin crawl."

"Talk to them," I said. "You'll calm down."

He hung back. "Those mounts won't talk."

"Did you ever try?"

129

"Not really, but I think—"

I kept walking and stopped ten feet from a mount who lay on his stomach with his face buried in his paws.

"Get up, you lazy son," I said silently.

The mount's head shot up and he looked around at me in amazement.

"I said get up."

He made no move to obey, just continued to stare while surprise and confusion had a fight in his mind.

"I'm your boss," I said.

"How can that be?"

"Am I a gib?"

"No."

"Am I a dreen?"

"No."

"What am I?"

His thought processes were rapid but uncertain, he had pride without real cause, he was like the dreens who had raised him, cocky because he had never seen anything better. I knew a mount who could show him a thing or two. Hell, even Volcano was reliable compared to this little bit of fluff.

He trembled before he answered my question in a whisper, "I don't know."

"Yes, you do. You have archetypes, the same as everybody."

"Who are you?"

"A jak."

Now he trembled more earnestly. "Please go away."

"Listen, mount, you have no choice, unless you're stronger than any mount I ever saw. I say you'll come to me."

"There is a strong thing within me, and it prevents me from agreeing to do your bidding."

"But you feel what I am, don't you? What you really know, in your mind, is that I'm a rider who could take you to places faster than the wind, and there would be no stopping. Do you see it?"

"I see traveling without pause, I hear eternity in my ears and I feel perdition threatening. With you on my back I would hunt for glory and I'd know a freedom more perfect than any other. You are what

130

I want, but I cannot come to you willingly. Perhaps you have the power to force me. Do so, and I will die. I am left with no choices."

I pulled him a little and he started to scream. He did it silently, without moving his mouth. Quickly I released him and immediately gave him a second gentle tug. He buried his face in the grass and sobbed.

Leaving him and the other mounts, I walked toward the guards by the gate. "Hi," I said, pausing in front of them.

The one on the end, a cold-eyed youth, spoke. "Good day," he said.

"Does that mean hello or good-bye?"

"Would you like to look around?" he asked.

It wasn't the nicest conversation I'd ever had. I didn't answer him, turned and walked back to the mounts. Beyond them, on the summit of a low hill, I stopped and looked into the valley. The village there was the most uncolorful one I'd yet seen on Gibraltar. All the buildings were painted a dull yellow and all were built along the same lines, low and rectangular with sloped roofs. They lay in neat rows that stretched toward more hills in the distance, one little boxlike house beside another exactly like it. In front of each house was a white mount. Some stood while others sat, but none moved away from their buildings. They reminded me of the cars parked in front of the gibs' homes. I wouldn't have expected a gib to take his car inside with him, but a mount was as good as a person and I didn't like the idea of the dreens treating animals as inferiors.

I knew full well I wasn't going to learn any more about the dreens than I already had; at least not here. It would do me no good to go down there and look in the houses. There wasn't time for me to examine them all, and I couldn't guess which ones were their science labs, schools, hospitals, et cetera. With Hinx beside me, I could have read the buildings right down to their atoms, but now I couldn't see beyond the doors.

Maybe the dreens would have answered my questions. There was simply no inspiration in me to ask any. It was a most depressing place. The sameness, the stillness and the lack of movement in that village made me want to get away fast.

"Let's go," I said to Arnet.

"Why did we come here?" He looked lost and bewildered, and I felt sorry for him.

"Don't you ever use your brains?" I said. "You see things and they mean nothing to you. This is the land of death but you don't even know it."

Shivering in the slight breeze, he looked away from me. "I don't understand you."

"Nor anything else. You shut your best eye and made yourself blind. The keenest jink can be had when you meld with a mount. On this planet only dreens meld with mounts. That fact ought to reveal something to you. What do you see down there in that village?"

"Buildings."

"I see a flat lack of imagination. The dreens are narrow-minded to the point of being deadly dull."

His voice lowering to a whisper, Arnet said, "I don't like it here. Please, Jade, let's leave."

A bushy shrub adorned with purple flowers sat beside the patch of grass where the mounts rested. As I passed by, my attention was caught by a big gray thing skulking in the shrub. Two yellow eyes glittered out at me, and as one of them slowly shut and opened again, I looked away. Valdar was uglier in shade than he was in sunlight. I walked on and didn't look back. Instead of going out by the gate, I climbed the fence and exited the same way I had entered.

"I've never done that in my life," said Arnet. "I'm glad I did. The dreens have the most beautiful property in the world."

"Is there some place I can find a map of Gibraltar?"

"No."

"What does that mean? City people always make maps."

"I'm sorry," he said. "We simply don't have any. No one travels, so there's no need for them."

It took us a long time to get home and my bed felt good when I finally climbed into it. I ought to have remained awake, as I had a bad dream.

"Jade," said the machine connected to my head. "You are asleep. We will continue last night's discussion. I call it a discussion because, even though you submit no verbal responses, your mind reacts to everything I say.

"I have decided to introduce myself at last. You call me Dead Eye in your mind. My real name is Rulon. I want you to start thinking of me as a different person. No longer am I the instructor who has been teaching you all these weeks, nor am I the enemy who tried to strike you down. There is no friction between us. I am Rulon, at first a stranger but one who will become a beloved friend after you learn all about me. Listen and know.

"I, Rulon, am a leader. So great are my responsibilities that at times I grow infinitely weary. I need a companion. It is my desire that you become that companion. The dreens are losing too many good traits because of their inbreeding. We need new blood. I will tell you why you have been chosen to be the mother of the new race of dreens. You have qualities that will be passed on to your children. Among these is your physical strength. You are large and beautiful. You are unlike other jaks in that you are not bound by spatial restrictions. Surely you are unaware of this talent, and it is my wish that you remain so. I will reveal it to you in good time. I brought you to Gibraltar in order that I might study you."

The monotony of the voice in my dream put me into a deeper sleep and I knew nothing more until morning came. At the first opportunity I hunted for Valdar, found him in a spacious hole in a thick wall behind the house.

"What were you doing in the dreen camp?" I asked.

"If you stand there talking to a wall, people will become alarmed."

Sitting beside the hole, with my back against the wall, I looked around. No one was near. "Answer the question," I said.

"Not at this time." A gray snout emerged from the hole and yellow eyes glared at me.

"Then let's talk about sex."

133

He groaned and his snout went back in the hole. "Adolescents are pains in the neck. I hate them for impersonal reasons. How many books have you read so far?"

"About a thousand."

"A third of them were classics, the remainder were trash. I wanted you to savor every type." A mouthful of teeth popped from the hole and grinned at me. "You should be an expert on sex by now."

"I'm tired of your kidding," I said. "I need to know about sex because the damned dreens are planning to—"

"I know all about it!" yelled Valdar. "Nothing on this planet I don't know." He stopped yelling and said, casually, "Curiosity was the reason I came in the first place, and it's satiated."

"You mean you're leaving?" I stuck my arm in the hole and closed my hand on his ear. It was the first time I had ever touched him. His fur was fine and soft. I felt his face, and his long eyelashes tickled my hand.

"I thought maybe I'd found a friend in you." I said. "I can understand why you don't want to stay here. If you get caught and put in a zoo, you'll be a prisoner for the rest of your life."

He laid his head on my arm. "Not worrying about that. Am worried about Rulon and his gonads."

"There's no need for that kind of worry. I can take care of myself."

"It sounds out of character for him to have sat down with you and discussed such a subject."

For the first time since I met Valdar, I had the feeling that he was fishing for information. I patted him on the head. "I want to thank you for everything you've done for me. Anytime you feel like sneaking a ride out of here with a dreen, go ahead. Don't hang around on my account."

"Is that how you think I got here? By hitchhiking?"

"Never mind what I think."

He came out of the hole, stretched and shivered, puffed out a little in the belly and rose into the air, about a dozen feet over my head. "Used to be, when

134

I talked to you, the conversation was light and easy. Don't enjoy it too much these days. No offense, but wish I'd never laid eyes on you."

"Good-bye, Valdar. If you ever run across any books about varks, remember me. I have a big curiosity."

There came a faint screaming sound as hot air met the atmosphere, and he shot away like an arrow, up into the sky, and in a few moments he was hidden by the buildings on the next block.

That evening, Arnet wanted to quarrel. "Why won't you talk jink with me?"

"Because it's difficult to do when there isn't a mount around, and you're not practiced enough."

"You talk jink with everyone and everything except me. Rocks, trees, the ground, you talk to them."

"No, only to a vark."

His eyes were slightly red. "Do you love me, Jade?"

"I'm pretty sure I'm about fifteen years old now. Jaks aren't mature until they're almost thirty."

"Meaning you don't."

"Meaning people experience all kinds of love and I feel practically every type for you, but there's no use your wanting me to feel grown-up love."

"I'm a mature gib."

"You don't look it."

He got mad and stomped away.

At dinner, I began to develop a liking for Otho. "Does an adolescent gib feel true love?" I said, ignoring Arnet. Cedron had his face in his soup and probably didn't hear me.

"He has an itch in his britches most of the time," said Otho. "Mostly it's just boredom." He looked at me from the corner of his eye. "If Arnet is pestering you, show him your bicep."

Arnet got up and left the table. I kept my stare on Otho.

"I'm curious about things," I said, and waited for the familiar blankness to come into his eyes. When it didn't come, I added, "Hypothetically speaking, I think it's possible for an organization to become corrupted because of a little internal rot."

"Really?" Otho ate rapidly and watched me like a bird, wide-eyed, unblinking.

"This idea is just imagination, I admit, but what if the dreens are a great deal brighter than is supposed?"

"I always did believe they were."

"They're either going to take over Gibraltar or abandon the planet altogether."

"Still hypothetical?" he said, not pausing in his eating.

"Yes."

"They'll probably abandon it. The place is fit only for robots."

"What happens to the gibs when the dreens leave?" I asked.

"There'll be a big noise, at first, but eventually order will be restored. The majority of gibs won't simply give up."

"Assuming the dreens don't hold too vindictive a feeling toward you."

Otho ducked his head and ate faster. He didn't want me to know that the same idea had occurred to him.

I sat back and studied him. Fat, mean little man. Could he have been born to better things? Possibly. He obviously had understood gib philosophy from an early age, otherwise he would now be engaged in slave labor, as was Cedron. It was stupid to condemn a man for being clever. Otho wasted his life in a society that demanded everything or nothing. Premature death due to exhaustion was Gibraltar's alternative to a leisurely existence.

I glanced at Cedron. He was too tired to hear what we were saying. Cedron didn't worry about dreens, didn't think of the future, worked his heart out and remained oblivious while his world, like a foundering ship, headed for the rocks.

Otho caught my attention and I was brought up short by the expression on his face. There was a hint of tears in his too-bright eyes, a helpless tension in the angle of his shoulders.

"Man, why don't you get out while there's time?" I said softly.

Getting to his feet, he walked away from me and from everything I had said. I did some more growing up in the next few minutes that I sat there and thought.

136

Chapter XIII

"How do you do?" said Dead Eye. Correction: Rulon. He came up behind me as I sat and tried to relax in the neighborhood park.

"Hi."

He lowered himself to sit beside me. "How do you like this section of Gibraltar?"

"Fine."

"Do you never smile?"

I smiled, stuck my feet in the make-believe creek in front of me, tried to imagine the touch of water. The entire park was a simulation. The area was about a mile square and was made of green and brown papier-mache. There were phony trees with phony fruit, artificial grass, rocks, bushes, even a creek that I wanted to wet my feet in. The water was made of glass.

Looking down at Rulon, I smiled again. He was small, wiry, sharp-featured, and his brown eyes were lazily alert. One of his hands lay on my knee. He moved it, put his arm around my shoulder.

"Why don't you sit on a rock?" I said. "You'll be taller that way." When he stared at me I made my eyes go round and immovable.

He did it, got to his feet and picked up an artificial rock, placed it beside me and sat on it. His arm went around my shoulder again.

"Gibs are fools, aren't they?" His voice was as smooth as genuine clover. His little Adam's apple jutted out to a sharp point. The hair on his head was a cap of tiny black snails. All the dreens had curly hair.

"They are," I said.

"They've ruined their world."

"And they gave up their freedom."

"Yes," he said, squeezing my shoulder. He tried to see down the front of my shirt, changed the subject by saying, "Are you happy with your bosom?"

"No, actually. I've been thinking about plastic surgery. I'm too flat. A pair of big ones would be more attractive, don't you think?"

"Of course."

"I'd have it done right away if I felt well enough. I'm simply too sick most of the time."

Squeeze, squeeze, one hand on my shoulder, the other on my knee, and I could feel his breath on my cheek.

"Poor little girl, it's only space illness. When I feel you're ready, I'll take you out for a brief skip. But it will be purely therapeutic. I'll want you to be in a proper frame of mind when you have the plastic surgery. It wouldn't be a bad idea to add a little padding to your thighs."

"Yes. Men like that sort of thing."

His little ass squirmed, his hip came against mine. "You're doing wonderfully. The nightly conditioning I gave you has taken a solid hold." He turned my face to his and made a little dive forward and downward so that his lips brushed mine. Chuckling, he used all his strength to put me down on my back, after which he slid on top of me and kissed me long and hard.

"That's enough for today," he said, sliding off me. I stayed where I was, and he stood over me. "There are certain chemicals we can use to soften you up, make your body sleek and feminine. You'll want that."

I watched him walk away. His uniform fit him snugly, his black boots shone, his snail-hair gleamed; he was a man who owned the world.

That night, Valdar flew onto my windowsill and hunched there like a vulture. "You look dead. What's the matter?"

"I need help."

He leaped down to the floor, came over to the bed and got in beside me.

138

Laying a hand on his head, I said, "If anyone can help me, you're it."

"Your wish, my lady."

"Meld with me. I know you can do it."

His muzzle lowered to relax on my chest. Wicked yellow eyes winked and blinked. "I'd do that only to save your sanity."

"It's my viscera that's in danger."

"Practically the same. Okay, we meld. But slightly." My mind lurched toward his, and he gave a yelp.

"You crazy kid, don't do that."

"All right. Gently. That better? Let's forget who we are. I want you to help me dream up a real man. A jak."

"Anyone in particular?" he said.

"No, no, hurry up, just go along with me until I get him to looking real. I can't do it by myself. I've been trying all day. I'm desperate, really stuck on a cliff, and in another minute—"

"Shhh. Mouth shut, eyes closed, throat relaxed, back like cotton, legs gone, you're a disembodied ego and I'm about to grab what little there is of your mind. Aha. There he is. That's a jak, for sure. Ugly, from a distance. Let's get him closer. Uh-oh."

"Yes, oh, yes, he's real enough," I said. "I don't know how I can dream up a stranger, but he's the one, the jakest jak I've ever seen."

"I really and truly hate adolescents for impersonal reasons. I want you to put that one out of your mind. He isn't the right one, isn't a proper—"

"Shut up," I whispered, and pinched the soft snout buried in my hair. "I wanted a real live jak and that fellow is the one. Help me to see him better. Ah, god, he looks good to me. Big, stringy build, huge hands, big nose, awful mouth, ugly yellow eyes; I like everything about that jak and I want him right next to me, close enough to touch. That's great."

"Kid, we don't want that one, can't you understand?"

"Hold your mind still, idiot."

"I have a bad premonition about this, and I want to state—"

Through my teeth, I said, "He's close enough now, the realest jak I ever created from nothing; something familiar about him, but his face won't come clear, but I don't care because his aura is powerful enough to knock me over. Hey, you, jak, you beautiful ghost, come here and save my soul. I've a terminal illness of the esthetic senses and only you can heal me."

I dragged poor Valdar into it. He hadn't a chance, once he gave me the inch I required. His mind melded with mine and I approached the jak in my head as if we were both standing on solid reality.

I could smell that fellow down to the ventricles of his heart, feel him down to the fine hair at the corners of his eyelids, hear him breathing, know his brain. I jinked that jak's body and I needed him to touch me and bring me out of my shock.

One of his hands gripped me by the shoulder, the other jammed me in the back, his breath fanned my cheek, yellow eyes bored into mine, I was flat against him and kissing him as if it were going out of style and I'd never get my share.

We lay side by side on a patch of grass, my arms around his neck and his around my waist, and he said in my ear, "I like them just the way they are, and I like this and that and that and that," and lordy how we kissed.

"Let me out, let me out, damn kid, rotten little seducer, I hate brats, never did trust them, wish I'd never laid eyes on you, if you think you're going to get your hooks in me you have plenty of thinks coming, nobody's going to tie a rope on me, aim to skip and ride and go to glory and never have a care in the universe. Get your hooks out of me!"

I sat up. Valdar was standing on his hind legs, screaming, and if he hadn't been doing it jink-style, the whole household would have been awakened.

"What's the matter?" I yelled. "Come out of it. It was just make-believe, you darned fool."

He gave a gasp, rolled his eyes to the ceiling, came down on all fours, glared at me from the corner of one yellow orb. "You're dangerous. You're a menace."

"And I'm happy. Anytime you want to hang out a shingle, I'll be all for it. You're the best psychologist I ever met. You cured me. There's no rotten taste in me anymore. I feel fine." I stretched my arms toward the ceiling and wriggled.

"Quit it, quit it. Oh, hell."

"It was Rulon. He did that same stuff to me today. Had me flat down and was feeling me—"

"Shut up."

"But why? He's the one who drove me to you, made me so sick I thought I was going to die. I mean, he didn't like my breasts and he said my—"

Valdar jumped off the bed and made a try for the windowsill, did it badly and had to claw his way up to it. He teetered there, cussing, and lashed the sides of the window with an angry tail.

"You're not leaving?" I said, surprised.

"Damned well am."

"If that's the way you feel about it, go ahead. But I wish you hadn't broken off that vision when you did. I enjoyed it immensely. That jak and I were about to proceed to something important. I can't figure out what it might have been, except I know it promised to be better than the kissing, and that kissing was so good—"

Valdar disappeared into the night with a rush of hot air.

The next day Otho the doomster said a terrible thing to me. He was painting a picture and I was annoying him by telling him how bad it looked.

He said, "Get accustomed to looking at my lousy work. It's the closest you'll ever get to the outside worlds. You'll never leave Gibraltar because you have no mount."

I went away and brooded. Practically everyone I knew here had told me I'd never get away from the planet. No, Valdar had never said it.

For some reason, Otho's words that day hit me hard. Suddenly I wanted my mount with a fierce wanting. I had to have him, needed him there beside me. I doubted if there had been an hour when I didn't jink that little planet where he was held captive, and though my jink had grown weaker I knew exactly where Hinx was and also knew he remained unavailable. The cloak the dreens laid over that world was as impenetrable as ever.

But I needed Hinx.

Going back to Otho, I said, "I came to say goodbye."

He jerked around and stared at me. His face finally broke and he gave me the sweetest smile I had gotten from any gib. "You lend me faith in the human race. Go to it. Always stay the way you are. Make up your mind and go after what you want. I'm so goddamned sick of people who do nothing but wish."

The conscience seemed a burdensome thing to me as I walked down the road with my thumb out. Right then and there I decided it was a thing to be suspicious of. If you did what was right and the nagger in your head started yammering, it meant the nagger was off base. Put another way, if you planted your feet on one road and refused to take any forks, the possibilities lying along those forks were wrong directions or choices for you.

What was I going to do about Gibraltar? It never entered my head that there wasn't a great deal I could do. That was what I meant about putting one's feet on a single road and refusing to be lured onto forks.

I decided. Whatever there was for me to learn on Gibraltar, I'd already learned. Anything else that came to me would be repetition.

What would I do about the people here who had left their mark across my path? Valdar—he was like a brother, a sister, a father, a mother. Which? I couldn't make up my mind. He was someone close. Arnet—there was no need to worry about him because he was going with me. Nobody his age should be murdered in the way he was being murdered. Cedron and Otho—to my mind they were similar, not externally but in more important ways. One worked and one loafed, with the same purpose, for a wrong cause. Both were tied to this planet. Cedron wanted to see the coming of heaven while Otho longed for hell. Heaven and hell were alike. Neither offered freedom, because freedom gave a person the right to leave. They were full of ropes and fences. And what of Rulon? The answer to that was easy. If he behaved himself I'd let him live.

142

Never make the same mistake twice. Possible? I could sometimes do better than that. By predicting mistakes in my mind, beforehand, I took steps to avoid them before they occurred the first time. Problem: The dreens intended to keep me on Gibraltar. They wouldn't sit back and watch me go. They trusted me more than I trusted them. That was their error. They assumed I couldn't use their mounts and there was no doubt in my mind that they were nearly all the way correct. A dead mount would do me no good and that was what I would get if I pulled one against its will.

I had never gone into the dreen camp via the gate. Up over the fence I climbed that day, waved to the three guards, after which I began meandering around. I stopped beside the resting mounts and took my time choosing one.

She had a chewed-up ear and no tail. I would have recognized her anywhere. Rulon had been riding her when he tried to kill me. At the time, I hadn't gotten a good look at her and assumed she was male.

Now she looked lonely and forlorn, with good reason. Dreens rode only the best-looking mounts. Rulon had dumped this one out to pasture because of her injuries, and she may have been wondering if she were about to be put out of her ugly condition, permanently.

I went over to her and hopped on her back. "How about a ride?" I said, jink-style.

"I can't. You're not a dreen."

"I mean just walking around."

"Like the dreen children?" she said.

"Right."

She stepped out, left the other mounts and took me along the left ridge of the low hill above the village. The guards at the gate looked after us for a moment before resuming their business of chatting idly.

"I'm sorry about your ear and tail," I said. Her curly back felt strange under me, and she was so small my feet nearly touched the ground.

"What do you mean?"

"Don't you remember me?" I said.

"Dreen mounts have short memories. Inbreeding has taken its toll."

"I'm sorry to hear that. Let's head for that little patch of woods."

Being the only natural spot for miles and miles around, the camp was quite beautiful, but it didn't compare with the wilds of Earth or the thousands of jungle planets I had visited. The trees here were dwarfed and unreal-looking. The dreens weren't content to manipulate themselves and their mounts; they had to do the same thing with their plant life. Even the flower beds were sickly. There was no room for them to spread. Around each was a ditch that prevented it from growing wild. Like people. Put a fence around them and they couldn't answer the call of their own nature.

"What's your name?" I said to the animal under me.

"Otilla."

"All right, Otilla, you can stop here."

She came to a halt beside a small shed. Hopping to the ground, I tried the door, found it unlocked. Inside were gardening tools. I shut the door and climbed back onto the mount.

"Let's go."

Through the dwarfed trees we walked, and I looked for more sheds.

That night, I slept on a grassy hillside. The dreens didn't come around to bother me, and in the morning Otilla was back with the other mounts. She had chosen not to stay with me.

I ate fruit for breakfast, took a bath in the mounts' stream, mounted Otilla again and spent most of the day walking through the streets of the village. Actually, it was more a metropolis. Many more people lived inside the fences than outside, and contrary to popular opinion, the dreens were intelligent, rigid in their philosophy and too proud of themselves.

Rulon had taught me about his kind, while I slept. I wasn't supposed to have remembered it. There were many things I wasn't supposed to have remembered. Bury ideas in the subconscious and everything which the conscious mind picked up would be sculpted so that it fit neatly around the buried ideas. That was how conditioning worked. It was no good if the conscious mind recognized it for what it was. If you didn't want to be conditioned, you either had to have a mind that was mostly conscious all the time or you needed someone to recondition you on every point. I was fortunate, or peculiar, in that I'd had both.

Call it religion or philosophy, the primary purpose of the dreens was to persevere. They believed that reproducing was one of their most important responsibilities. The species must survive and the best way to ensure this was for them to have lots of babies. Women were made to be subservient, otherwise they might decide not to get pregnant except when they wanted to. Here lay another significant difference between jaks and gibs. I knew practically nothing about conception, but I was aware, through plenty of hearsay, that a jak became pregnant only when she wanted to. Gibs had no control over their internals and could reproduce once a year whether they desired it or not. Jaks had to spend a deal of time thinking on the subject before they became fertile. If, after the baby arrived, it proved to be a nuisance, the parents could drop it almost anywhere, knowing full well it wouldn't be abused.

Had the outside world been aware of the true dreen population, there would have been alarm and confusion. Down in the village, below the hill where I stood, people were packed inside the houses like beans in a pot. How did I know? Rulon told me in my sleep. Rulon was a lazy sort, wanted me to hear everything without being able to ask questions. It had been intended that I love him and the dreens so much that nothing I learned about them would seem unattractive.

Anyhow, this morning I kicked Otilla in her rear and climbed aboard, and at the same time I knew the guards at the gate were paying no attention to me. The first place the mount and I walked was into the trees. The camp was about three hundred acres and it took me about an hour of poking along to reach the shed I wanted. It had one small window in it, plus a variety of paints, brushes and cleaning liquids.

Inside, baffled, Otilla wanted to know what I thought I was doing by bringing her into a building.

"Going to kill you," I said, and she laughed.

"That door behind you is locked," I said. "This window is just big enough for me to crawl through."

I was careful where I poured the solvent, didn't want the entire place booming. Through the window went most of the paint and cleaner. It would be beyond the heat. What I wanted was a fast burn, but not too fast, as I didn't intend cooking. Neither did I expect Otilla to cook, but that was up to her.

"Mankind isn't to be trusted," said the little mount. She was moving nervously about the shed, peering up at the window, hurrying to the door and grabbing the knob in her teeth.

"Dreens aren't to be trusted," I said. "You can trust a jak not to hurt a mount. We love animals."

Her laugh carried an hysterical note. "But you're going to kill me."

"I'm only doing it to save your soul. That's a remark that should sound familiar to you, as you've been hearing it all your life from your masters."

"Let me out. Open the door."

I swiped a match across my thigh and tossed it into a corner. The solvent caught fire. Leaping up to the windowsill, I hauled myself up and out through the narrow opening. Otilla cried aloud. I walked away from the shed and stopped in a little clearing a hundred yards distant. Flames shot up in front of the window and I couldn't see past them.

"You're going to die," I said, jink-style.

"Why?" she screamed.

"Because you're too stubborn to come out of there."

Bewilderment, terror, desperation, these I read in her mental broadcasts. "How can I if you don't unlock the door?"

"I won't answer that. You know already, and so do I, and if you want to end as an idiot, it's your business."

"Ahhh, I die, I die."

I was locked in on her tight, and I knew she wasn't that close to it. I let her squirm. She ran around and tried to stay away from the flames. The walls began to glow. They were mostly tough plastic but the inside linings were made of paper and wood. In another minute the whole place would go.

She began shrieking. "I can't. I don't know how. I skip only with dreens."

I let her get warmer. She ran, stumbled, rolled across a blackened strip of flooring. Flames probed for her.

"Help me. Blank out my mind."

"No."

"I don't want to die."

That wasn't the right response. I started sweating. Stupid mount. No negatives now, you fool. Think positive in the next few seconds or you'll look like a piece of toast. I didn't say these things to her, just thought them to myself. It looked as if I might have made a mistake. She wasn't tough enough to forget her conditioning, would rather die than give herself to anyone but a dreen.

She wasn't really damaged yet. The heat inside the shed wasn't too intense, the fire was still pretty well confined to the walls and adjacent flooring. What terrified her was the fact that the ceiling was an orange spread of color. Made of fibrous material, the roof was rapidly being engulfed. Another moment or two passed and patches of sky appeared. Air poured in and shoved the flames downward. Big evil tongues reached for Otilla. Now she knew she hadn't a chance.

"I want to live," she screamed.

That was a good response, but I didn't want any reneging, so I made no suggestions. My mind was breaking from the fear that I had doomed a mount to death. Hold on one more moment. If I could bear to. She was so little, so scared, so much in my charge.

"Pull me, jak! Save me, save me!"

She was all mine, would rather live than die, and I yanked her damned fast, just before the roof caved in, and by the time it splashed all over the inside of that shed, Otilla was moving through D-2.

I had a smoking mount under me and she was a willing mount who answered the call of her nature with no compunctions whatever. Her conditioning had been blasted to hell, and she did it all by herself.

For the first time ever, her mind had no rocks closing up its passages.

With a whoop and a holler, we were one and inseparable, and I let out another yell that drowned out hers. My god, the glory of it, and I didn't even feel a prick of conscience at the fact that it wasn't Hinx who was giving me that big pleasure. A jak I was, a mount Otilla was, and never the twain should part, at least not right then.

"Hang on, you crazy mount, we're about to do some traveling!"

"You're the one who had better hang on, you insane jak, or you'll lose your seat."

In and out of D-2 we skipped, without going anywhere but simply staying where we were, but how we played with that hunk of sod. Up and down in giant leaps we went, until we were so far up we were in the clouds.

"I lead you," I yelled, while I took her away.

Arnet felt me coming. He was so scared he started to run. He'd been in the park, with his feet resting on glass that was supposed to be water. His jink couldn't have been too dead because long before I set Otilla down, he was up and speeding across phony grass toward phony trees. I was yelling at him with my mind, but he was too frightened or too unwilling to recognize me, or maybe he knew what was coming and couldn't bear to think about it.

Otilla and I stopped beside the artificial creek, parked there, and I let my feet dangle while I sat back and relaxed. My mount raised a hind leg and casually scratched her ear.

"Dumb gib," she said.

"Arnet, come out of those danged trees," I said.

He stuck his head around a papier-mache stalk and blinked at me. "Go away," he croaked.

"For once in your life be free."

"Jade, please go away. Leave me here."

"To corrode?"

Tears trickled down his face. His skinny little body was racked with shudders. "I knew this was going to happen. The first time I saw you I knew you were

148

going to clobber me. Don't you understand that I'm not like you?"

"Nope."

Stepping from behind the tree, he said, "You haven't much time. As poor as my jink is, I can sense them coming."

"Unimportant."

"Jade, there are so many of them."

"But not yet aboard their mounts. Besides, I don't care. Can outrun 'em."

"You sound different."

"Never changed. Go get him, Otilla."

We disappeared, came back into view beside Arnet. He was on his knees, too weak to stay on his feet.

"Get on in front of me," I said. "Don't trust you behind me. You might faint."

His face dead-white, Arnet reached up with a shaking hand. "Never did it before. Don't know how. My heart is going to stop in another second."

"We don't have time to wait and see it happen," I said, and grasping his hand I hauled him into my lap. No sooner did his rear touch Otilla's back than his body went limp. He had fainted dead away.

Certainly, Rulon must have suspected he wouldn't catch me, but he tried anyway, led about thirty mounted dreens across space after me. He may have entertained the hope that if they came at me in a tight circle I would feel so fenced in I'd lose my head. Ha! He tried to grab Otilla's mind—I could sense it—but the mount had one-track ears by then. A rider couldn't afford to have her mount halfway with her and I had mine captured all the way. And I heard no complaints from her.

Otilla, Arnet and I simply went away, fast and far. To my knowledge no one in the galaxy could keep up with me when I skipped, and the dreens surely didn't, that day. Maybe somewhere back in space Rulon's profanity was drifting around in the ether. To hell with him. If I ever saw him again I'd stomp on him a little.

Chapter XIV

I was hunting for the planet of the varks when I came across a jak in limbo. She had abandoned her mount and both were well on the way to dispersing.

"Am committing suicide," she yelled, after I'd inquired as to what in hell she thought she was up to.

"Oh," said I. "Mind saying why?"

"You mean you ain't heard? There's no Doubleluck. It's all a lie. Ain't nothing to skip for, nowhere to go, no place to need."

"You're an idiot. I know for a fact that there's a Doubleluck."

She let out a shriek, pulled her mount to her, solidified as much as D-2 would permit. "Say that again."

"Not only is there a real, true Doubleluck, there is also a way to get through the barrier around the galaxy."

"Tell me, tell me, tell me, tell—"

"Shut up. Find the planet of the varks. They have all the answers in reality."

"Don't believe you," she said. She was about two or three hundred, gray of hair, the tallest and skinniest jak I'd ever seen. Must have outlived her mount, as the animal under her was no more than an infant.

"You have no right to doom a mount of that age," I said. "Kill yourself, if you like, but that mount has the privilege of making her own decisions."

"Mind your business. But if you must know, this mount is blind of eye and also is daughter to my old mount that died. Won't part from me, and if I take a notion to kill myself, I can't hardly see how I can do without her company. I mean—"

"Never mind," I said. "Where did you hear there was no Doubleluck?"

"The word is all over. Expect you're the only one who hasn't heard."

"Been hearing such tripe always, but that doesn't make it true."

"Prove to me it's a lie."

Scowling and snarling, I said, "You're alive and need no proof of anything else. Kill yourself or hunt for what exists."

Didn't know if she continued her suicide or not, as I left her in a hurry and took Otilla to the nearest planet.

Reality was changed. Alterations had crept into my world while I'd been on Gibraltar, and those changes had spread and become more serious while I ignored everything and went on the hunt for varks. Arnet was in the Ridge Cluster, living with a bunch of babies on an innocuous little planet. He was barely surviving and I believed he belonged with infants. His emotional level was about on a par with theirs. With them, he wasn't required to compete with anyone who knew anything. Those babies looked, saw, wondered, they listened and explored, they absorbed stimuli like sponges, they saw young mounts and argued with them; all were ignorant and new and Arnet was exactly like them. If he didn't revert and become completely stupid, at least for a while, he would probably die. I expected the babies to make him one with them and teach his mind all over again until he turned into a normal human. Or a jak. Both words meant the same.

How he had blubbered when I'd left him.

The Land of Ectri committed suicide. This was a group of jaks who liked living together on a planet that had a huge volcanic crater on its surface. The people skipped, same as everybody, but they always returned to Ectri to eat and sleep and quarrel. Inside the crater was fertile ground and plenty of food, and there were dunes inhabited by intelligent insects who provided for the jaks by picking fruit and depositing it in piles every day. Probably the insects

151

made the food donations so their dunes wouldn't be raided by the jaks.

Anyway, the Land of Ectri was well known throughout the galaxy because the jaks who lived there were fortune-tellers. Everyone wanted his fortune told, at least once in his life. I had been to the planet more than a few times, and discovering that they had all killed themselves came as a shock to me. The crater-planet was now off limits to everyone but the crass or overly hardy. The atmosphere around the Land of Ectri was literally peppered with jak dust. A rider could jink the dead pieces of humanity floating in that atmosphere, and if he was normal he turned and went the other way in a hurry.

Since I wasn't normal, I landed on the planet and had a peculiar kind of conversation with the insects who had already moved out of their dunes and were spreading all over the planet. They sang, and it took me a while to interpret the little squealing sounds. They told me the jaks had decided to end it all because there was no Doubleluck. The fabled planet was the only thing that had kept them attuned to life. Nobody could get out of the galaxy, and with the promise of Doubleluck gone, there was nothing to keep them in this sphere. They skipped into limbo and dispersed.

No more fortune-tellers now, no more of approximately four hundred jaks and as many mounts; only a befouled atmosphere that glittered and glistened and chased riders away. The only jak family I knew of—gone.

How could one jak tell all her relatives that a race of people called dreens were beginning to spread poison? The damned dreens had decided not to wait for Utopia to create itself. Why? Because of me. I wasn't natural and the dreens were afraid of unpredictables. Were there more unpredictables than just myself? Well, where you found one weed, you were likely to find another, and another, and so on. A terrible thought: hundreds or thousands of Jades.

I was asleep on a hill of grass, under my best friends, the stars, when I received a call from an old acquaintance.

"Honeypot, can't you hear me? I wish you'd wake up and pull this poor, lonely mount. I'm about to die from homesickness."

"Um, um, um. Howdy, Hinx."

How that beautiful black monster mourned in my dreams. "I could wait until you wake up, but I can't stand it now that we're so close to being together. Honey, won't you quit snoring and listen to me."

"Can't," said my sleeping mind. "You're on that blocked planet and we can't communicate. Am stymied about what to do. Been figuring, but haven't come up with any ideas."

"The varks solved it," said Hinx.

"Didn't know you knew any varks."

"Know one called Shaper."

"That's impossible," I said.

"Agreed. But he was always nuts, wasn't he? You see, tonight a thing flew down onto this world, and it was ugly and gray and was blowing a lot of hot air around. It lit on my head and damn if it wasn't a vark. Said he was Shaper. Said he switched carcasses with a vark. Said varks are omniscient. What that means is they're egotistical to the point where they stick their noses everywhere. Anyhow, Shaper said Big Jak sent him. Shaper melded with me and Volcano, and the three of us blew away the rays left by the dreens. So here I am trying to wake you up so you can pull me and all you want to do is snore."

"I quit snoring practically as soon as you opened your head. Am alive and alert and awake."

He whispered, "Pull me, love."

"Don't want to underestimate the dreens. Rulon, that's Dead Eye, is sure to be on my trail, and what better way to do that than keep an eye on you?"

"You can pull so fast we'll be gone in a second," said my mount, and there was anxiety in his mind.

"You were always an impatient sort. Relax for a minute. Want you to give yourself a thorough inspection and see if there's anything plastered to your hide, like maybe—"

"Shaper already inspected me. He found a funny-looking leaf stuck on my belly, and another one was

153

in my ear, and there was a burr in my tail, and a few more in the hair on my neck."

"What did he do with them?" I said.

"Buried them. Said he didn't know how they could be dangerous but he wasn't taking any chances. He gave me a clean bill of goods, said I was in shape for traveling. You don't have to do a lot of explaining. Know where you've been and know all about Rulon."

"How could you? Shaper didn't know any of it."

"Sounded like he did," said Hinx.

"You haven't seen Big Jak?"

"No. Are you going to pull me?"

"Shortly," I said. "First I have to do something else."

What I had to do was take Otilla on a trip, which I did. Grabbing a tent of oxygen, I hugged it around both of us and we headed for the Ridge Cluster and Arnet.

Arnet was babysitting infants and little mounts. He looked like a slightly older infant, and that was the only difference between them. He cried right along with the rest of them, ran away and hid behind a rock when I landed and he wouldn't come out, though I called and called.

"I'm leaving you here," I said to Otilla. "The next time you travel, it will be under that gib over there behind the rock. At least that's the way I wish it."

"I'll do what I can. I knew you weren't for me permanently, so I didn't let myself become too attached to you. But there was a fair amount of feeling between us."

"There was and there is. Good luck." Looking up at the sky, I yelled, "Hey, Hinx, time for you and me to get together."

He came skidding on his big rump out of nowhere, his legs clawing empty air. Right beside me, he stopped. While he was unscrambling his legs, I leaped for his back, settled into my old comfortable niche, gripped his sides with my legs.

"See that rock way way up there?"

"Sure do."

We went, screaming and yelling, a pair of hedonists who were doing that which gave the most exhilara-

154

tion. To hell with all else, a jak and her animal was a dual thing that was simply following its own nature.

This time it was a little different. Somewhere along the way we picked up a hitchhiker, and he wasn't asked if he wanted a ride. One moment I was sailing through D-2, in the next moment I was settling down on the surface of a little asteroid, and then I felt something touch my back. There was a vark sitting behind me. There he was, for about a second, and then he was perched on Hinx's head, teetering on four trembling legs and grinning at me. Two crossed blue eyes tried to focus on me and failed.

"Hi," said Shaper. "I've changed, ain't I?"

"You wanted to skip so bad you had to steal a varmint's skin?"

"Don't want to talk on this dead place. Let's go find a pretty planet."

"These dead asteroids get passed by, so they're safer to rest on. I don't want to meet up with any strange travelers. I'm suspicious of everybody. Don't aim to get kidnapped again."

We stayed on the rock and talked. Or rather, Shaper did most of it. First of all, if it was a vark body he was in, and obviously it was, why were the eyes crossed? This was the first question I asked. Shaper couldn't answer, other than to say that his was a most powerful mind and he had dragged into the vark body more than just his mental factory. My own thought was that the vark who switched bodies with him had possessed an odd sense of humor.

Shaper and Big Jak had been abandoned on a gray world of dust and cactus. Because of the planet's dense and cloudy atmosphere, even the sun had looked gray. They'd walked and walked but found nothing except more dust and cactus. The wind never stopped blowing and moaning. At nightfall they lay down in their tracks and slept. Morning came, they woke and found themselves surrounded by dozens of varks who did nothing but sit and grin.

It turned out that varks weren't much like they were supposed to be; that is, hearsay claimed they were such and such when they were not. If a vark

thought he could learn something from you, he would
trade information with you. If there was one thing a
vark wanted to do, it was to travel off his home
planet. None ever had. Because of their inner pipe-
workings and their perfect control of body temperature, varks could fly; in fact, they were a regular
jet set, faster than birds, but they hadn't the power
to leave their world. This made them tedious to associate with. They sulked, often refused to respond to
queries, assumed condescending attitudes, et cetera.

The varks began to communicate right away with
Shaper and Big Jak, said it was obvious the two jaks
had no mounts, and would they kindly explain why.
Talking to a vark wasn't like talking to a mount or
another jak. With those two, you knew the communication came directly from their head. Either the vark
was zany and did it deliberately or his mind was so
scrambled that it didn't know which way to go. Anyhow, when talking with a vark you were liable to discover that his thoughts came from the end of his
tail, or his ears, or his nose, or from any part of
his anatomy. It was disconcerting.

Varks had an insatiable curiosity, wanted to know
all, so they began swapping ideas with Shaper and
Big Jak. There were creeks to drink from and there
was tasteless catcus to eat, and this was the extent
of the food supply on the planet, which was another
reason why the varks were anxious to travel in space.
They were sick and tired of their diet.

Long before, the varks had acquired the ability to
exchange minds with other organisms. They did it
in order to learn all they could about a variety of
life forms. When a vark swapped psyches with a different species, something happened to the vark brain.
Its composition altered. Spatial reality became easy
to manipulate. The alien mind in the vark's body was
able to perceive D-2 as a narrow corridor and it was
possible for the alien to travel within that corridor.
He didn't need a mount and he could retain a breath-
able atmosphere around him while he skipped. For
the first time in millions of years, a living creature
traveled through the void without a vehicle.

Occasionally there had been opportunities for a

vark to trade minds with a jak, but doing it once didn't teach the vark all there was to know about jaks. The latter were unlike beasts. The differences between two jaks could be great, and so each mind exchange taught the vark something more about the species.

It had always enraged the varks that other species could skip alone through D-2 after a mind trade, while the vark mind remained chained to its home world. Perhaps with these two unique, unusual, peculiar jaks, this unbearable situation could be corrected. Would the jaks please concentrate on the problem and help the varks learn how to skip?

First of all, Big Jak wanted to know if varks could meld with mounts. The answer: Varks were allergic to mounts, became victims of hysteria and fell in a paralyzing swoon off animals.

An important thing Shaper learned was that he also was allergic to mounts. He could talk with them, he could ride them in D-3, but trying to meld with them, which was essential for skipping, sent his mind into shock. The varks discussed this with him and suggested that he be psychoanalyzed. Something prevented him from giving over his volition to an animal. This mental surrender lasted only a moment before the jak took control of the skipping situation, but Shaper was incapable of it. And of course there were no psychoanalysts in the galaxy. This the varks readily admitted, when Shaper asked where he could find such a healer. Had there ever been? Indeed there had. When? Impossible to say. Very long ago.

The varks possessed many such useless bits of information. If Shaper could find a psychoanalyst, of which there were none, he might be able to discover why he distrusted mounts. The varks thought it was the result of some childhood trauma. Perhaps a mount had bitten him or dumped him on his head.

What of Big Jak? Where was he? Oh, well, of course he had gone his own way almost immediately, was mad because Shaper wasn't anxious to get back to the planet where the forge lay collecting dust. Big Jak was eager to get on to making more hats, but Shaper was not.

All jaks had one-track minds and Big Jak was no exception. Other galaxies existed across the impassable pit but nobody could get to them because of celestial static. This was a fancy name for an ordinary phenomenon. Solar wind, gravitational influence, electronic impulses from dense stars—the ever-present garbage of the galaxy—created interferences that inhibited jink. The normal jak could only skip for short distances. The debris in space dimmed faraway objects. A jak instinctively demurred from aiming for an obscure destination, needed to have it clearly and substantially in his sights. He couldn't jink another galaxy because of the debris in between.

This had always been Shaper's theory, and he thought he was unique in his belief until he'd met Big Jak. It wasn't the pit or distance between the home galaxy and the next that kept jaks at home. It was Shaper's idea that jink couldn't be muffled by very many things, but that celestial static could. If he could find the right metal and make a hat and put it on his head, he might thereby stifle enough celestial static so that he could "see" into the next galaxy. Of course Shaper disregarded the fact that he couldn't skip a mount from one planet to another. That problem was supposed to solve itself somewhere along the way.

Now Shaper was no longer interested in working with the hats. He was allergic to mounts, there were no psychoanalysts to heal him of this disability and it appeared that he would never be able to skip like other jaks. He came up with another idea. What was it? None of anybody's business. As to Big Jak's whereabouts, he was probably on the other planet making hats.

I finally got a word in edgewise, and I said to Shaper, "You aren't figuring to keep a vark body and skip that way, are you?"

"Nothing is any of your business, except I'll say this much: These are the worst bodies in creation. The varks are starved for something to eat besides cactus. They can't eat anything else. This body I'm wearing has practically no guts in it; it's mostly ther-

158

mal tubing. Feels hollow. Feels awful. I ate a bunch of fruit and nearly died. Sure I can skip now, can go any-place I want, except where I really want to go, which is to another galaxy. I'm limited in the same way jaks on mounts are limited. Short jumps are all I can take."

"How did you catch up with me?" I said.

"Kept an eye on your mount."

"Now what do you aim to do?"

"Why, I don't know what you mean."

"You're lying," I said. My mount and I skipped in a hurry, left Shaper behind. Not on the asteroid. He skipped after me like a shot, but he had handicaps and Hinx and I lost him with our first hop. It was a long jump and Shaper couldn't make it.

"What do you think his plan was?" said Hinx. We were parked in D-3 on the moon of Earth.

"I don't think he had anything really sinister in mind. Probably he would have tried to talk us into skipping to a particular planet where he had a jail prepared for me."

"When are we going to do what they're all planning to keep us from doing? When are we making our try for that galaxy over there? I can see it when we're skipping. Your mind gives me a glimpse of it. I know you're thinking about it all the time."

I shivered. "Hate responsibility. Want to go and will, but not right away."

"Scared?"

"Always have been. Saw distant places from the time I first skipped with you. Took all these years to understand what those places are."

"Show me," he said.

I let him have a look. He fell on the ground and hid his head in his paws. "Oh, god, how far. I thought my mind wouldn't get back to my body. It's death, honey. We'll never make it."

"I won't show it to you again for a while. Give you time to get accustomed to it. That actually was only the edge of it. Could have taken you into it deeper."

"They'll kill you. Everybody who has a soul wants to get there first. Sure Shaper had something sinister in mind, probably intended to brain you with a rock. All his lfe he's dreamed of making the trip first. As for Big Jak, he's worse. He'll do anything at all."

"He's the toughest, I agree. And don't forget the dreens."

Hinx took his turn shivering. "Let's admit it. The whole galaxy is against us."

"Maybe not all of it. Maybe the varks are non-partisan."

"But you don't know where they are."

"Wrong. A certain skunk I know leaked that information to me. He doesn't know it, but every time he thought of the vark planet I followed his mind."

Chapter XV

"Do you have any morals?" I asked.

"Possibly."

The vark sat in shadows so that all I could see was a double row of long fangs topped by two slitted yellow eyes.

"Are varks altruistic by nature?" I asked.

"As much as anyone."

"Fine. I'm glad we have the preliminaries out of the way. You're as greedy as a snake and it was honest of you to admit it."

"I didn't say—"

"I came here to talk to all the varks," I said. "Why are you the only one I can find? It's my understanding that this planet is crawling with your people."

"I have been appointed their spokesman."

"What's so special about you?"

"I'm two thousand years old."

"You're sure you aren't Big Jak in disguise?"

"If I were, I'd lure you to a place where you could be locked up."

"Why do you have so many teeth?" I asked. "You can't eat anything but cactus."

"They are evidence of virility."

"I need an opinion about something."

"You seek advice?" inquired the vark.

"I rarely ask for that. An opinion will be sufficient."

"What do you want to know?"

"About Doubleluck."

He raised his head and howled with laughter.

"I have a variety of motives for wanting to find it," I said. "The dreens are spreading the word about

Earth. As far as I've been able to determine, they haven't told anybody where Earth is. But they're going to. Jaks are already committing suicide without even collecting proof that the legend of Doubleluck is a lie. Once they begin to skip to Earth and see for themselves, they'll start dying in droves."

"Do you believe Earth is the legendary planet?" said the vark.

"I believe many things about it, but it isn't the city of gold."

"You believe in El Dorado?"

"Jaks think they're familiar with everything in the galaxy, but only a few know about Earth and only a few know of Gibraltar. Why can't there be another place no one knows of? I want to find Doubleluck and squelch the plan of the dreens."

"So everyone will see the city of his dreams," said the vark. "What will that solve? Will it do away with the bottomless pit? Will they then be able to fly away?"

"It will settle them down long enough for me to reason with them. Nature is trying to get us out of this galaxy. If jaks will only be patient—"

Said the vark, "You can travel to the next star cluster now. Why don't you do it and leave the problem to nature?"

"Because I wouldn't feel right. I think my kind are a pack of hedonists with no sense of responsibility. The dreens hate us and want us to die. They say we ruin everything. In a way they're right."

"What do you plan to do about the dreens?"

The question made me mad. "You sound as if I've taken all creation onto my shoulders. What do you think I am? I can't do it all."

"If there is no other to do it—"

"Listen, I don't want to talk about that. I'm interested in Doubleluck."

"For your own purposes."

"That's one reason, yes. I told you I had a variety of reasons for wanting to find it. I want to see the greatest thing in the galaxy."

"And what if the greatest turns out to be the smallest?" asked the vark.

"How can that be?"

"What if the brightest is the dullest, the most powerful the meekest, the terminal the original, the highest the lowest?"

"Please."

"For a price," said the vark. "Teach me."

"I'm way ahead of you," I said. "You're promising to tell me where Doubleluck is if I swap bodies with you for a while."

"I have already told you of its whereabouts."

"And I'm not reneging, because I didn't promise in the first place. I'll simply say I wouldn't live in your body even if it was the only one around."

"You find me repulsive?" he said.

"The truth is more brutal. I don't trust you."

"You are a thief."

"I'll make a deal with you," I said. "I'll teach you everything I know about my own mind. Used to be, I thought only jaks were fit for the good life. But there are mounts, and I consider them worthy. Then I met a couple of gibs who seemed as good as jaks, and now I discover that varks have to be included on the list. Someday someone is going to go to glory. That's skipping out of the galaxy. In my opinion, that someone should be a whole group of all kinds of people. We should all go at once."

"Why?"

"Only that way will we realize the next fellow is entitled to his existence. Till now, we've only tolerated each other."

"The golden rule," said the vark.

"What?"

"It died a long time ago. Lo and behold, at this late date it is resurrected. I am bemused, astonished, dumbfounded. Go away immediately. I wish to ponder."

"On what?"

"Jade of the galaxy."

"Wait a minute, I came here—"

"The varks will let you know," he said. And that was all he would say.

Hinx and I left the planet and went away. We skipped to the Ridge Cluster, landed on the right planet and spent some time trying to find Arnet. He found us, came skipping out of D-2, right over our heads and settled down on the ground beside us.

He didn't say anything, just sat astride Otilla, a little smile on his face.

"I'm glad you made it," I said.

"I came close to suicide a dozen times before I climbed on Otilla's back. And I damned near got stuck in limbo, about a hundred times. I'm getting the hang of it."

"Good."

"I've been drifting in and out of D-2 for days, waiting for you. And dodging dreens and varks and jaks."

"They're looking for me," I said.

"I know." He paused. "I went to Gibraltar."

"It's your world."

"What you're saying is that it's my problem."

"Do you want me to do anything?"

He shook his head. "At the moment I'm just observing."

"What are the dreens doing?"

"Killing people. It's all coming out into the open. The gibs are learning what the dreens really are."

"How bad is it?" I said.

"My family is all right. So far. It doesn't look good. Gib intelligence isn't what it should be."

"Why don't you come here once a month? We'll talk."

I had to leave him then, didn't dare linger. If he showed up in a month's time, I might be able to talk everything over with him.

I needed to do my thinking in privacy; it had to be deep thinking and I wanted no interference. Besides, I aimed to find what I was looking for. On Earth.

"Hinx, what's lower than a snake?" I asked.

"Ground."

"What's duller than an idiot?"

"A corpse," he said.

"What's meeker than a has-been?"

"Nothing."

"Let's go find Doubleluck."

We went to Earth. We skipped, or rather skimmed, that little world. Through D-2 and D-3 we went, and while we traveled we took a good look at man's starting place.

Just a few places were polluted, the worst being the area I had first visited. It seemed a lifetime ago that Big Jak had tried to snare me with his rope.

We finally settled down at the base of the mountain that lay on the other side of the deadlands where the creeks and lakes were corrupted and where the air was unfit to breathe. We waded in a rotten creek and wondered why it was rotten. There was no obvious reason why this section was so unpleasant.

It took me a solid week of smelling bad odors, walking in stinking mud and worrying about being found by one of my enemies before I found a box. After more hunting, I found many boxes. They were all the same, three inches by three inches, black metal with a screen for a top. Out of the screens drifted a green gas which was thin but not so thin that I could clearly see inside the box. From the few glimpses I managed to catch, I guessed that little lumps of material caused the fumes.

How old were the boxes? They showed no signs of corrosion from having been immersed. Who had placed them in the water? I couldn't answer without knowing the age of the boxes. I knew, though, that the lumps were responsible for the pollution of the air and water. About fifteen square miles of the planet were contaminated. Almost in the center stood the mountain.

As soon as I took the third look at it, I called it the brooding mountain. I sat beside Hinx and stared up at it. It made me feel bad, took away my optimism and forced me to think about the state of humanity, which was the most pessimistic subject ever invented. A mountain was strong and reliable, changeless and uncringing. Of course, it was also dead as hell.

That mountain; something odd about it. Jink revealed only solid rock to me. What was it doing here, anyway? Such was the trouble with nature: always on a rampage; would plant a river or a ridge wherever she took a notion and never mind if it was all alone and sticking out like a sore thumb.

This brooding mountain was a single big nose on

a flat face, with no pimples of rock around it. Was it really the source of melancholia? Maybe if I hunted for and found a laughing brook, I would soon be laughing right along with it.

Oh, Earth, whatever did you think you were up to when you made us?

I talked out loud to Hinx, but he said nothing back to me. It wasn't necessary, for he was as much inside my mind as I was inside his.

"If I found Doubleluck, would I take a look at it all by myself? My conscience rumbles when I think about that. Who owns Doubleluck? Finders keepers, losers weepers? How does one person say that to a hundred billion jaks?

"Now I'm thinking about Big Jak. The storyteller. He has a rare eye; that is, he's seen things no one else has ever laid eyes on. Maybe he didn't want to look, but he was forced to because it was his job, and he didn't want that, either.

"There's an old saying that one jak's meat is another jak's poison. Also, all that glitters isn't gold. Do those sayings refer to the fact that reality consists of opposites? Good and bad have to coexist because without both there can be neither. People who long for Utopia want nirvana. If there is a Doubleluck, and I know now that there is, it represents both sides of reality. It contains good and bad. Something for everyone."

I smacked the ground with my fist. "By damn, I think it's time the thing was unveiled."

As I said that last part, I turned to look at Hinx. He wasn't there. He was gone.

Whoosh! Where had I heard a sound like that before? I obeyed my instincts and fell over on my side. So did whoever was behind me. The rope missed me and as soon as I saw it I knew who had sneaked up on me.

He reckoned without Hinx. My mount had been alerted by intuition, had run off and hid. Now he came into view, fast and growling like thunder. No jak ever lived who could outmaneuver a mount. Volcano tried to interfere and took a deep bite in the

166

flank. With his next motion, Hinx had Big Jak flat on the ground on his back.

"Shall I tear out his throat?"

"No, but don't let him up, either."

"Can't watch Volcano when I'm in this position."

"Hold up there," I said to the big gray mount. He was getting ready to sink his teeth into Hinky's back. When he paused and looked at me, I said, "You wouldn't want your rider to be missing an arm or a leg. He wouldn't be able to hang on when you skipped. Now back off and sit down and shut up."

Volcano dropped onto his haunches.

"You're too close," I said. "Start backing."

He scooted on his rear a few yards.

"More. Okay, that's enough. Now lie down on your belly."

He did as I said, rested his nose on his paws and watched me with glazed eyes.

"Thought you and my mount might be friends, since you were stuck together on that planet for so long," I said.

"He doesn't know the meaning of the word," said Hinx. "I hate him and he hates me."

Kneeling, I grinned down at Big Jak. "Hi, Valdar. I was expecting you so I pretended to be thinking about nothing but talking. Sensed you snooping around two days ago. Let a little alarm leak from my mind so my mount would hide. How have you been?"

"Never mind that. Tell your beast to put his fangs back in his mouth."

"Can't. You're untrustworthy."

"I was all right on Gibraltar, wasn't I?"

"Because I represented no threat there and because you wanted to use me. You're a great user of people. You swapped bodies with a vark because it suited your purposes. You brought me books and taught me a lot of things about reason and philosophy so I wouldn't fall for the conditioning Rulon fed me every night. I might as well tell you that I wouldn't have fallen for it anyhow, but I did enjoy every bit of the learning I got from you. You did all of it because you hope I'll relieve you of the responsibilities your father dumped on you."

His yellow eyes were slitted and gleaming. "Didn't know you'd guessed all that. Maybe I underestimated you."

Again I grinned. "You never underestimated anybody or anything. Now, suppose you tell me why you let yourself get caught. Or do you want me to do some more guessing?"

"Wanted to ask a favor of you. Want you to forget all this and go back to making mud puddles or whatever it was you were doing before you began sticking your nose into my business."

To Hinx I said, "Watch him; don't let him wiggle."

"Right."

I walked over to Volcano, grabbed him by the ear, twisted as hard as I could. "Be good," I said. I waited. He didn't bare his teeth or attack me, which meant Big Jak was telling him to behave. There was no use trying to meld with that mount. He was a one-jak beast who listened to no one but the cranky cuss on the ground.

I picked up the rope that had been intended for me.

"Don't do what you're thinking of doing," Big Jak called.

"Have to."

"First let me talk."

"Listening to you is a fool's pastime. You'd better make your move right now, if you're going to. Tell your mount to rip me up, or shut your mouth." I tied the rope around Volcano's neck.

"You're wrong," said Big Jak. "I came here to see you. Just wanted to know what you were doing."

"Liar." I led the gray mount to the nearest tree. It was a huge dead growth that jutted from one of the creeks. Over my shoulder, I said, "You'd do anything to keep me from finding Doubleluck. As far as I'm concerned, you're an obstacle in the way of progress. Why don't you get out of the way and stay out?"

Volcano was tied to the tree and I was confident that he couldn't be pulled. I headed for the base of the mountain.

"You're making a mistake," yelled Big Jak.

I went back to him. "Why are you such a hog?"

168

"That ain't exactly it."

"You're afraid for people to find Doubleluck."

"It's in my charge." He glared at Hinx, who growled into his face. "Nobody can see it until its secrecy isn't important any longer."

"You're so close to the mine you can't see the gold."

His eyes hot and intense, he said, "Be careful, gal. Unveil Doubleluck and you take away the only thing jaks have left to hold on to."

"Jaks are leaving the galaxy. Not just one big one with yellow eyes, not just one with crossed eyes, not just one with yellow hair. All jaks are leaving the galaxy. Before they go, they're going to see Doubleluck."

"How are they going to go?" he shouted.

"Every which way."

"Nobody can leave the galaxy except—"

"Go ahead and say it," I said softly. "Nobody can leave the galaxy except Jade. Me. The first time I realized that, I felt pretty good. Imagine being such a rare person. But I soon realized something else. I can't be the only one like me. Where there's one weed, there's another. There must be many. Maybe they're too little to skip yet, maybe they're being born right this minute. In fact, it's possible that someone has already kissed this galaxy good-bye and lit out. But the jaks who are here right now are headed for freedom."

"You're a goddamned do-gooder!"

"I'm simply an adolescent jak. But do you know what you and Shaper are? You're jak infants. You're cases of arrested development."

"You're an asshole brat!"

"I'm glad we understand how much we love each other."

"Remember those books I lent you. What's dangerous about people who are so sure of themselves that they won't listen to advice?"

"Don't bother me," I said and walked away.

"Jade."

Pausing and looking back, I said, "Now what is it?"

He was staring up at Hinx, writhing and swearing.

"What do you want?" I said.

He turned his head to look at me, said, "What?" His eyes began to widen. "Who are you talking to? Goddamn!"

I looked around at the sky, at empty space. "Who's calling?"

"The varks." It was the damnedest voice I'd ever heard, sounded as if it came from an endless tunnel.

"I hear you," I said aloud.

"We have decided to share some of our knowledge with you."

"In exchange for what?"

"You must allow us to travel from the galaxy with the jaks."

"You already know I said you could. But it really isn't up to me. I'll help all I can and won't interfere with anyone, but I don't see how I can help all of you. Some can ride on mounts, but too many of your people are so allergic—"

"The varks wish to skip independently."

"How?" I said.

"You and a vark will meld. We must find the way in this manner."

"I promise to consider the proposition. That's the best I can do."

There was a pause, then, "Agreed. Now I impart knowledge to you. The gibs have done as you anticipated. Rulon and his men have visited at least fifty planets. They are spreading the word that Doubleluck is the planet Earth, that it is the birthplace of humans and mounts and that it is an insignificant little disappointment."

"What's the reaction?" I said.

"Rulon showed them where it is. Lo, the jaks are melding with their mounts. They intend to see for themselves before they die."

I raced to the mountain wall, frantically searched the naked surface in front of me. I'd never make it. It was too big to examine in a few seconds, which was all the time I had. The inhabitants of fifty planets were going to be hitting Earth's atmosphere. They would be slowed by their numbers, but not much. Of course, I could kiss them off, let them come and see nothing. They wouldn't believe anything I told them.

They would go away and commit suicide, and then I'd have ample time to find the opening into the mountain. The jaks who came after would be all right.

"There's a big white hole," yelled Big Jak.

Why would I believe him? For no reason. But I looked for the big white hole. It was a hundred yards to my right, about two feet up the granite wall. It looked like a natural concavity.

"Kick it!"

I did. The mountain suddenly grew a line down its middle, and the line grew into a crack and the crack became a wedge. I fell back on the ground, astonished at first and then scared enough to scramble away. I couldn't get far enough. The mountain was about two thousand feet high. The opening in it got wider every moment, and I knew it wasn't a natural phenomenon. This thing was a noiseless, mechanical monster.

The mountain no longer seemed to be giving me a huge, sideways grin. It had ceased smiling and now its two separate parts were sliding and descending into the ground.

The sky was almost dark but I could see what the mountain had hidden. Before me, above me, dwarfing me, was the lost city of Doubleluck. Here was the treasure for which humanity hunted forever and ever.

There must have been an automatic timer somewhere in the underground mechanisms. The city stood completely naked of its granite coat for approximately three minutes and then the lights came on. What was the city made of? Glass? Was it really tinkling? On Gibraltar I had seen chandeliers made of thin strips of glass, and the slightest movement of air sent the strips to swaying, and as they touched they tinkled. The city didn't sway. It was made of different parts, but all the parts merged into a single glistening, many-tiered monument. Inside its heart was a miniature sun that rose at once to full intensity. No hesitation, no preening of solar feathers, the sun within Doubleluck turned on and "illumination" suddenly acquired a new definition. The buildings were made of a transparent material. Viewed as a whole,

Doubleluck was pale green on its outermost surfaces, became a darker green just inside this layer, once again became lighter and burst toward the center in a blinding rush of pure yellow. Golden was the heart of Doubleluck.

This huge jewel was more beautiful than the most beautiful jewel in existence. It wasn't nature on a rampage; it was nature taken into a pair of hands and molded to suit the sculptor; it was the presentation of a multitude of masters, a drama enacted before an audience of neophytes.

The builders of Doubleluck had created an ideal, a record to be broken. They had known nothing of the talents of those who would come after, and so they had created the best they could. They might as well have hung a sign over the city: "See if you can do better."

I had been everywhere, to thousands of planets. I had heard everything. There was no need of my visiting places others had seen. If they told me a planet was worth seeing, I went and I saw. Had it been worth it? It hadn't been startling.

There was just so much beauty in sunrises, oceans, ridges or fields. In the city of man there was endless beauty. Lying on my back on the sod of Earth, I admitted what I couldn't help but admit. This was the greatest achievement of humanity. To deny it would have been to lie. For the first time in millennia, man possessed a standard. Now he had something to work for. Now the jaks had a road ahead of them. They owned a heritage.

The rainbow in the sky took away the darkness. Little drops of sparkling light fell from it: diamond-rain. The air was full of perfume. From any point on the ground, a visitor could ascend to any part of the city. A wide yellow grill encircled the base and after stepping onto this, a person was elevated by air drafts. Controlling ascent with slight body motions, the visitor was able to step into the building, through one of the many doorways, whenever he pleased. Passage inside the city was accomplished in the same way. Along the walls of every room and beyond every doorway was an elevating grill. A visitor could ascend

172

to the room directly above him, he could walk into the room adjacent to him or he could ascend to another room by simply stepping onto the outside grill.

I stood in a room of statues. Made of a variety of stone, rock, clay, glass, metal, paper and wood, the images ranged from tiny pieces to boulder-size works. All were covered with a thin glittering shellac that kept them ageless. In another room were paintings; different styles, muted or vivid colors, strange shapes, faces, bewildering lines, startling contrasts; the works of masters. Still another room: the contents were naked people. Imagine delivering yourself to being stuffed? These people had, when there was nowhere else to go but into the grave. There was a man astraddle a great fish, there was a woman with bird wings strapped to her back, a bespectacled man seated inside a small spaceship, a woman whose skull had been replaced with glass so that her brain was visible. She represented the beginning of independent travel; her brain was her vehicle. Beside her was another woman who stood looking upward while her hand rested on the head of a large dog. All the subjects in this room showed signs of extreme age. Their presence told a story. They came from the sea, stood upon the ground for a brief moment and then leaped into the air. Above the heads of the petrified men and women was a spinning cluster of little twinkling stars. Over the galaxy hovered a black cloud; the unknown; mystery; the unexplored.

I was about to step on the grill outside the room when somebody took me by the shoulders, lifted me up and turned me around.

"Hi, Valdar."

His mind wasn't bedazzled, he wasn't starry-eyed, sweat didn't drip down his face and neither did his mouth hang open. Like mine. Like all the jaks who moved through Doubleluck. I hadn't realized what I was doing, hadn't noticed that the place was full of silent people. Only when I looked into the strained face of Big Jak did I come down to Earth. He had seen everything so many times; he didn't need to respond as the rest of us did.

"You went ahead and did it," he said.

"I had to. You should be glad. There's nothing holding you to the ground any longer. You can fly like any hedonist."

His eyes drooped and his mouth went grim. "That's right, but I'm not glad. What do you think the dreens are going to do now?"

"W-what does that mean?"

"Why look so surprised? Don't tell me you overlooked something?" He pointed and I saw. In the room behind us, amidst a throng of jaks, moved a little man who had curly dark hair and who wore a white uniform. He shoved jaks aside as if they were nonentities. I could see his face, suave and handsome, and his eyes were wide and glittering. The mind of Rulon sped, plotted, conspired, considered the beautiful surroundings. Without being able to read that mind, I knew what Rulon was thinking. He was constructing fences.

I turned to speak to Big Jak. He was gone.

Chapter XVI

"Now we meld," said the vark.

I shrieked because her brain cavity was so big. The enormity of the empty space threatened my mind. I felt as if I were about to become lost. Parts of me floated away into endless tunnels, and I tried to follow them, took wrong turns, couldn't catch up. The rest of me wandered away onto detours. I felt parceled out, dispersed. This was like death, where one's atoms separated to fly in different directions.

"We're still melded," said the vark. "Release me."

"Not on your life. You have my body."

"This was not part of the bargain."

"Sorry. It's an involuntary defense mechanism."

"Which must have its origin in your subconscious," said the vark. "How can you commit a voluntary act with the involuntary part of your mind?"

"Never mind that. Help me gather myself. I'm scattering like dust."

"I will, in return for a favor. Remove from your brain the sentinel you left behind. If this is to be my property for a while, I want it free and clear, with no squatters peering at me."

"First we have to take care of me," I said.

We spent half a day discussing our moving-in problems. Time passed but we were unaware of it. The vark body and the jak body sat in six inches of fine gray dust, on the vark planet, surrounded by approximately one hundred other varks. The remainder of the population went about their business and stayed tuned in to the goings on by mental telepathy. Varks had no privacy at all except when they ordered others to tune them out. Sometimes the others did this and sometimes they didn't. One of the conditions I had insisted upon was that all varks were to mind their own business where my thoughts were concerned.

Elda was a very old specimen of vark, and she had volunteered to meld with me when the older male vark, with whom I had spoken earlier, changed his mind. He said he hadn't traded bodies with anyone for a long time and would rather monitor Elda's impressions.

Nature fits a brain to a body, and the mind fits the brain, so everything works automatically. A mind that transfers to another body must first learn to live in the brain and then it has to familiarize itself with the rest of the habitat.

Elda's brain cavity was so different from mine that it took me hours to settle down. Afterwards, I took a look at the body and at first it seemed weird to the point of being incomprehensible. Most of me was a series of pipes and examining them consumed a long time. I grew aware of my four legs, tail, organs, feet, nails, fur, and I knew there was a gnawing hunger in my belly which lay in one of the pipe junctions.

Other than the fact that I was shorter now, the external world appeared the same to me, except for the jak seated beside me. She was me, but she didn't look like me. Self-image was more a projection than I had supposed, and the jak was more strange than familiar. For one thing, she looked like just another jak. Her mannerisms were ordinary, her voice was common. She wasn't bad-looking. But, damn it, she was me, so why wasn't she outstanding in several different ways?

"I look like a vark," said Elda, staring at me.

"I look like a jak," I said, staring at her.

"Uniqueness is mostly in the mind. It resides in chemistry."

"More or less," I said. "If the body you're wearing committed an unusual act, it would be more noticeable."

"To change the subject for a moment, the sentinel still watches me."

"I brought everything with me that I could," I said. "Shall I come back and try to remove it?"

176

"No, it might be an asset later. Now I want to examine reality through the eyes of Jade of the galaxy. I must function through your brain. By doing so, I hope to learn things that will be beneficial to varks."

"Well, go ahead and function."

"I see a vastness that has no boundaries. Its perimeters extend to no terminals, but rather toward limitless space. This is good. The other jaks who were tested had fences in their brains. Jade sees no end to reality."

"You have fences in your brain, too," I said. "I feel them."

"Because varks cannot skip."

"That isn't exactly true. A jak called Valdar or Big Jak visited Gibraltar in the body of a vark, and I'm sure he came independently. Also, a jak named Shaper joined me in naked space and he had no mount."

"But they were varks in body only."

That strange human face of mine; Elda stared at me for the longest time, obviously waiting for me to say something else, but I already knew I would learn nothing from her unless she felt like imparting information. Besides, varks didn't always think in the same manner as people. They followed a line of thought to a certain point and then abruptly ceased communication while they silently considered alternatives. When they finally did voice a conclusion, they were so far off the original track that what they said made little sense.

Elda was mulling something over in her mind, so I did the same, thought about jink and how mine had been affected by the mind transfer. Hinx was beside me, but my jink was strong without him. This wasn't too much of a difference. The only times I hadn't had strong independent jink were when I had the metal hat on my head and when I was a prisoner on Gibraltar.

I jinked the crowd of varks around us and discovered they were as blank-headed as always. Only when they gave me a direct thought could I read them. The big old male vark who had opted not to switch with me sat to my right, and I walked over to him and stared him in the eye.

"Something familiar about you," I said.

"Archetypes. You have a vark body, so you're picking up echoes."

"Where did varks come from?"

"The past, same as everybody."

"Why didn't you want to switch with me?"

"I already explained."

"But I think it wasn't true."

Before he could answer, I turned away and skipped into D-2. All by myself. It was the same as skipping with Hinx, but not quite. My destination wasn't pulling me, rather I was impelled by my origin. The planet pushed me and I could easily overestimate the force behind me. This was what the varks wanted to do, this was why they wanted me to switch minds: they longed to skip.

I zoomed back to D-3 and the old vark, landed beside him. "I know a jak named Shaper. His obsession is no different than anybody's; he aims to skip out of the galaxy."

"I believe I've heard of him," said the vark.

"He had an idea that a metal hat might muffle celestial static so his jink would have a farther reach. I think he gave up the hat idea, partly because he found out he was allergic to mounts and partly because of something else. Would you like to know what I think that something else is?"

"I am not truly interested."

"Don't believe you. But he switched bodies with a vark and found he could skip all by himself. That was great, but the drawback was just as great: If he wanted to continue skipping, he had to keep the vark body. What if he could learn how to transfer the skipping talent when he reclaimed his own body? Wouldn't it be nice if he could skip independently as a jak?"

"Astonishing possibility," said the old vark.

"Not to anyone who knew Shaper. It would be the next logical thought for him."

"For a jak."

"For anyone," I said. "Know another jak named

178

Valdar. He's a big ugly fellow with yellow eyes like yours. Like most jaks, he can't skip too far in one hop. He's been working on the hat idea with Shaper. Now he's working on the same idea all alone. I figure he doesn't have any faith in Shaper's second idea, or maybe he's using the hats as a red herring to keep another jak named Jade off the scent."

"Or maybe your imagination is out of control."

"I like your eyes. They're weird."

"Thank you," he said.

"Have you ever seen Doubleluck?"

"Often."

"Glad you said that. Too many lies in one package make me sick." How bright and eager and intelligent I was. I should have quit while I was ahead.

I skipped. Hedonist that I was, I had to do it in a pleasurable way, so I leapfrogged from solar system to solar system, for about ten minutes. When I came back to the old vark, I noticed something missing.

"Where am I?" I yelled.

"Standing before me," he said.

"That isn't what I mean, and you know it. Where's my body? Where's Elda?"

He didn't answer, just sat on his skinny rear with his long forelegs neatly together and his angular head hanging. He grinned at me like a mindless devil.

"Ever since I first met you, you've been suckering me," I said. "Think I don't know who you are? Think I'm too. dumb to realize you've never let me out of your sight? First you're my enemy, then you're my friend, then you're my enemy again."

"All this is in your own mind."

By then I was shaking all over. "Valdar, be like you were on Gibraltar. Know you were using me there, but you were kind to me. You wanted to keep me sane. Please stop trying to kill me now."

"Haven't laid a hand on you."

"Where's my body? Don't want to stay a vark. Don't want you taking your revenge this way."

"I told you once I'd never harm a child to get what I want."

"I'm not a child. Thought I was, but I'm not. I had to bring Doubleluck out in the open to save the lives of a lot of people. I didn't want the responsibility, but nobody else would do a thing. Jaks are little children, like you think I am."

I got down on my belly and licked his feet. "See what I'm willing to do to get my body back?"

Leaping away, he growled, "Don't do that."

"Why not? It's the way you want everybody to treat you. Kissing your feet is the only way a person can please you."

Big Jak jerked his head around. "Get her out of here, damn it. She's too much to tolerate."

"I want my body," I yelled.

The varks closed in on me. I tried to retain my position beside Big Jak, but they wouldn't let me, squeezed between us by the dozens, and in a few moments he was lost in the crowd. My instinctive reaction was to skip into D-2. They wouldn't allow that either. I was pinned to the ground and held there and when I tried to pull Hinx I found that he was tethered to a huge cactus.

Nobody was making any noise but me, so when Big Jak's voice sounded its warning, we all heard it clearly.

"Goddamn it, you took too long, they're coming."

Then I knew why only a hundred or so varks were present. The rest were in hiding while these stayed in the open and faced the enemy. They had volunteered to be expendable.

Out of the sky came a swarm of dreens, hundreds of mounted Dead Eyes with scowls on their faces and weapons in their hands. It wasn't difficult for me to guess where the weapons came from. The dreens had heat guns on Gibraltar, and they were pretty effective, but little bolts of heat were no good when the intent was to slaughter a planetful of people. For that, a man needed bombs or blasters. The dreens had chosen the latter. Each had a blaster and the guns came from the only place in the galaxy where good and evil coexisted: Doubleluck; El Dorado; everything a person could want, and since some people wanted evil, Doubleluck had it.

A blaster discharged a pellet that exploded on contact. Around me, varks exploded. I tried to run, tripped over a vark, rolled aside and watched as he popped into a thousand flying red pieces. Twenty varks leaped on me, covered me, provided the dreens with a fat target. Bodies burst and flew away from me.

I screamed for Hinx in my mind. The dreens weren't shooting at him. He was all alone beside the cactus, unable to do anything but watch what happened.

More varks covered me with their bodies. None of them tried to run. They all stayed close to me and when one group was blasted, another group protected me. I was drowning in vark blood, scrambling through mounds of bloody chunks, screaming and trying to escape from the horror around me.

If only the varks had allowed me to skip, they might have lived. They could have sent the dreens after me. Instead they did it their way, died under me, beside me, over me, allowed themselves to be slaughtered like garbage. There was one vark who never let go of me, grabbed me by the legs when I tried to crawl, swarmed on top of me every time I felt clear air above me, hid me from the sky, grunted and sobbed and never let me become a dreen target.

When the shooting ceased, he was sprawled on my back, weeping into my neck. Too exhausted to protest, we both lay still while the dreens turned us over with their boots.

I looked up into Rulon's face. Turning my head, I looked at Big Jak's vark face. His snout was gone, blasted away. One of his eyes was badly torn. The other glittered at me through a film of tears. Reaching out and touching my muzzle to his ear, I kissed him.

"I goofed," he whispered. "The damned varks promised they wouldn't sacrifice you, and I believed them."

"This one is Jade," said Rulon, nudging me with his boot.

"You going to kill me?" I said.

He didn't answer, aimed his blaster at Big Jak's belly. "Please tell me where her body is."

"Why ask him?" I said. "He's nobody and he knows nothing."

Rulon transferred his hateful gaze to me. "We'll find it if we have to kill every vark on the planet."

I trembled, shook like a leaf, gagged. Big Jak prodded my side with a paw. "Nobody knows where they are. Tell this bastard to go—"

Rulon hit him with the long stock of his weapon. Before he could draw it back again, my teeth were deep in his leg. Another dreen knocked me in the head with something and the conscious world went to sleep with me.

They took me to Gibraltar and chained me inside a small cage. The first thing I did when I woke up was hunt for Hinx.

"I'm in Doubleluck. So are a lot of dreens. I can't get out, but they can. They're in and out all the time. They're moving their whole population here. At least it seems that way. There are hundreds and hundreds of dreens here. They say they're going to kill—"

That was the last I heard of Hinx for a long time. Something or someone had cut him off. I was left to finish his last sentence, and my imagination made it a humdinger. If Rulon killed all his enemies, he would have to wipe out the galaxy. Could he do that? Did he have that much power now? First he could eliminate the varks, though they weren't particularly sinister; he might decide to ignore them. It wouldn't be too difficult for him to kill a mess of jaks. They were probably visiting Doubleluck in droves, and if Rulon picked them off as they came . . . but naturally he couldn't kill that many people. Could he?

What had I done to El Dorado but open it to a pack of thieves? And what had I done to Big Jak?

Every night, after the dreens went away and left me alone in darkness, I tried to communicate with my body. I felt insane doing it, but I did it anyway. Elda had said I left a sentinel behind in my brain. I had no idea what it might have been, but it couldn't hurt to try and learn what it was.

Every day Rulon came and talked to me.

"I can't do the future dreen population much good in this body," I said. "Why don't you let me go?"

His handsome face screwed into an exasperated

scowl. "We'll find your real body." Suddenly he smiled. "It's quite superior to the one you're wearing."

"The mind hasn't changed, though. I still can't see you for dust."

"As if that matters," he said, and went away.

I had expected to find Gibraltar razed by bombs, but my jink revealed no major destruction. Neither did it reveal the presence of too many gibs. There were a few stragglers just inside the limits of my mental awareness, and I guessed that since the cities were now occupied by dreens, the gibs had fled to wherever they thought there might be safety. What the gibs were doing or how they were surviving, I couldn't say. Likely, they weren't surviving too well. So many of them were below normal in intelligence and those who were bright enough were too uninformed to defend themselves.

I thought of Cedron. His head had been buried in the sand for most of his life. No doubt the world looked bewildering to him now. As for Otho, if there was any way of surviving, he would take advantage of it. But he, too, was ignorant. What did he know about wholesale war? Did he realize that he and the hordes of gibs with him were going to be left to starve by the dreens? What did any gib know about operating, organizing, supervising, planning? In the long run, a great many of them would live—if the dreens left them alone.

My body remained elusive. Like a specter that hovered just beyond one's vision, my genuine self floated on the other side of a shadow somewhere on the planet of the varks. I knew it was there, but out of reach, and I couldn't touch it.

"I think it's only just that the dreens are inheriting El Dorado," Rulon said to me.

It was morning and gray daylight came in the single window of the shack that was my prison. There was nothing else in the shack but my cage. The chain around my neck was light but strong. Sometimes, at my request, the guard outside would come in and transfer it down to my belly where it felt more tolerable.

"You make it sound like something that happened out of the blue," I said.

"What if it had?"

"I wouldn't call it just. Either way, it's a travesty."

"A travesty of an abstract," he said. It was warm in the shack and the hair on his forehead was damp. He looked tired, as if he had been up all night. No doubt he had. Wasn't it in the dark that evil men did their conspiring?

"The principle of the survival of the fittest has always applied to every living creature," he said. "Do you know how my people were persecuted by the gibs? The first dreens were called conscious subnormals. They were a little bit different, asked too many questions, were dissatisfied with moving on a treadmill. Those first dreens were confined in mental institutions. Each one that was released left the cities, and when there were enough of them, they started their own civilization. The gibs laughed at them, called them atavisms. All because they weren't content to live for their reward in heaven."

"I know all about it," I said.

"But do you understand?"

"That the dreens were inevitable? Yes."

"Then why condemn us?"

"You didn't have to go the way you went. You can change now. Join the jaks. Let the gibs go."

He frowned at me. "We're letting them go, but we won't join the jaks. Never again will anyone tell us what to do."

"Then live by yourselves in peace."

"Humans are natural predators. Others won't allow us to live in peace."

"Don't attribute your own qualities to others without a reason," I said.

Reaching through the bars, he stroked my ear. "I'll be a good husband to you."

"Will you be kind?"

"Of course."

"Even when I misbehave?"

"I'll see that you don't."

"You won't beat me?" I said.

"No."

"Not even when I throw up? Because that's my reaction to you. It's really uncanny, totally involuntary. The second you come near me, I want to up-chuck my cactus."

My ear got a savage twist before he stalked out of the shack.

A so-called physician came around the next day and took some of my blood. The guard brought in a table and the medicine man set up his equipment next to my cage. He was the thinnest individual I'd ever seen. I had already learned that skinny dreens were the most fanatic kind, were so dedicated to the cause of dreen superiority that they had no interest in the flesh. This man simply didn't take the time to eat properly. Fortunately, or not, he wasn't the most reticent of dreens and talked freely to me. He needed blood because Rulon wanted to learn more about vark anatomy. Varks had turned out to be one of the un-predictables in the experiment of taking over. Taking over what? How much did the dreens want of reality? Those were my questions, and they evoked only a smile from the medicine man, who then went about his business of making holes in my hide.

He told me that after my real body was located he would be back to run some of the same types of tests on it. Rulon wanted me to be drained of my strength. I asked the medicine man how an individual of my size and heritage could be made weaker than a dreen, and he hemmed and hawed and admitted that if the adjustments worked, I would be pretty much of a mess.

How would it be done? Extra jak female hormones didn't make a female jak weaker. They just botched up her metabolism. If she received too much, she died. How did the dreens know this? For years they had been kidnapping jaks and using them as guinea pigs.

What the medicine man intended to do to me, once I was united with my own body, was to bless me with a good dose of dreen hormones. If I didn't die, and chances were good that I wouldn't, I'd begin to sprout female dreen qualities. The more hormones I received, the more I would revert. Eventually my bone structure would lighten and my musculature would become altered. My genes would remain unaffected.

Rulon visited me in order to do some boasting. They had discovered that the varks could fly. Odd creatures, the varks. Anyhow, the dreen soldiers had scoured the planet's surface but with no success. The varks weren't hiding in mountainous or underground caves. So much for that. However, the knowledge that varks could fly had given Rulon other ideas. There were forests of tremendous cacti on the planet, ancient and dead growths that stretched hundreds of feet into the sky. The dreens hadn't bothered examining these forests, for varks had no claws with which to climb. There seemed to be no apparent way for them to get up the plants. Now there was. Rulon believed the varks were hiding in the top branches of the giant cacti.

I brooded about it after he left me. Was my body still in one piece or had the varks dropped Elda when they tried to fly her aloft? Evidently they had succeeded in hiding her, since Rulon hadn't found my corpse.

Again I probed with jink for my jak carcass. It was the only time, in all my searching, that I found it, and this was because my body was on its way to me.

I sensed it, probed more intently, located it, recoiled in my cage and began to curse. My body was slung over the shoulder of a cross-eyed jak who was even then speeding through D-2. Shaper had no mount under him. An independent traveler had to be a body with someone else's mind in it. Right? Wrong. I knew, before Shaper arrived in the shack beside me, that it was indeed he and that he was traveling free-style.

"That's the most traitorous smile I've ever seen on the face of anyone," I said as he materialized.

He was a happy jak. Right then I considered him an ugly, mean one. He made Big Jak look meek. Landing gently on his feet, he lowered my body to the floor and gave me another smile. "Nobody has to kick me in the rear end anymore. Have decided to be as exasperating as everybody else and speak whenever I feel like it and not just when I'm spoken to."

"Hello, Shaper. I'm not sorry you've found what you wanted."

He came over to the cage and looked at me and his smile disappeared. "You were always fair. I know you don't begrudge me my victory. I knew, soon as I switched bodies with a vark the first time, that I'd find another way to get to glory."

"It didn't take you long."

"Yes, it did. Have worked on nothing else for months. It ain't easy, but I'm persistent. The secret was in getting outside myself. It made me see that I was as relative as everything else. Once I could look at the situation objectively, I saw that jink is something every living thing comes into the world with and that it's as natural as breathing. Melding with a mount isn't at all necessary. Melding is love, and when a fella is loving, everything is easier to do."

"Meaning you have no use for love?" I said.

"Meaning I put it in its proper place. I love you, but that has nothing to do with my traveling. I could love a mount but simply don't want to. Don't desire to love a thing because I need it. I had to find another way of getting to glory."

"What did you do with Elda?"

"Nothing. She's still in your body. I just knocked her out."

"Nobody can fool the varks," I said.

"Maybe not, but I took the body off the top of a cactus and ran, and they didn't try to stop me."

"Why did you do it?"

"I thought the dreens aimed to kill you. Then I learned Rulon wants you for his wife. That changed the situation. Would never have allowed them to hurt you."

"I see. It's all right for me to wed a dreen."

"Sure," he said. "Death's final but marriage is just a pain in the ass. Won't do you any lasting harm."

"And your conscience is clear. You can try to skip out of the galaxy—"

"Not try. I will."

"How far can you skip now?"

"Better than an ordinary jak, but I'm lengthening the distance between hops."

"Like swimming underwater?" I said. "The lungs hold only so much air."

His eyes crossed violently and he stamped a foot in agitation. "Shut your mouth. I'll get to glory first, see if I don't."

"You're a traitor."

He opened his mouth to cuss.

"Where's Big Jak?" I said quickly. "Is he alive?"

His mouth shut with a click. "Don't know," he said sullenly. "That big skunk is a lying, treacherous opportunist. I hope he ain't dead, as I want to see his face when I skip to glory and leave him my dust to eat."

"Shaper, listen to me—"

At that moment the door of the shack opened. Rulon stepped in, saw the body on the floor, saw Shaper standing there—

But Shaper wasn't there anymore. In the space of a brief second, a dozen varks zoomed from D-2 and appeared in the room, each of them grabbed a piece of Shaper's lanion skin in their teeth, and then they took him away. The sound of his screeches faded away until nothing was left but faint little yelping noises.

Interesting: The varks had gotten their wish, had learned how to skip independently. Or maybe they had always known how to do that and had lied to me and everyone. Interesting: They came to Gibraltar and stole Shaper. Not me. Not Elda. Why Shaper? There was only one possible reason: He had learned how to skip, he was good at it and getting better every day, and he was threatening to leave the galaxy.

Me? Here comes the bride.

Chapter XVII

"Beware the House of Joseph."

Elda said that to me just before she and I traded back into our own bodies. Rulon promised not to kill her, after he threatened to kill us both if we didn't make the switch. Rather than have him use Elda for his experiments, I asked if I could have her for a pet. I knew he wouldn't let her go, and I knew it would please him to see a superior organism loping about on a collar and leash. Elda, plus myself, made two pets. She was mine and I belonged to the dreen whose day it was to mind the animals. Instead of wearing a collar on my neck, I wore a tight chain on my right wrist. The guard held the other end of my leash and I usually held Elda's leash.

"After your therapy, there will be no more of this nonsense," Rulon said to me.

"It isn't necessary to give me hormones," I said. "I'm civilized. I know how to worship my master."

"You're not a slave."

"Of course I am. If I were free, I'd be gone."

"If you insist on thinking things like that, what choice have I but to chain you?" he said.

"If you can't see the holes in that statement, I see no point in trying to reason with you."

Rulon spent most of his time in Doubleluck and he was in a hurry to get back there. I was surprised when he told me I was going with him. He didn't trust anyone else to take care of me. Thankfully, he was postponing the marriage until after I had been primed with hormones, and as he was too busy to supervise the medicine man just then, the transforma-

189

tion of Jade the jak into Jade the freak would have to wait.

That was fine with me. Elda and I were tied together with strong ropes, placed on the back of a mount and dragged through D-2 by Rulon and a dozen soldiers.

Jaks were playing hide and seek in Earth's atmosphere. They popped into view, dreens chased them, they popped into D-2, and so it went. Had those jaks swarmed over the dreens in the beginning, they wouldn't have been outside looking in at this moment. Jaks were too passive to leap before they looked. They liked answers first. This was unfortunate for them because now they couldn't get into Doubleluck and more than a few of them were getting blasted by the soldiers who chased them with guns blazing.

I was relieved to discover that Rulon hadn't found a cache of super-weapons in Doubleluck. My relief didn't last long. One of the first rooms he showed me, in the city, contained more super-weapons than a mount had hair.

"Nobody ever helped us," he said, looking around the room with a fond eye. "Only our ancestors. They left us these and all the other treasures."

"They were my ancestors, too. And the gibs'."

"They left this city for the brightest of their posterity."

"How do you know who they left it for, or why they left it?" I said.

"Don't argue with me, don't contradict me," he said. He wasn't irritated. I think he really did like me, that I was more than a symbol to him. By marrying me, he was stealing from the enemy, by taking me against my will, he was proclaiming his superiority over me and my kind. Rulon would always need to feel superior. Never would he understand jaks, or varks, or gibs; more important, he would never understand men, and men had built Doubleluck.

The weapons: all large enough to be used by an individual but so small that they were obviously trinkets or toys. Men had intended for them to be looked at and understood. Tiny blasters, rays, molecule-freezers similar to the one Big Jak had used to destroy the hat stuck on my head; there was a thing Rulon called an atom attractor; aim it at an object and three points of light lured atoms in three different directions. Maybe atoms were conditioned like minds: when they moved out of their normal positions, they went mad. The object began to whirl and fly and before it disappeared through the wall it was whirling so fast it was almost invisible.

There was a tube that produced sound frequencies destructive enough to make a stone collapse and leak across the floor in a wet trail. Another instrument, when aimed at an object, created an air pocket around it. Pressure could be increased and held within the pocket. Also, the shape of the pocket could be controlled. The object could be moved up, down or to the side.

Doubleluck was an effect. The glittering beauty of the floors, walls, ceilings and furnishings, the faint tinkling sound that was almost like music, the sweetness of the air, the promise found in another corridor or behind a closed door, the huge rooms and the small ones, the eternity of the things within the city—all these were a single effect, and the response to it was that of awe. In this place the word "artifact" had no meaning because everything had the touch of a master; a race of masters. Light, color, substance were enhanced by the perfection of their shape and position.

I walked through halls so bright and sparkling that the space ahead of me looked like solid light. Pale green shades swept so rapidly into darker green that the former seemed an illusion. No matter where I looked, color smashed me between the eyes. Walls that seemed as high as mountains became frozen stalks of white ice streaked with green. Through them peeked darker mountains. Behind them all blazed a sun that was never reached, only felt. Doubleluck was warm and silent, cool and still, peaceful and patient. It was an effect, and maybe it truly existed only when there was a mind to behold it.

Fabulous room: clear, transparent pipes two inches in diameter and two inches apart decorated the walls and ceiling; through them ran fluid gold. They met

191

in the center of the ceiling, and the gold poured down like a waterfall into a swirling yellow pool carved in the middle of the floor. The pool sides were inlaid with jewels, red, blue, green, white, and the spattering drops lunged into a narrow gutter, were sucked into the pipes where they began their endless race to the ceiling and down again. It was cold in this room. One felt a reluctance to approach the pool. There was intense coldness here, and that was strange. It seemed natural to associate wet gold with heat, but this room was an alteration of the natural. The gold was wet, it ran and chuckled and gurgled through the pipes, fell with a great splashing, and it was because of the weird coldness in the pool and in the pipes.

Usually it was Rulon who led me around on my leash, and I often nagged him to let me ride up the outside of the buildings on the air lifts. For me it was like skipping to glory. I rose up the sheer cliff-buildings and back down again as many times as I could get Rulon to take me. Naturally he wouldn't let me go alone.

I loved Doubleluck. I was glad it existed. If the day ever came when I was free of all my friends and enemies, I'd come back to the House of Joseph and . . .

I was sitting in my room when that particular thought came to me, and it startled me so much I yanked on the leash holding Elda to my chair. If I could have unlocked our chains, both of us would have been long gone.

"Elda! Are you putting ideas in my head?"

She was lying at my feet, and when I spoke, she rolled her eyes upward and yawned. "If I talk, you can hear me. But I'm not talking at the moment."

"What's the House of Joseph?"

"You've asked me that fifty times and I've told you I don't know. Said nothing about it to you."

"Are you sure?"

"Am sure."

I sat back in my chair and tried to relax. "Well, something invisible is talking to me and it's giving me the spooks."

Elda shivered and moved closer to my feet. "Better listen to it."

Looking down at her, I said, "Why do you say that?"

"No special reason."

Again I brooded. It was easy to do in my room of light. Waving bands of pastels danced across the walls. Sometimes they flashed to the left, at times they went down or up. I think Rulon put me in that room in the hope that it would keep me partially hypnotized. The secret was in viewing the colors and movements as a whole. If you watched a particular wavy band of light, followed it all the way, you ended with your psyche dashed against a wall or a floor or the ceiling. Or your psyche plunged into the band, swirled along with it and became diffused. Hours could pass while your mind swam through the labyrinths of aqua, pink, yellow, rose.

The House of Joseph. I had read about people named Joseph, in the books Valdar had given me while I'd been on Gibraltar. There were books here in Doubleluck, too, innumerable volumes that nobody had time to read. The only significant Joseph I remembered reading about was a man who became a dream interpreter; he once owned a coat of many colors.

"Doubleluck is the coat of many colors," I said, vaguely aware that Elda's head shot up into the air. "The dream interpreter wears it."

"What?" she said, and she trembled from head to toe.

"Joseph. He told the king what his dreams meant." This time I noticed Elda's uneasiness. "Tell me," I said. "I want to know all about the varks. There's no point in keeping secrets from me now. If Rulon wins, you and I will probably die. If he loses, the galaxy will be free. I think he's going to lose."

"How do you know?" she whispered.

"I think it. Do you know what dreams are? They're confessions of the soul. You are what you dream."

"Don't stop. Go on."

I smiled. "Rambling, you mean? Let's change places and you do the rambling."

"You're better at it."

"Which may be one of the reasons why you dog my footsteps. Or is it the only reason?"

Vark ears went forward, back, forward. Alarmed, Elda refused to look at me. But then, it wasn't Elda, anyway.

"Valdar," I said. "Big Jak."

For a long moment there was no response. Then, "Is there no way to keep a secret from you?"

"What happened to the old vark? His body was in bad shape."

"I think he's going to be all right."

"You switched bodies with Elda. You lived in my body. Don't you get tired of sticking your nose in my business?"

"No. It's my job. I'm a Watcher and take my orders from the varks who are the overseers of the galaxy. The people who built Doubleluck chose the varks because they're so objective and have a keen sense of justice."

For the first time in a long time, I felt myself truly relaxing. "Tell me all about it. What's the purpose of everything?"

He gave me a sad grin. "Nobody knows. The builders of Doubleluck were preparing to change their style of life. They were going to skip, had developed the talent, and they were afraid of what skipping would do to them. If a person doesn't work with his hands, what will become of him? The varks were old friends of men, knew a good deal about the galaxy because they traded bodies with every alien that came to their planet. They made a deal with man: if people took the wrong track in the future, the varks would interfere.

"As it turned out, it wasn't that simple for the varks. The human race had split up. At first there were gibs and jaks, then there were dreens. There were already Watchers, who were my own personal family. I'm the last of that family, so far. The varks couldn't make up their minds whether jaks had gone to hell or were still in the process of growing up. On the other hand, the dreens were making fools of the gibs and were threatening to become powerful enough to

194

influence conditions external to their world. Again, the varks couldn't make up their minds. Would the situation on Gibraltar soon change, and if so, what changes would occur? Of what significance were the dreens? How did they fit into the picture of one big happy galactic house?

"The varks finally got it into their heads that a house full of children has shaking walls. If they interfered, they might destroy something potentially good. It looked to them as if the jaks were getting ready to run off to another galaxy without cleaning up the problems behind them. There was a young kid who had a skipping talent like nobody else, and she was hot on the trail of Doubleluck. There was a cross-eyed fella who had learned about celestial static and was planning to make a hat to cancel it. There were all sorts of unpredictable people popping up. The only Watcher left was a fiddlefoot who couldn't stick to his job of keeping people away from Doubleluck."

Big Jak stopped talking, shook his head and gave a sigh of resignation.

"If it hadn't been for me, things would have stayed the way they were for a while," I said.

"That's right. People would still be hunting for this city and they'd have no end to their road."

"Then I'm glad I came along. It was time for a change, and there's no end to the road. It wasn't even a road. It was a rut."

"You feeling proud of yourself?" he said.

"Everything I did came naturally. I'm not afraid of the future. Men shouldn't have been afraid either. What made them think they could build a highway to forever?"

"Well, the varks—"

"What will they do now?"

"I don't know."

"I do," I said. "They won't do anything. They're objective and an objectivist is an observer who doesn't take sides. He sits back and watches what everybody else does. If the varks have any sense, they'll forget their promises to people who have been dead for millions of years."

"Forget and do what?"

I grinned. "Do like me; visit new places."

"I think you're an optimist. You're sitting there in chains, planning to skip."

"To glory."

"What about the dreens?"

"To hell with them."

"What about the varks?"

"To hell with them."

"What about me?"

"To hell—"

"Uh uh. I'm not gotten rid of that easy." Big Jak wouldn't say any more. He sprawled at my feet, with his chin on his paws, and soon he went to sleep.

When Rulon came to get me for dinner, he found us both out like lights. Later, he told me the supplies they had brought from Gibraltar were almost gone. He had sent a detachment to bring some more. The detachment hadn't returned and Rulon was irritated because he had to eat leftovers. There were no kitchens, dining rooms or bedrooms in the city, which ought to have attracted the attention of someone besides myself.

Several million dreens lived here now, so there was no such thing as privacy; not that the city was laid out for close living. Doubleluck wasn't a domicile, had never been intended as such. But dreen families had come in astride single mounts, and Gibraltar had nobody on it now but gibs and a few thousand dreen guards. Rulon told me, quite calmly, that he hadn't made up his mind about the gibs. He might kill most of them. Whichever way, some of those who survived were destined to become body slaves for the dreens in Doubleluck, while the remainder would have to be farmers on Gibraltar.

In a way I was worried and in a way I wasn't. Like most jaks, I was more concerned with where I was going to go tomorrow. I knew where I'd go, but I wasn't sure when the appropriate tomorrow would arrive. I knew where my mount was. The varks had him. Big Jak either didn't know or wouldn't tell me how Hinx had gotten from Doubleluck to the vark

196

planet. Rulon had little to say about it. Plainly he didn't care. I couldn't go anywhere with a chain and leash on my arm, so what did it matter where another mount was? I asked Hinx about it and his reply was that the varks had threatened him if he let me pull him. He didn't elaborate and I didn't question him further, as the varks had forbidden him to talk to me. When the time came, I would make my move. All I had to do was wait and hope Rulon didn't decide to get the marriage over with.

We had been living in Doubleluck exactly one month when the first dreen died. His scream could be heard all over the city.

His death unnerved everybody but it didn't come as any great surprise. For the past several days he had been acting crazy, running up and down corridors, yelling his head off, cursing and keeping people awake. Rulon had him examined by a physician. There seemed to be nothing wrong with him. When he was quieted with a tranquilizer, he said he had been having bad dreams, that he had trouble getting to sleep and was feeling apprehensive. He apologized for his behavior and Rulon let him go. A few hours later, he was riding the air drafts up and down the city's exterior, and he was yelling again. A city with several million inhabitants is usually noisy, but it was early morning when the dreen died, so nearly everyone heard his last scream. He simply fell down in a corridor and didn't get up.

He was being examined for the cause of death when the second dreen took the very same route, started screaming and acting insanely. Before the week was out, thousands of people were trying to see the physicians. They couldn't sleep. No matter how quiet their surroundings were, they had great difficulty dropping off. And when they finally did, they had nightmares.

"Tell me what it is," I said to Big Jak.

"I don't know what you mean."

Maybe he didn't. He and I and Rulon were strolling down an avenue of gold, somewhere toward the rear of the city. Rulon was no more familiar with the surroundings than I, and if it hadn't been for Big Jak, we would have gotten lost many times. Big Jak had enough sense to play dumb and appear to do things the right way by accident. Rulon was quick, though, and I knew he disliked my vark companion. His dislike would eventually change to suspicion, but I hoped to be free before then. I hoped a lot of things.

Again I spoke to Big Jak. "You have to know what's ailing the dreens. How many have died so far? About a dozen?"

"The little fellow leading you like a slave has pretty fair jink. Don't you think you ought to save your questions till later?"

"Quit stalling. The brain of a vark is a blank wall with a sponge behind it. You're grabbing everything I say before any of it can leak out."

Rulon suddenly came to a stop, and I knew a moment of alarm. But he wasn't interested in us right then. His head was up and he was staring at a small green door far up the wall to our right.

"I don't recall seeing that door before."

"There must be hundreds—" Big Jak began.

"Don't interrupt, vark," said Rulon.

"What do you want to do?" I said. I had never seen the door before, either, but then there were many places in Doubleluck that I hadn't visited. The green door was so high up the wall that it seemed to be almost directly over our heads.

"I want to take a look," said Rulon.

"Do you think it isn't occupied by about a hundred dreens?"

"I don't care. I want to see it. This is my city. I'm making it my country. I intend to learn to know it intimately."

"Hope there are no corpses in it," I said. He gave me a black look and did a poor job of masterfully dragging me over to the wall. The three of us stepped onto the grilled gutter and let an air draft capture and carry us into the air.

There were no people living behind the green door. There was nothing in the little room but a green statue. Two glass windows in the ceiling reflected

198

light and shed it on the head of the figure. It wasn't sunlight but the odd, fierce light of Doubleluck, rich and golden rays that bathed the statue's crown of hair and seemed to make the entire figure glow from within.

The statue was a woman. She was tall and sleek, long of leg and arm. Her hair flew wild, her eyes were large and alert. Her arms were flung up, not toward the ceiling or to the sky, but to the void and the unknown space beyond.

"This is the most beautiful piece of work in the city," said Rulon. He had spent many minutes walking around the statue and viewing it from different perspectives. "I have to admit that a genius constructed it. Do you notice the expression on the face? It is dead matter, frozen forever, but the expression of pride and compassion was stamped there in the beginning and will never fade. A fine, lovely masterpiece."

"What do you think she represents?" I asked.

"The value of the human soul. To the sculptor it was worth more than any substantial treasure. The statue is made of jade. What a trial and a tribulation it must have been to make this huge work."

"What did you say?" I said.

Rulon looked at me with irritation. "You didn't understand me? You want to quarrel with my analysis?"

"What did you say it was made of?"

"Jade." All at once, Rulon started. "Your name, by heaven! How did you come by it? Who gave it to you?"

"How does anyone get a name? From someone who loves them."

The vark beside me laid down on the floor and groaned.

Rulon said, "Thank the powers that the artist who made this statue wasn't blessed with your acquaintance. You're nothing like this eternal woman. See how soft and feminine her body is? Note the fine, full breasts, the normal hips? This is a mother of people, not a hedonistic adolescent who will grow up to be a caricature of a female. All jak women are

199

reluctant to submit to a male. They don't know how. They deny their own nature and can never experience total fulfillment."

Still flat on the floor, Big Jak gave another groan. I laughed. Rulon flushed.

"The dreens have preserved many values from the past," he said harshly. "Men were not completely inferior."

"Why don't you relax and stop trying to lord it over me?" I said. "Because I'm female doesn't mean—"

Rulon waved me silent. "I know I'm not exactly free of prejudice. I will learn."

"Hmmm. What kind of male insists upon having a woman who doesn't want him?"

He did something I had never seen him do. He trembled. "This is a terrible life, full of uncertainty and danger. I want my kind to survive."

"Do you mean your posterity or your uncertainties?" I said.

"I mean my people. With all their imperfections."

"Do you want them to be exactly the same in, say, a thousand years?"

He fingered his brow, glared at me with hot eyes. "Will it be wrong if someone can point to one of my descendants, in a thousand years, and say, 'This is a dreen'?"

"I think so."

"Why?"

"Following his true nature, a human combines himself with everyone else."

"What does that mean?"

"A jak is a truer person than a dreen. He or she is a descendant of free man and free woman."

"Damn it, this is what comes of arguing with a female. Insults."

"The unreason of the testes," murmured Big Jak, and received a booted toe in his ribs.

"Why not kick me?" I said. "I've been more frank than the vark."

"I can't strike a woman."

"I can strike a male," I said, and I hit Rulon, which may have meant that I was every bit as unreasonable as he. But from the moment I first met him, he had been telling me that no matter what position my body pretended to assume, it was, theoretically, flat on its back and being worked over by him or any other male dreen. I was growing up, and I didn't mind the idea of being worked over by somebody of my own choosing, but at the same time I would have to be doing some working over of my own, otherwise I simply wouldn't be interested.

Too, I owed Rulon a lump. He lost his hold on my leash as he went flying backward to slam against the statue of Jade.

"Yay," said Big Jak, but it wasn't a cheer. It sounded glum. "That's the way you're going to be as an adult. If a fella says something off-color, you'll plant him among the flowers."

"You've been reading too many books."

"You haven't read enough. You think men and women have settled their old quarrel?"

That really surprised me. "You mean they haven't?"

He hadn't moved an inch and now he gave another groan, louder than before.

Rulon slumped at the foot of the statue, fingering his cut lip with one hand and the back of his head with the other. Little cries of rage came out of his mouth. He kept trying to get his feet under him.

"Hit him again before he sounds an alarm," said Big Jak.

"I can't. He's too little."

"Don't be dumb. He's as big as you are and twice as rotten, though that last part is hard to believe."

"I don't care if you love me. I'm going to glory and to hell with the whole pack of you."

"I wouldn't want you any other way," he growled. "But what makes you think I love you?"

"You named me after this statue. You think I'm beautiful and courageous and proud and—"

"Damn it, slug him."

I didn't enjoy it. I didn't hate Rulon and never had. And he wasn't as big as I. Poor Rulon. His face was ghastly as I picked him up by his fine white jacket. I had read about emasculation, but I actually saw it in his eyes as I drew back my fist and aimed it at his jaw. He was a damned fool for feeling that way.

201

Maybe he didn't feel it, just before I put him to sleep. Maybe during that last moment, he realized we were merely two foes. I hoped so, for his sake. As for me, I didn't really give a damn. He was, finally, in my way, and if he couldn't tolerate defeat, it was his hard luck.

"If we get caught, we're dead meat," said Big Jak. "Try and get this collar off me."

"Why are we dead?"

"Nobody can live in Doubleluck. It's a monument. It's dead as hell. It's pretty to look at but if you try to set up housekeeping in it, it'll kill you."

Chapter XVIII

I had no sooner succeeded in getting the chain off my wrist than I realized Big Jak was gone. I didn't believe it. I even looked behind the statue. He had told me to start working on the chain, that it was only a puzzle-link and shouldn't give me much trouble. So I did. And he deserted me, took off in an independent manner and left me blinking in disbelief and sniffling, more in anger than self-pity. He loved me. He wouldn't leave me in the midst of my enemies.

Of course I got caught. I was too big to hide for long. I spent a deal of time running down avenues, riding air drafts, et cetera, but there were too many dreens and they finally cornered me and overpowered me by leaping on me and holding me down.

I did have one consolation, though, during the few minutes when I was speeding down an avenue with about fifty dreens behind me. Big Jak made an appearance for a little while. He burst from D-2, directly above the avenue, and I and my pursuers stopped long enough to watch.

The big gray vark carcass with the degenerate soul of Big Jak encased in it came screeching, literally, into view, and behind him came half a dozen other varks. That they were chasing him and that he was alarmed was plain. He didn't have a chance. The varks knew their bodies and had him enclosed in a circle before he could pop out of D-3.

"Help. Goddamn it, let go."

The varks had their teeth in his tail, ears, belly, backside, arms, legs. He looked as if he were about to be eaten. But they weren't cannibalistic, just determined to capture him.

That's how I got caught. I shouldn't have taken the time to enjoy the spectacle.

"Hang him high," I yelled. "Dump him back in his own ugly hide and string him to the highest cactus you can find."

They took him away, the dreens jumped me and pounded my head a little, I was chained to the statue of Jade and left to brood over many things. Rulon came around to strut and threaten me, but in the end he sat down on the floor and stroked me, petted me, kissed me, made me scream in exasperation. Finally he gave me one last affectionate squeeze and went away.

The varks; what were they up to? It was fine that they had taken Shaper and Big Jak prisoners. But they had left me in Doubleluck where people were dying. Shaper and Big Jak couldn't skip to glory, but neither could I. They would live while I might not.

The next time I saw Rulon, he wasn't so gay. "There's a curse on this city," he said. He was haggard, his uniform was filthy, he didn't try to hide his fear.

"Why tell me about it?"

"You seem to know all the answers. Besides, I don't want to be seen too much. My people are turning against me. They're waiting for me to tell them what to do, and I have no suggestions."

"I can tell you what I think."

"Go ahead."

"Okay. You'll never be able to stay here. The whole place is a killer."

He got down on the floor beside me. "It's my imagination. Everyone is sick. I, too, feel ill."

"I don't."

"Why do you think I'm here?" he snarled. "You're immune to everything."

"Not to things that disgust me. Why don't you set me free and both of us can go our own way?"

He shivered. "My men are searching everywhere. We'll find the source of the illness. The air is being analyzed. We'll find out what's causing it."

"You already had the air analyzed, and I thought it

was a waste of time then. I still do. The air is the same stuff that's outside. It's Earth atmosphere and it's perfectly good."

"Shut up."

At that moment the door flew open. A soldier, his face pinched and deathly white, staggered inside. "Commander, help us," he gasped. "We can't endure."

Rulon screamed his response. "I have to learn what's causing it. Get out of here and don't come back."

The soldier sank to his knees, hobbled across the floor, placed weak hands around Rulon's neck. While Rulon shrank, frozen in terror and stupefaction, the soldier tried to strangle him.

"You made so many promises. You said we'd control the galaxy. Now we're dying and you don't care."

With a cry, Rulon leaped to his feet, dragged the soldier to the door and threw him onto the avenue below. Back to me he came, cursing. "The rotten wretch. Why didn't he leave me alone?"

"You're losing your mind, Rulon. Don't you know? Can't you see? First people have trouble sleeping, they have nightmares, they're edgy and impulsive. This city is a banking board for the conscience. The fears of your people are rebounding."

"What's that supposed to mean?" he shouted.

"The House of Joseph. Maybe the engine that gives power to the city is the source. I don't know what that power is. Maybe it comes from the sun. Whatever it is, it's giving off something that is everywhere in the city. The entire area is saturated with that influence."

"What influence?"

"I don't know. The builders were at the pinnacle of technological success. They left it all behind because the mind was greater than artifacts. But they were proud and didn't want anybody cluttering up their city. Too, they didn't want the human race to fall back to depending upon machines. Everything on Earth except Doubleluck deteriorated, and that was their intent."

Again Rulon sat beside me. "I don't believe you. You're lying."

"Shut up. Joseph was a man who had the power to interpret the dreams of a king. The king and all his people would have died if he hadn't listened to Joseph and taken his advice."

"What the hell has that to do with—"

"I told you to shut up. The builders left a message behind, and if you ask me how they did it, I'll kick you, even if I am chained up. I heard the message. It said, 'Beware the House of Joseph.'"

"You relate that to a stupid character in a work of fiction?"

"He was the only Joseph I read about who was really meaningful to men. Try to imagine men who were so technologically advanced that they could build a machine that absorbed thoughts, dreams, thinking patterns. Suppose this machine could redirect those mental creations right back to their source? How would you like to have the monsters in your subconscious talking to you? Think of just one thing you're afraid of? How about an example: You're alone in the whole universe; everybody has that sensation at one time or another. Say you go to sleep and your dreaming mind acts out this fear. The drama is absorbed by Doubleluck and then is played back into your mind. A fear which you already have is taught to you in your sleep. What's your automatic reaction? Fear, fear and more fear."

Rulon shuddered, shivered, shook his head, pinched my leg until it was blue.

"The dreens are great for conditioning," I said. "They have little machines that teach propaganda. Those machines are toys compared to this city. Take another fear as an example: What if you're afraid you're inferior; or depraved? The city bounces this junk right back at you. What if you suspect you're evil? During sleep, Doubleluck gives you the whammy. Your suspicion is reinforced. Then you begin to realize you can't sleep. The city reinforces the realization. You start thinking you're crazy, start to believe you're losing control—"

"Shut up, shut up, no, no, no."

"Okay," I said. "Don't believe it."

"But the machine isn't bothering you."

"Not yet."

Eagerly, he said, "But you're worried?"

"Thanks a whole lot. Put seeds in my mind. Yes. Nuts to the machine, but I'm worried. I don't want to lose my marbles. The longer I stay here, the more I'm in jeopardy. This place would make a hell of an execution chamber. Chain your worst enemy to, say, a statue made of jade, and then leave and come back in a few weeks and laugh over her corpse."

Rulon was on his feet and gazing down at me with a triumphant expression. "Talk about hitting a nail on the head! There's a galaxy of jak women out there and I'll bet my boots I'll find others with your talents. But they won't have your deranged personality."

"Speaking of derangement, I can see you've made your neat decision, but I'd like to know if you simply thought it up as a reasonable way to deal with me or if you're just plain nuts and don't know daylight from dark."

"Oh, I know what I'm doing. I'm affected by the force in Doubleluck, but for a long time I've been plagued with the subject of Jade. I can thank you for showing me the solution."

"You're going back to Gibraltar?"

"We have to. We'll get rid of the gibs and live on the world our forefathers claimed. We'll use it as a home base from which we'll carry on our vendetta against the jaks."

"A word of advice. Don't try and loot this city."

He sneered. "Why not?"

"Remember those damned men. They could have given the dream treatment to every artifact here. You wouldn't want to take away a souvenir that could drive you out of your mind."

He blanched so obviously that I laughed. He leaned down and took my face roughly between his hands. "You could have been a queen. Enjoy your independence, girl. Die with it."

They went away and left me there alone, the whole pack of them, dreens and mounts, and when the last sounds had died away and the only noise was made by my beating heart and the tinkling that was like little musical feet running through Doubleluck, well,

I sat chained to my stone monument and figured out a few things. Like: The tinkling sound was probably the way dead men killed live jaks and dreens; that is, it was probably some kind of conduit to the human psyche; it touched all the right chords and eventually the mind or soul or conscience turned inward and began to consume itself. How to turn off the sound; how to stop my beating heart? There was only one way. The first would stop after the second stopped.

Like: How long did I have? Not for a moment did I believe I was immune to the tinkling of Doubleluck. Truly, all that glittered wasn't gold. In a way, those men of old had loved me. They'd built this grand city so that I could come and see it and stand in awe of it. Was it possible that the spite and jealousy I'd seen in Rulon and his kind were qualities inherited from those men of old? Had everything they did carried a hidden motive? Was it their subconscious wish to kill the people in the future?

Like: That damned Big Jak and that crazy Shaper wouldn't remain prisoners of the varks forever. As soon as they found their freedom, they would have a race to glory, Shaper with his newly discovered talent for independent skipping and Valdar, the rat, with a dumb hat on his head. Both would likely end up dead. And I knew better than to fancy they would come and give me a helping hand. This was a predicament I had to get out of by myself. Such was the code of the galaxy. Or someone's code. Mine, maybe. Served me right.

I sat and thought and listened to the gentle tinkling of a monster that had no form. What was its nature? Perhaps it was like the little electrical brain stimulators Cedron had spent so much time showing and explaining to me. Everything in the brain could be inspired by an electrical stimulus. Tap a section, titillate a cell cluster, diddle with dead experience and it was resurrected. The tinkling sound could work in that manner. Why couldn't noise do the same as an electrical probe?

The tinkle tinkle of Doubleluck worked on my psyche as I sat beside the statue. My imagination was boundless. I created monsters unlike any I had ever seen. They paraded through my head in legions, they devised exquisite tortures for a girl named Jade, they hated me for no damned reason that I could see, yet this didn't lessen their influence.

There was something else in me that wasn't extinguished by my fear: I loved this city. I sat and jinked all its sweet parts, admired what I saw clearly and what I saw vaguely. It was the loveliest thing I'd ever seen, and to hell with the monsters and the tinkles, the dreens, Valdar, and the varks and the other et ceteras who had interfered with my life. I had seen Doubleluck. It was real, it had been worth it, and I didn't regret having found it. Best damned place I was ever in.

I opened my eyes and was surprised to discover that I had slept. I felt refreshed. Stretching, yawning, sitting up, I heard the tinkle, tinkle, tinkle of little shadows of yesterday. I liked them.

"I'll never cease to be amazed by you," said a voice. "Or maybe you haven't heard about the jinx on this place."

There was Arnet, and he smiled at me and kept his hand on Otilla's head so she wouldn't bolt.

"I heard about it. By damn, I'm glad to see you. Was going to worry about breakfast after I got fully awake. Now I don't have to."

He hunched on his heels and regarded me with a grave expression. "I think you may be one in a million. Do you suppose you could live here and stay healthy?"

"I think so. Had a nice dream last night. Talked to the men who built it. Did you know they were whimsical? I met about half a dozen of them and they talked to me for a long time. Told me how they wanted Doubleluck to be our precious jewel. I got the notion they intended us to kind of worship it. That's not what they said, but I believe it was in their minds."

"And?" said Arnet.

"It's touching. And too bad, because I ain't staying in the galaxy to worship anything. Hey, what are you doing here?"

"I wanted to tell you about the dreens."

"Rulon? I hope he didn't kill Otho and Cedron."

Smiling, Arnet said, "He killed nobody. He couldn't even get onto Gibraltar. Every gib who could hold a gun was ready for them. Our radios sent out the message, and they heard it while they were still at a safe distance. We told them that every dreen who tried to land on our world would get blasted."

I started to laugh. "You don't mean—"

"I mean the dreens have been banished from Gibraltar. The last we jinked of them, they were headed away in search of another planet. They'll never be welcome again. Gibraltar belongs to the gibs."

"And what will the gibs make of it?"

"That problem will be handled the same as any other. We'll do the best we can."

"And your family?"

"Otho's a general now. My father is his personal physician."

Again, I laughed. "Poor Rulon."

Arnet looked at me with a wry expression. "You're a pushover for anyone who loves you."

"Not exactly. Let's just say I make room in my head for them. Get this damned chain off me."

I personally closed Doubleluck to the naked eye, stood at the foot of the mountain and stepped on the little green eye in the center of the grill. Did I feel grief as the big ugly mountain began to close like a mouth around that glittering vision? Briefly. I had places to go and excitement was building to a crescendo within me.

"Need my mount and then I'm off. Good-bye, Arnet. Maybe I'll see you sometime."

He sat aboard Otilla and there was sadness on his face. With a salute, he said farewell to the city that slipped silently back into its cocoon of rock.

"Yes, well, I guess I'll go witness the vark marathon before I go back to Gibraltar," he said.

"What's that?"

"What's what?"

"A vark marathon."

He shrugged. "Haven't the faintest idea, but word of it is everywhere. Probably isn't important, since varks have no imagination, but I'm a little curious. Well, good-bye, Jade. I want to wish you good luck and—"

"Wait a second. What's a vark marathon?"

Laughing a little, he said, "I just told you I don't know."

"What's it all about?"

"I don't know."

"Then why are you going to see it?"

"Because I don't know anything about it," he said, his exasperation beginning to show.

I looked at Doubleluck, but it was gone, hidden in the mountain. I jinked my stomach and found it to be damned empty. I needed a bath. I needed my mount. Suddenly I was crabby as hell.

"Hinx," I hollered. "Don't care what you're doing but want you here right this second."

"What the heck kept you?" he said in my ear, and I fell all over him with hugs and kisses.

"How come the varks let you go?" I yelled.

"Never had me for the last several days. They're up to their dirty ears planning the marathon and had no time for stray mounts."

"What's a marathon?" I said.

He scratched an ear. "Don't know."

"What do you mean, you don't know?"

"Just what I said. Heard a lot about it, but no one told me what it was."

"So long, Jade," said Arnet.

"Hold on. Wait a moment. You say you're going to see what the marathon is?"

"Yes."

Turning to Hinx, I said, "The varks aren't holding anything against me?"

"Don't see how they can have time. I tell you, they're busy."

"They have Valdar and Shaper imprisoned."

"That's funny. I seen both of them and they looked pretty free to me."

"Hell, I have to go see what's going on," I said. "Am too curious for my own good. But will only stay a minute, just long enough to find out what the hell they think they're up to. Then we'll skip."

I walked right into their waiting arms. Hinx was innocent but Arnet wasn't. The varks had sent him
after me.

We had our mounts skipped, and naturally I jinked
around and ahead of me. I should have gone the
other way as soon as that aura of strangeness entered
my consciousness. It was so odd and I was so curious.
And oblivious. The aura emanated from about a billion or more jaks who were waiting out in the void,
blanking out one another's jinks so I wouldn't pick up
their presence. A piece of my mind was aware of
that blank space. Usually there was someone somewhere. The other piece of my mind was occupied
with feeling the vark planet, and the situation there
had something to do with my dismissing the emptiness of the void as just a coincidence. The varks
weren't doing a damned thing, which seemed more
curious to me, seeing as how they were planning a
marathon, whatever that was.

I couldn't find Big Jak or Shaper or Elda or anyone I knew, just a bunch of varks sitting in a circle,
grinning at something in the center. That something
was invisible.

First I landed and then I waited. All a vark had to
do was look at me sideways and I would take off.
They didn't look at me. Finally I relaxed.

There they sat, all those insane varks, doing nothing but grinning at something I couldn't see. Completely unconcerned by then, I dismounted and approached the circle. I still couldn't see anything for
them to be grinning at. Maybe it was a very small
object. If so, I wanted to look at it. Stepping between
two varks, I slowly, cautiously walked toward the
center of the circle, peering at the ground as I went.

There I was, in the center, but nothing lay on the
ground. To make sure, I bent over for a closer look.
Still nothing. Straightening up, I looked at the varks.
What the hell were they grinning at?

Those damned varks grinned and grinned. At me.

"Hinky, I think we better get out of here," I said
silently. Gulping down my nervousness, I got ready to
pull him.

He wouldn't pull. I tried to walk out of the circle, but my legs wouldn't move.

"Hinky."

"I can't help it. They're all sitting on my mind."

People I knew began stepping from the shadows cast by rows of giant cacti: Big Jak, Shaper, Arnet, a lot of jaks and a few varks I had run into a time or two. Big Jak and Shaper walked close together, forced into that position by a circle of varks who kept snapping their teeth and looking ferocious. The two were escorted into the big circle, and then the three of us were side by side, stupidly staring at each other.

"Knew you were involved in this, soon as I saw I'd been suckered," I said.

Big Jak scowled. "Am no more involved than you are. No, I take that back. We're all in it up to our ears. Incidentally, I'm gratified to see you're alive. My conscience was bothering me about you, but not a whole lot."

"What the heck is that thing on your head?"

Grinning, he patted the thing with his palm. "I'm an expert haberdasher. Me and this skinny hat are skipping out of the galaxy. Oh, yeah, my mount's coming, too."

Shaper started hollering. "Mine ain't. Don't have one, don't need one, and something else I don't need is a lot of interfering beasts. You varks clear out and let me go."

The biggest vark I ever saw came meandering toward the outer circle. He was grinning up a storm, and it finally dawned on me that no matter how pleased he looked, this vark was mad as hell. Even Shaper sensed it and shut his mouth. Big Jak took a few steps backward and collided with me. I was doing likewise.

The circle opened to admit the big vark. In a leisurely fashion he walked over to us and stopped. "Nobody skips before anyone else," he said.

Naturally we expected him to say more. When he didn't, I forgot how forbidding he looked and started complaining.

213

"Everytime I turn around, someone locks me up. Don't care who you are—"

"I am the overseer of the galaxy."

"Oh." Blinking and gulping, I said. "Don't know what that means, but really don't care. If you'll step aside, I'll be on my way. That is, if your people will kindly release my mount."

"I know all about you, girl. Watched you grow. Got onto your tail when you were five years old and took your first skip."

Blink, gulp, blink, gulp, I had to keep stuffing my feet in my mouth. "You thinking of sending me to Bounding Winter? Because if you are it won't do you much good. Besides, I don't recognize your authority."

"Or anybody else's," growled the vark. "The same as any jak, or gib, or dreen, or mount. Maybe it's a disease. The galaxy is a one-room schoolhouse with everyone eager to break out." He turned away from me and faced his own kind. "So be it. Today is breaking-out day. Varks were given the job of watching over the children of men. We don't want the job anymore. It's too tedious."

The varks did an astonishing thing. They all cheered. In fact, they brayed, cussed, leaped up and down, thrashed their tails, kissed each other. They made a thunderous din. Meanwhile, their old leader stood silently, with a cynical grin, and waited for them to quiet down.

To Big Jak, Shaper and me, he said, "The varks have decided to hold a marathon. You can skip, anyone can skip, to wherever you please, but we're holding you to doing it together. No one goes before the others. Agreed?"

"Now look here," said Big Jak.

"Just a minute," said Shaper.

"Not by a long shot," I said.

"Shut up," said the big vark. "The next individual who speaks out of turn can't go."

"But the thrill is in being first, damn it, can't you—" I said, but quickly broke off as he turned on me with an enraged glare.

"No one goes first. Didn't you hear me? Maybe

214

you'll learn something if you do it together, though I doubt it."

"Sir," said Big Jak.

"Speak, Valdar. From the side of your mouth. With forked tongue and crossed mind, tell me your thought."

"I apologize for being so much a jak. We been friends for a long time, so I know you're a fair individual, same as all varks. Am I to understand that you're reneging on your promises to men?"

The vark's eyes flashed red. "No, not exactly. If I say we varks can no longer tolerate the children of men and that we don't care if you skip off a cliff en masse, what makes you think we're breaking our promises to your fathers?"

"Sorry, sir, but you told them you'd take care of us," Big Jak mumbled.

"The fact of the matter is, we're not certain holding you in is the best policy. We varks respect law and order, we like things organized and we demand logic and reason in and for whatever we do. Obviously, jaks aren't like varks. We've been going along, doing nothing but observing and trying to keep the fringes neat. Now you're dead set on spreading your lifestyle to the outer reaches. Much as this goes against vark grain, we've decided to adopt a hands-off policy."

"You mean we're free?" I said.

"That's what I mean."

"Then get out of my way."

How evil is the grin of a vark who enjoys his power over children. Actually, that "children" business was sticking in my craw. It was my rotten suspicion that he was right.

"I'll get out of your way in just a moment," he said. "We'd like you to remember a few things. For instance, remember your birthplace and have a little respect for it. Try and recall the people who came before you, and once in a while, if it isn't too much effort, consider how hard they worked to make a decent reality for you. Remember that all creatures live for a purpose and that the purpose is always internal and never external. Try, goddamn it, to grow up."

He was the maddest vark I ever saw. So great was his anger that his eyes brimmed and' threatened to spill over.

"Okay," he roared. "No more lectures. Line up. Get in front of me and prepare yourselves. I want you to station your mounts under you and I promise that if you dare skip before my signal you'll be hauled back here and held till doomsday."

Hinx was under me. How did that happen? Had I called him? Didn't know. Was too excited and confused to think straight. Was I really going to get to . . . ? Were they turning us loose amidst all that danger out there? How would we ever make it? How dare they not let me go first?

"I know what you're thinking, and my advice is to forget it."

Big Jak said it. I turned my head and stared at him. Right then, he looked beautiful, even with his silly hat that hid his ears and damn near covered his eyes.

Joyously, I said, "Anyone cheats around here, it won't be me. This is my meat. Soon as that vark gives the signal, I'm going to create a lot of dust for you to eat."

Shaper was screaming. "Look at me, everybody. No mount. Just my own two feet. I'm going to glory all by myself."

"I'd like to travel behind you," said a voice, and I whipped my head around and there sat Arnet on Otilla. Her little head was up and every muscle she owned quivered with anticipation.

"If I had any sense, I'd warn you not to do it," I said. "Won't say anything, because I'm too busy concentrating. Except, what about Gibraltar?"

"I'm a jak. Ever since I first skipped. Can I take a hand from you if I need it?"

"What if I say no?"

"It won't matter."

"Then come along and hang on the best way you can."

The varks didn't make a sound, except for the leader. He stood in front of us, blinking his angry wet eyes and smiling. Yes, smiling.

216

"It's a long way to the next galaxy," he said. "Does one of you have a piece of it fixed in your mind?"

Four voices: "No."

"Fine. I'd consider any other response insane. Does any one of you feel confident that you know what you're doing?"

"No."

"So far, so good. Please concentrate. Jink hard. In the proper pecking order, peck that galaxy."

"We're pecking."

"Is it hazy?"

"Yes."

"All right, I'm going to count to three and when you hear my shout, you're free of all your responsibilities in this sphere. Ready?"

"I'm scared," Arnet gasped.

"Oh, god," Shaper gasped.

"Come on, Volcano," Big Jak gasped.

I said nothing. I was too busy jinking.

"Good-bye, Jade," whispered Big Jak. "Remember I love you."

Startled half out of my wits, I broke my concentration and looked at him. What did he mean by saying good-bye? Was he afraid he wouldn't make it? Why, if he wasn't going to be there—

He succeeded in doing what he intended, got me rattled and put himself one up on me. I didn't even know the vark had finished counting, was unaware that he was shouting his lungs out, that the signal had been given. All I knew was that Big Jak flashed me a wicked grin and disappeared. Shaper disappeared. Arnet disappeared.

"Goddamn," I screamed, and disappeared.

He was ahead of me. "I'll get you," I howled, and Hinx and I poured it on. Through D-2, like a couple of ghosts, we zoomed. Behind me someone cried out. Arnet. I sent back jink, felt him, hauled on him. Lordy, he was heavy and weaving like a snake that had no end.

"Come on, Volcano," yelled a voice, and I had the enemy pinned down.

"Thy kingdom come, thy will be done." That was Shaper, talking to himself, revolving in black space, threatening to disperse. I sent jink in his direction. He screamed, "Get away from me, damn it, you'll kill me." I didn't kill him. Instead I gave him a needed shove.

"Jade, honey, where's our destination?" cried Hinx.

"I forgot to pick one out."

"As usual, we're clicking on all rotors."

Arnet. Lordy, he was heavy, and he kept losing his air pocket. I kept tucking it in around him. Otilla was singing a little happy song. I was sure she had lost her mind.

"Jade, honey."

"Yeah, Hinx?"

"I didn't say nothing."

"Jade, honey."

"Valdar? Is that you?"

"Yeah, baby. I'm cutting out. You'll have a better chance."

"What you mean?" I screeched. "You're lying again."

"Not this time. Knew I never had a real chance but had to try. My jink isn't on a par with yours. I'm kind of like the last of the old guard. You belong up there with the youngsters."

"No, no, no, don't want to go without you."

Shaper yelled. "What the hell's the matter with you two? You think one of us can drop out? You'll kill the whole species. You never did understand varks. You damn fools, jink way behind you."

We did, and we didn't believe it. Across the void came a wagon train, an endless stream of mounted jaks and independent varks.

Yelled Shaper, "They're traveling on our power. The varks gave them permission."

"Nobody goes without the other!" This was Arnet.

No wonder he seemed so heavy. I wasn't just pulling him, I was pulling the galaxy.

"You can't drop out," I shouted at Big Jak. "For the first time in your life you have to finish something you started. There are only the three of us. You, me and Shaper. Jink is making a single column of force behind us, but it's coming from the three of us."

"In that case, we better find a destination!"

"Already have one. See it?"

"Hell, no."

"Hinx, do you see it?" I yelled.

"Sure do."

"The farthest ever!"

So we did it. Big Jak, Shaper and I skipped for dear life. For the very first time, maybe in history, Jakalowar cooperated and did a thing together.